Wuthering Heights Revisited

Wuthering Heights Revisited

G. M. Best

ROBERT HALE · LONDON

© G. M. Best 2011
First published in Great Britain 2011

ISBN 978 0 7090 9364 0

Robert Hale Limited
Clerkenwell House
Clerkenwell Green
London EC1R 0HT

www.halebooks.com

2   4   6   8   10   9   7   5   3

Printed in the UK by the MPG Books Group

Contents

Prologue

Ellen Nussey was Charlotte Brontë's most long-standing friend. She died in 1897 in Moor Lane House in Gomersal in Yorkshire. Following her death, her possessions and letters were dispersed at auction, and many of Charlotte's letters eventually made their way through donation or purchase to the Brontë Parsonage Museum in Haworth in Yorkshire. What follows is a document that never became part of that collection or any other, one that has only recently been uncovered. If it is genuine, it totally changes our understanding of Charlotte's character and, in the process, reveals the shattering truth about Heathcliff Earnshaw, the most powerful figure in her sister Emily's novel, *Wuthering Heights*, and how he ultimately destroyed the Brontë family.

1

Meeting Charlotte

I was puzzled to receive Charlotte's letter in December 1836. It was so full of self-loathing. She, who had been my friend for five years, seemed to think I was ignorant of her true character. She said that her heart was a hotbed for sinful thoughts and that she yearned to be like me – a person who could aspire to be one of the saints. I did not recognize myself in this description. It was true that even then as a young girl I looked to my Redeemer for guidance, but I was no paragon of virtue. The letter seemed totally out of character. Normally Charlotte was full of how talented she was and how one day she would become a famous writer. What had brought her to such a depth of misery that she could only describe herself as being destined for damnation? I had no doubt that some people were, but surely not my dearest friend, not Charlotte Brontë.

It is now almost sixty years since I opened that letter. It lies in front of me as I write this. I read again its opening lines: 'If I could always live with you, and daily read the bible with you. If your lips and mine could at the same time drink the same draught from the same pure fountain of Mercy – I hope, I trust, I might one day become better, far better, than my evil wandering thoughts, my corrupt heart, cold to the spirit, and warm to the flesh will now permit me to be.' Did she truly mean that? I would like to think that the letter was written in a genuine moment. Or was it penned simply to evoke my sympathy? The truth is that our friendship mattered far more to me than to her and for many years I was happy to bask in her shadow. I knew nothing of the guilty secrets that lay in her past and which made her feel one of the damned until circumstances led me to seek the truth about her.

The prospect of my death has made me feel it is time that I wrote about what I uncovered so many years ago and my role in the tragedies that ultimately destroyed the Brontë family. After Charlotte's death I was accused of betraying too much information about my friend to her biographer, Mrs Gaskell, but the truth is that I hid so much, so very much, from that gifted writer because of my love for Charlotte and her sisters, Emily and Anne. I feared that their literary reputation would be forever ruined if I disclosed the real truth and that my own standing would be seriously impaired. Such is their fame now that I am sure it will survive. As for me, I no longer care what people will say.

My name is Ellen Nussey and my own early life can be told very briefly. I was born in 1817, the twelfth child of a prosperous cloth merchant who lived in Birstall, near Gomersal in the West Riding of Yorkshire. My parents wanted to provide me with a good education and I attended a small local school. My father, who was a kind and generous man, died when I was only nine years old and my brothers took over the family business. My mother ensured that I progressed first to the Gomersal Moravian Ladies Academy and then, in January 1831, to the newly opened and more fashionable Roe Head School, outside Mirfield. This was a kind of finishing school for young ladies and it was based in a fine, three-storeyed eighteenth-century mansion, which still stands alongside the road that leads to Dewsbury and overlooks the beautiful parkland of Kirklees Hall. Its headmistress was a clever and kindly woman called Miss Margaret Wooler and her four able sisters, Catherine, Susan, Marianne and Eliza, assisted in the running of the school. Miss Wooler took a motherly interest in all her pupils and I was to count her as not just a mentor but also a close friend until her death when she was in her nineties eleven years ago.

It was at Roe Head that I first met Charlotte Brontë, who was a shy and nervous fellow pupil. She had arrived just eight days before me. On first showing she had little to commend her. She was small for someone approaching her fifteenth birthday and her dumpy figure was dressed in a dark, rusty-green dress that was patched in places and distinctly out of fashion. To this had been sewn what was obviously a homemade lace collar and cuffs. She was very plain of face because she had an overhanging brow, a large nose, and a mouth that was slightly crooked. It did not help that her head was overly large for her body and that her dry, frizzy, brown hair, which was screwed into tight curls through the use of heating tongs, emphasized this defect. She also seemed to be constantly staring at everyone through her reddish-brown eyes. Only later did I discover this arose because she was extremely short-sighted.

Charlotte was terribly homesick, far more so than any of the other girls. I learned that her Irish father was a curate in Haworth and that her family had faced a triple tragedy – not only had her mother died ten years earlier, but also, in 1825, so had her older sisters, Maria and Elizabeth, who were then aged only ten and nine. They and Charlotte had been sent to a newly opened school for the daughters of clergymen at Cowan Bridge in Lancashire. Charlotte had not only hated the over-crowded dormitories and inedible food, but also resented the ruthless cropping of her hair to which all the girls were routinely subjected. Her outspoken desire to return home had led to her being constantly vilified and she was cruelly made to feel that her mother's untimely death must have been God's punishment for her sinfulness. When Maria and Elizabeth contracted consumption, all three returned to Haworth, but then Charlotte was forced to watch her sisters die. She had looked on helpless as gobbets of blood had trickled out of their mouths from their failing lungs. She told me that the sound of their tortured breathing still gave her the most appalling nightmares.

There was, of course, nothing in our school that was remotely like the harsh environment of Cowan Bridge and I tried to encourage Charlotte to take pleasure in its oak-panelled rooms and its sweeping lawns and sweet-scented rose garden and apple orchard, not to mention the fine panorama over meadow and parkland. Unfortunately I was unsuccessful, partly because she found the school's structured day very irksome but mainly because she missed her family too much. Following the deaths of her elder sisters, she had understandably grown much closer to her brother, Branwell, who was just a year younger than her, and more protective towards her younger sisters, Emily and Anne, who were aged thirteen and ten. It was in one of our conversations about them that Charlotte gave me the first hint of that self-condemnation whose cause I was later to discover. She told me there were aspects of her character that she had to strive to conceal and suppress and that I should understand that her brother and sisters were far worthier than her.

Some of the girls teased Charlotte because of her ugly and stunted appearance and her squinting eyesight, and others were amused at her ignorance of some very basic skills and social graces and mocked her occasionally Irish accent. She took to staying apart from their games, preferring to read books, but the sight of her squinting at these only caused further mockery. She would hold each book so close to her face that it would almost touch the tip of her nose. The girls thought it unnatural that she should desire to possess knowledge of poetry, art, literature and politics and were resentful of her easy grasp of things that were beyond their range of thinking. However, my mother had taught me to be kind and so I took pity on her and comforted her as best I could, as did another girl called Mary Taylor, who was the elder daughter of a cloth manufacturer in Gomersal. She shared a bed with Charlotte in our dormitory and was stunningly beautiful, so much so that I still remember how our headmistress, Miss Wooler, used to say that she was too pretty to live for very long. The three of us became great friends, though we were dissimilar in appearance, aptitude and temperament. Gradually Mary and I persuaded the other girls to look on Charlotte with greater kindness. It helped that one of Charlotte's gifts was story-telling and that all the girls began to look forward to the tales she would spin at bedtime.

I soon discovered that Charlotte was far more academically gifted than me. I was judged dull by comparison. She soon moved from being bottom of the junior class to the top of the senior one, outshining all except Mary, who was not only highly intelligent but also more assertive. I was a conformist, keen to obey the school rules and do what society deemed appropriate in terms of dress and behaviour, but Mary encouraged Charlotte to challenge accepted behaviour and opinions. I remember her saying to Charlotte that she must think of a life beyond the confines of her home. 'It is better, Charlotte,' she said, 'to try all things and find all empty, than to try nothing and leave your life a blank by burying your talents in your home in Haworth.' Then she laughed and joked, 'Do you want to take each gift and deposit it in a broken-spouted teapot or shut it up in a china closet among tea things or

smother it in piles of woollen hose or hide it in a tureen of cold pota-
toes, to be ranged with bread, butter, pastry and ham on the shelves of
the larder?' Many years later Charlotte depicted Mary as the feisty Rose
Yorke in her novel *Shirley*.

In one of her more open moments, Charlotte informed me that she
had been sent away from home not only so she could acquire the skills
to become a governess but also in order that she would spend less time
with her brother Branwell. Her father had judged the intensity of their
relationship inappropriate. The bright spot of her week was always when
she received a letter from Branwell, though she never shared its contents
with me. Once I managed to get hold of one of his letters whilst she was
out, but I found his handwriting mostly illegible and the little of the
contents I could vaguely decipher confusing. I once also sneaked a look
at the contents of Charlotte's homemade, stitch-bound notebooks,
although she had banned any of us from reading them. They were filled
with a virtually illegible script, and seemed to largely be about imagined
adventures in Africa and in a kingdom called Angria. Only years later
did Charlotte talk to me about the fantasy worlds she and Branwell had
created and how, whilst at school, she had secretly transformed me and
other girls into characters within them.

On one occasion Branwell turned up at our school, having walked
sixteen muddy miles to give his sister a birthday present. Given
Charlotte's rapturous idealization of him, he was a huge disappointment
to me. It was obvious that he was not accustomed to being in polite
society and he was quite short in stature, unpleasantly thin, and far from
good-looking. His forehead was bumpy, his nose was overly large, and
his slightly retreating chin conveyed weakness. It did not help that his
face was freckled and that his reddish hair, which he had tried to brush
into a Byronic style, was thick and matted. Because he shared Charlotte's
eyesight problem, he also wore unattractive spectacles and, even worse,
rarely looked you in the face. Instead he tended to stare at his feet or
hands. His physical failings were matched by clothes that were dirty and
sweat-marked and too small for him and by a strange manner that was
far too excitable and impetuous and unpredictable for my liking.
Nevertheless, I could see Charlotte was completely overjoyed at his presence.

When I tried to ask Branwell questions about his sisters, he answered flippantly. He said that I had to understand his sisters were honoured to have him as their brother. He described Charlotte as a broad, dumpy thing, Emily as a lean and scant creature, and Anne as an absolute nothing. 'What?' I said. 'Is she an idiot?' 'Next door to it,' was his joking response. Charlotte took no offence at these remarks but laughed and then took him away. It was obvious that she had no desire to share his company with us and we saw little of them for the rest of the day. Once he had headed back to Haworth, she could talk of nothing but his visit. She said with total conviction that her brother was destined for greatness. It was not until the next day that she repented that she had not asked him more about her sisters and about her aunt, Miss Elizabeth Branwell, who had come from Cornwall to care for them all after their mother's death.

By the summer of 1832, it was decided Charlotte's education was complete enough for her to cease attendance at Roe Head. She and I agreed to remain in contact via letters. When term ended and the time came for us to separate and return to our respective families, she wept. She, who had once desired nothing more than to return home, now bemoaned that she was to be confined to the monotonous life of Haworth. Her new role was to simply pass on what she had learned to her sisters, Emily and Anne – a task she was to fulfil within the parsonage for the next three years. In July 1832 she wrote this in a letter to me:

An account of one day is an account of all. In the morning from nine o'clock till half past twelve I instruct my sisters and draw, and then we walk till dinner. After dinner I sew till teatime, and after tea I either read, write, do a little fancy work, or draw, as I please. Thus in one delightful, though somewhat monotonous course, my life is passed. I have only been out twice since I came home.

I invited her to come and stay with my family in our house, the Rydings, the following month in order to cheer her up. Her father was quick to grant his permission but he made it a condition of her visit that her brother Branwell should accompany her. He loved my home, particularly because it had mock battlements that appealed to his military tastes, and he compared walking in our lovely grounds to a stroll through paradise. Charlotte was equally taken and I am proud to say that years later she based Mr Rochester's home in *Jane Eyre* on the Rydings and Briarfield Church in *Shirley* on St Peter's, the church that my family attended. For three weeks we all thoroughly enjoyed each other's company and both Branwell and Charlotte were therefore loath to return home. Charlotte promised that she would persuade her father to invite me to stay with them.

I first visited the small, grey parsonage at Haworth in July 1833. The large village had nothing to commend it. Its bleak main street was lined with dismal buildings and I had to cover my nose with my handkerchief because of the stench that arose from the damp, soot-soaked air and the effluvium that flowed from privies and open cesspits. As I rode in a gig up the steep hill, dirty, unwashed people gathered in many of the doorways to stare at me, their hostile and prematurely aged faces showing not the slightest hint of welcome. At the top of the village, there was an ugly mix of cottages and back-to-back houses that were obviously hugely overcrowded. I saw a number of people queuing to get water from a well, but what they were collecting looked green and putrid. It was safer to drink alcohol and I was not surprised to hear the sound of drunken revelry from each of the three public houses that we passed, especially the last, which stood at the foot of the church steps and was named the Black Bull.

From what Charlotte had told me, I knew that Haworth suffered from a very high death rate – worse even than London – and having seen the squalor of the place I was not surprised. Not that I had seen the worst because there were places where entire yards were filled with a stinking combination of rotting rubbish, discarded offal and the refuse of privies and where, when it rained, the foul mix found its way into those damp cellars where the poorest families had to live and work. I found it hard to understand why Charlotte had yearned to return to such a miserable place. The graveyard bore evidence of many new graves and, during my stay at the parsonage, I was to find it depressing that it was rare not to hear the 'chip, chip' of the mason cutting fresh headstones in a nearby shed or the toll of the funeral bell. However, I also came to appreciate that the parsonage was almost the last house at that side of the village and so it overlooked miles of moorland. This vast open space was Charlotte's real love and she and her sisters seldom ventured into Haworth itself.

A cobbled lane led, via the graveyard, to the parsonage and church. I did not regret my journey when I saw the excited smile on Charlotte's face as she stood waiting for me at the gateway. She had heard the sound of the gig as it neared her house and hastily come to greet me. Once I entered the house, Miss Branwell appeared, dressed all in black. This did not surprise me because Charlotte had warned me that her Aunt Elizabeth always wore the colour of mourning, despite many years having passed since her sister's death. She was small and stout, plain in feature and in form, eccentric in manner and, to my young eye, very antiquated in appearance. She wore wooden patens instead of shoes, a gown that was obviously old, and a jacket that had long been out of fashion. On her head was a frightful white frilly cap that stood a quarter of a yard broad around her face. This served only to emphasize her unattractive upturned nose and her dormouse cheeks, and it also drew attention to the fact that she was obviously wearing a false-piece of auburn hair. She offered me a pinch of snuff from a gold box – a habit that had long ceased to be fashionable. I courteously declined but I appreciated that it was her way of treating me with all the care and solicitude due to a weary traveller.

Miss Branwell insisted that, after such a long journey, I should have something to eat, but what was provided was badly cooked and I could not help but notice the cheap cutlery and the darned tablecloth. Charlotte's father joined us and my first impression of the Rev. Patrick Brontë was not an unpleasing one. He had the bearing of a soldier and in his clerical garb he struck me as looking very venerable, with his snow-white hair and powdered white collar and small-lensed spectacles. Unfortunately, closer contact made me appreciate that he had none of the genial warmth that is the hallmark of the best of the clergy. Though his manner and mode of speech had the tone of high-bred courtesy, he was morose and he made no effort to engage me in conversation. He also made far too much of being an invalid, to the extent that his silk cravat was worn up to the edge of his lips to protect himself from any draughts. This focused attention on his piercing, pale blue eyes. To further protect himself, he insisted on the house being heated to an uncomfortable degree, on the shutters being drawn early, and on doors being kept shut, and he was very fussy about what he ate, claiming that he was easily prone to dyspepsia and indigestion.

The parsonage itself was elegant enough from the outside, possessing fine sash windows, a doorway with pilasters and portico, and a stone-flagged roof, but its garden, which consisted mainly of a few stunted fruit bushes and some lilacs and elders, was terribly neglected. Internally it was very austere with very little carving or ornamental plasterwork. It had some wooden panelling but there were no curtains at any of the windows (their place being taken by wooden shutters) and not much carpet anywhere, except for a few rugs on the stone-flagged floors in the sitting room and in Mr Brontë's study. Instead of being papered, the walls were coloured in a dove-shade tint, and there was only a small amount of inexpensive furniture. It made me realize how fortunate I was to live in such great splendour and comfort at my home. Later I was taken upstairs, where there were five rooms, all spartanly furnished. Mr Brontë shared one with Branwell, his sister-in-law one with Anne, and Charlotte one with Emily. The fourth room belonged to the servants and the fifth room acted as a kind of day room so that the family could undertake tasks without disturbing Mr Brontë in his study.

Despite his earlier visit to my home, Branwell kept himself much to himself. I thought him obsessed with things military and was surprised that he was still expecting his sisters to create imaginary tales about his toy soldiers. There were aspects of his character I found very unattractive. For a start, he showed little respect to either his aunt or father whenever he was out of their presence, poking fun at her Cornish accent and idiosyncratic manners and mimicking his father's Irish accent. He also, on this occasion, appeared unhealthily morbid. When I mentioned how taken aback I had been to see so much poverty in the village, he seized me by the arm and whispered savagely in my ear, 'What is the point of living, Miss Nussey? We are just wretched beings, tossed upon time's tide. We can see all life's rocks and whirlpools, but fate prevents us from escaping them. We are doomed from our first bitter breath to launch upon this sea of death without a hope. My father talks of the justice we will receive as our reward in heaven but that is just a delusion.

When we die, all that happens is that our corpses fester and decay. I shall never see my mother and older sisters again, whatever my father says. All I have to remind me of them is that last sight of their white and wasted bodies as I was made to kiss them goodbye.'

I soon appreciated that Mr Brontë, Miss Branwell and Charlotte's brother saw my visit as an unwelcome nuisance, even though they took some pride in Charlotte having acquired such a ladylike friend. However, the friendly reception that I was offered by Charlotte's younger sisters more than outweighed their coolness. We were, of course, all of a similar age. I was sixteen, Anne was thirteen, Emily had just become fifteen, and Charlotte was seventeen. I found Anne open in manner and gentle in nature but a little shy. She had a very pretty face, with a clear, almost transparent complexion, fine pencilled eyebrows, lovely violet-blue eyes, and attractive brown hair. She was very much treated as the baby of the family, although she was only a little younger than her sisters and already taller than both Branwell and Charlotte. As for Emily, few people could look and smile like her. She was a strange mix: at times wild and headstrong, at times very reserved, despite the fact that she physically dominated us because of her greater height. She had a lithesome, graceful figure and the most beautiful kind, liquid blue-grey eyes, but her complexion was poor and her hair was shaped into an unbecoming tight curl and frizz. What struck me most was her adoration for birds and animals. Unfortunately this meant her clothes were often dirty as a consequence of her keeping a small menagerie of cats, dogs and geese in the kitchen.

Seeing Charlotte in her home environment made me realize for the first time just how isolated an existence her family lived. It was to compensate for this that she and her sisters – and indeed her brother also – had got into the habit of constantly inventing their own imaginary worlds. They made up stories and acted them out, using whatever they could find to make improvized costumes. To my surprise Charlotte identified so much more with Branwell than her sisters that she often took the part of a male, painting a moustache above her lips. Even with me present as their guest, the four of them used to disappear to secretly write and draw, forgetting their duties as host. When they re-emerged, they would engage in weird tableaux or wild dances or enter into debates about politics or the latest book or magazine that they had read, much to my confusion. It was no wonder that Charlotte had felt so out of place when she had first entered the polite, refined circles of Roe Head. I was far too inhibited to join in their games and often felt socially uncomfortable amid their noisy banter. They jokingly dubbed me 'Your Ladyship'.

Breakfast each day of the fortnight I was there was awful. It began with a solemn prayer from Mr Brontë and then Charlotte's aunt insisted on turning it into an occasion when she could preach at us. The tenure of her talk was always the same. She hoped that we had not been thinking unworthy thoughts because, had we died during the night, we would have damned ourselves to eternal destruction in the fiery pit. She knew that Haworth was a barren desert but its soulless, godforsaken nature would not prepare us for the torments and horrors of hell. Mostly these tirades were met with a deathly silence, though I could see by the expression on Branwell's face that he was scornful of her fierce piety. On one morning Charlotte tried to remonstrate with her aunt, saying that she should be more charitable in the company of a guest, but this was greeted with a stern reprimand and an even longer lecture about the sins that so easily beset young girls. Teatime was little better. The conversation consisted mainly of arguments about religion between her and Mr Brontë.

My experience was no happier when I went to hear Mr Brontë preach in church. I soon realized that the people he served were for the most part entirely illiterate and therefore unable to follow the service book. When they assembled they did so with a stolid look of apathy fixed on their faces. Some took the occasion to go to sleep and a sexton with a long staff would continually walk round in the aisles to prod them awake. It was also his task to keep children from becoming too unruly. When Mr Brontë began to expound, it is true most listened but they took no pleasure in it. He spoke for about an hour as was his custom, and, to do him credit, I thought he preached quite well and with a dignified air. He did not rant or whine but spoke with the authority of a man impressed with the truth of what he was saying and who has no fear of consequences, but I am not convinced this achieved anything. Some looked as if for a penny they would defiantly oppose whatever he said, while others tried to look as if they understood what they blatantly did not.

What made my visit enjoyable was that both Emily and Anne were insistent that Charlotte should permit me to explore the countryside they loved and so the four of us went on delightful rambles, threading our way through the creep-holes in the dry-stone walls down into the glens and ravines that here and there broke the monotony of the moorland that surrounded their home. Branwell accompanied us as our protector, though he was no different in age. On these walks I could not help but notice that the close bond between Anne and Emily was far deeper than their relationship with Charlotte, whom they treated more like a substitute mother. Each of the sisters in her own way seemed to become another person once on the moor, more alive, more vivacious, more happy. I took pleasure in their enjoyment of nature and in the way they often lingered to appreciate almost every new flower, every fresh tint and shape in the surrounding scenery. Even just the fording of a stream by the use of a few stepping stones seemed to cause them an untiring excitement.

They took me on more than one occasion to their favourite spot, which they called 'The Meeting of the Waters'. It was a small oasis of emerald-green turf, broken here and there by small clear springs. Seated on a few large stones that served as resting places, we were literally hidden from the human world and nothing appeared in view but miles and miles of heather, a glorious blue sky, and the brightening sun. We laughed and made mirth of each other, and agreed that we would call ourselves 'the quartette'. Emily, half reclining on a slab of stone, played happily with the tadpoles in the water and then fell to moralizing on which were the strong and brave, and which were the weak and cowardly, as she chased them with her hand. Anne joined in and soon the two of them were almost oblivious of either Charlotte or me. The extent to which Anne's love of nature was inspired by Emily's was something I came later to increasingly appreciate.

When my visit came to an end, Charlotte and I agreed that we would try not to rely entirely on letters to keep our friendship alive and that, whenever circumstances permitted, we would meet up again in our respective homes. In 1835 Charlotte began teaching at our old school,

Roe Head, in order that Emily and Anne might also receive an education there. However, all three sisters saw no future for themselves but menial employment. They thought Branwell alone was destined for greatness either as a writer or an artist. Are not men's interests always put before those of women in the world in which we live? I, like them, assumed he was the most gifted. He had the ability to read a page at a glance whilst at the same time instantly committing it to memory, and so possessed an extraordinarily wide knowledge as a result of his extensive reading of newspapers, journals, magazines, and library books. Not only could he write imaginatively and well, but, if he chose, he could write two things at once, using both his right and left hands simultaneously, and that dexterity was equally evident in his ability to draw.

Unfortunately his sisters' extreme reverence for his talents convinced Branwell that he was going to effortlessly acquire greatness. That year he told Charlotte that his artistic gifts were going to be snapped up by the Royal Academy. In fact this was nonsense. His art teacher told Branwell that he had nothing in the portfolio of his work that was yet suitable and that he could never expect to become a famous painter without first showing greater dedication. Branwell's response was to say there was no point going to the Royal Academy if it would not take him solely on the basis of his flair and inspiration. He then pretended to his friends that he had gone to the Academy and left because it proved unworthy of his talents! Then he wrote arrogant letters to *Blackwood's Magazine*, almost demanding that its editor should employ him as a writer because he was so uniquely gifted. Needless to say, he received no replies.

I watched as first Emily and then Anne and then Charlotte all became ill from their attempts to prepare themselves for a life of drudgery, whilst Branwell merely dabbled in voluntary roles in Haworth, playing the church organ, teaching in the Sunday school, and for a time becoming secretary to the local Temperance Society. Through his father's influence, he was initiated as a Mason and I know it was Charlotte's view that this proved detrimental. The strange rites associated with the Masons led to a growing obsession with things fantastical. Branwell began writing more and more about increasingly bizarre fictitious worlds. What made matters worse was that the lodge met in the Black Bull and this encouraged him to spend time drinking there, with the consequence that his language grew increasingly coarse and his stories became obsessed with illicit passions and decadent living. In 1838 Mr Brontë paid to set him up as a portrait painter in Bradford, but this venture proved short-lived because Branwell took it as a personal slight whenever a potential client chose to go to a better-known artist in Halifax or Leeds.

Branwell returned to Haworth in February 1839 ostensibly to yet again devote time to writing a masterpiece. When I heard about this, I was not impressed. From my simple perspective, it was time Charlotte's brother stopped relying on his family to sustain him. How could he not see that his unemployment was placing pressure on his sisters to take up very uncongenial employment rather than additionally burden their father? In September 1838 Emily had been forced to take employment as a teacher at a terrible girls' boarding school at Law Hill on the high moorland overlooking Halifax. When she returned home shattered by that experience, Anne took on the earning role and in April 1839 became a governess to a family called Ingham, who lived at Blake Hall, near Mirfield. The following month Charlotte became a governess to a family called Sidgwick, who lived near Skipton.

By this time I was convinced that Branwell was not worth Charlotte's sacrifice of her own potential for greatness. Little did I realize that I was about to discover why the self-loathing expressed in her letter of December 1836 had validity. The pedestal on which I had set her in comparison to her brother was shortly to crumble in ways that I could not possibly have foreseen.

2

Unrequited Passion

Charlotte left me in no doubt from the outset that she found being a governess detestable and demeaning for a person of her intelligence and talents. She found it hard to repel the rude familiarity of her riotous and unmanageable wards and unreasonable that Mrs Sidgwick expected her, once lessons were over, to undertake hours of needlework hemming yards of cambric and making muslin nightcaps. She found it insufferable that she even had to make clothes for the children's dolls! I was not entirely sympathetic because I had offered Charlotte a route out of such misery by encouraging my brother Henry to propose to her in the March of 1839. I had been confident she would accept because my brother was a very eligible young man of twenty-seven who had newly become a curate in Sussex. She knew enough of him to know that he would be a good and kind husband. Moreover, Henry had intimated to her that, should they marry, he was prepared to have me stay with them so that Charlotte and I could enjoy our friendship to the full.

Yet amazingly Charlotte had declined his offer, saying that even the teaching she hated could not drive her into making a loveless marriage. Her refusal seemed madness to me, and, given her unhappiness as a governess, I hoped to make her rethink the matter that autumn. In October I borrowed Henry's carriage so that I could take her for a holiday to Bridlington on the East Yorkshire coast. Charlotte had never seen the sea before and she revelled in its rough roar and swirling mix of green and blue and foam-white, but I got nowhere on the subject of her marrying my brother. I am sure that was because in the summer her father had acquired a new curate called Mr William Weightman. This handsome and constitutionally cheerful twenty-three-year-old seemed a far more attractive proposition than my brother. He had found no problem in charming Charlotte's eyes with his rosy cheeks, blue eyes and fine auburn hair and in delighting her ears with his clever wit and his romantic tales.

I confess that I was also not immune to Mr Weightman's charms. I remember in particular a night when Charlotte, Emily, Anne and I all went to hear him speak at the Mechanics Institute in Keighley. He spoke not just with learning but also with wit and vigour, and then, on our long walk back to Haworth, he entertained us so well that the time flew and I could scarce believe it was midnight when we reached the parsonage. Emily teased me that she would have to become our chaperone if I continued to spend time with him. This annoyed Charlotte, who told me that she did not mind him finding troops of victims amongst young ladies as long as I was not one of them. I responded by saying that her interest in my feelings for the curate must indicate she had herself been smitten by Cupid's bolt. This she denied but not, I thought, convincingly. Perhaps to offset his charisma – and so perhaps weaken his impact – we took to nicknaming him 'Miss Celia Amelia' because he blushed very easily. Somehow calling him this made his presence among us seem safer. Once it became clear that he had no intention of seriously courting Charlotte, she took against him and began denigrating his character. I found this unsettling because he was a good man and I mourned his loss when he caught cholera from working among the poor and died in the September of 1842.

In the March of 1841 Charlotte moved to enter the employ of a family called White, who lived in Upperwood House in Rawden, near Leeds. Her experiences there served to convince her that she lacked the patience to be an effective governess and that she was not cut out to live in other people's houses. She informed me that Mr and Mrs White were civil enough and the children – a boy of six and a girl of eight – reasonably well disposed towards her, but this did not alter the fact that her role was inadequately paid. She felt her life was being wasted. I was not surprised to hear from Charlotte how she had begged her father not to make her return when she visited home that Christmas. She made much of the fact that Emily's health had collapsed as a result of her work at

Law Hill and of how equally unhappy Anne was. The outcome was that their aunt agreed to provide £100 from her savings so that all of her nieces could set up their own school in Haworth.

It was what happened next that made me realize how much I had let my love for Charlotte blind me to her selfishness. She rejected a kind offer by Miss Wooler to let her take over her school, though it had a good reputation and required little in the way of investment. Instead she persuaded her father that, prior to her and her sisters opening a school, he should permit her and Emily to go to Brussels, where they could improve their French and German. Thus Charlotte committed Emily, who had no desire to leave home, to go abroad and simultaneously condemned Anne to unnecessary months of further slave labour as a governess. Was not this shockingly selfish behaviour? Moreover, in the light of what subsequently happened, I do not believe that Charlotte ever intended creating a school. All she really wanted was to use her aunt's money to fund an adventure for herself.

What surprised me most was that she was also prepared to do this at the very time when her brother Branwell needed her most, because he was increasingly turning to drink to drown his sorrows at his blighted career. Far from securing a bright future for himself, he had been reduced, after a brief unsuccessful time as a tutor in the Lake District, to taking on the menial role of a booking clerk at Sowerby Bridge Station on the newly opened Leeds-Manchester Railway. He begged her not to leave him and yet she ignored him.

I disliked the selfishness that Charlotte had shown, but I still took pleasure in seeing her happy again and I hoped that her venture abroad might bring her the success that her talents warranted. Early in the February of 1842 Mr Brontë escorted her and Emily to Brussels via London. Charlotte wrote to me about their excitement at experiencing the capital for the first time. On their first morning in the city her father had taken them to see St Paul's Cathedral and, from its magnificent dome, they had been able to see the whole of London stretched before them, with its great river, its beautiful bridges, and its many fine churches and open squares. Charlotte said it was as if her spirit, long imprisoned, shook loose the wings that had been cruelly fettered and she, who had never truly lived, was able to taste life for the first time.

However, their stay proved short – just three days – because their father lost no time in booking them a berth on a steam ship bound for the Continent. A small boat carried the two sisters by night to where they could board it. According to Charlotte, the river was black as ink and a chilly wind blew in their faces so in her imagination it seemed as if they were being rowed on the River Styx to the Land of Shades. Nevertheless, she enjoyed every minute of the voyage across the Channel, feeling the sea breeze on her face, experiencing the heaving waves, watching the encircling sea birds, and gazing at the white sails of other ships in the distance. From Ostend they travelled by coach via Ghent to Brussels. Charlotte was later to recount her impressions of this journey in her novel *The Professor*, saying that such was her exquisite enjoyment of her new freedom that everything seemed picturesque, even though the landscape was flat, the scenery was plain, and the buildings they saw no more than hovels.

Once in Brussels their father enrolled them for half a year at a Catholic girls' boarding school or 'pensionnat' run by Madame Zoe Claire Héger in the Rue d'Isabelle, and then returned home. According to Charlotte, Madame Héger was a short and stout woman of thirty-six with strikingly blue eyes and a kind smile and her efficiently run school had much to commend it. The food was abundant and good, the lessons were arranged so as not to overtask any pupil, and there was time set aside for healthy recreation. Unfortunately, once the initial excitement wore off, neither Charlotte nor Emily were happy. They made the mistake of refusing to disguise their strong Protestant views and this led them to becoming as isolated as if they had been marooned on a desert island. In response they judged their fellow pupils to be unfriendly and selfish. Charlotte also complained to me that the girls were academically weak and lacking in self-control, and that her teachers were dull and unworthy. The one exception was Madame Héger's husband who taught rhetoric at the school and who had been a former professor at the Athenaeum.

Monsieur Constantin Georges Romain Héger was five years younger than his wife and just seven years older than Charlotte, and very much a man in the prime of life. From what I have been able to gather, his velvet black hair, piercing violet-blue eyes, Roman nose and delightful smile combined to make him very striking, though Charlotte, in her usual acerbic manner, initially poked fun at his appearance, saying he was a little black ugly being who totally lacked any social graces. She said his dogmatic Catholicism made him so very choleric and irritable that he reminded her of an autocratically insane tomcat. However, her dislike of his manner soon changed to admiration because his intellect shone in comparison to any previous man she had met. Then she viewed him through new eyes and realized that he had physical presence too.

Under his skilful tutelage both sisters made prodigious progress and I suspect much of their later skill as novelists arose from his teaching. Charlotte jokingly referred to herself as a cow that was being permitted to munch fresh grass again after months of eating only dry hay. It was not long before Professor Héger began offering Charlotte private lessons, though this generated spiteful rumours among her fellow pupils about their relationship. They saw that Charlotte, although far from beautiful, possessed a youthful attractiveness that the prematurely aged Madame Héger lacked and a mind that was infinitely more beguiling to a man of her husband's intellect. It did not go unnoticed that Charlotte began changing how she dressed, wearing more fashionable garments that she knew the professor would like. Understandably Madame Héger was not entirely happy about what was happening but she acceded to her husband's request that Charlotte and Emily should stay on and become assistant teachers at the school once their six months as pupils were over. I think this was because she was essentially a kind-hearted woman, but the decision proved very unwise.

Charlotte's correspondence with me left me in no doubt that she was ecstatic about staying on at the school. Nothing else mattered. She ignored Emily's heartfelt desire to return home and she appeared entirely unconcerned about what was happening to Anne and Branwell. So preoccupied was she with the professor that she was remarkably unaffected by the unexpected death of Martha Taylor, the sister of our friend Mary, when on a visit to see her, or by the news of William Weightman's untimely demise. I was taken aback by how very resentful she was when she heard the news of her Aunt Elizabeth's death in November 1842. Annoyance at having to return home outweighed any grief. Having paid their last respects, Charlotte wanted to immediately return to the pensionnat, but Emily made it clear she had had enough of Brussels.

Charlotte insisted she should return alone in January 1843, even though Branwell pleaded with her to stay. He was in a terrible emotional state. During her absence, friends of the family had secured his promotion to the post of stationmaster at Luddenden Foot, not far from Halifax, but he had been dismissed for a serious discrepancy in his station's accounts. I think incompetence rather than theft lay behind the loss, but that did not alter the extent of his public humiliation. Charlotte harshly rejected his pleas for her support, saying she had to perfect her French and further study German.

What Charlotte wanted, of course, was to get back to her professor. She instructed Emily to look after their father, whose eyesight was failing badly, and directed Anne to take responsibility for Branwell. Since the autumn of 1840 Anne had been working as a governess to the daughters of the Rev. Edmund Robinson, a country landowner at Thorp Green Hall, a fine mansion set in acres of beautiful parkland about six miles south-east of Boroughbridge and about twelve miles from York. It was not an easy post because his daughters were very demanding. Her painful experiences were to provide rich material for when she later wrote her novel *Agnes Grey*. It says much for Anne's capacity and good character in dealing with her awkward wards that her employer was prepared to take her brother on trust to educate his only son.

In March 1843 Charlotte wrote to me from Brussels, saying how much she missed having Emily with her because she was no longer able to intrude so often on the Hégers' private life. Only much later did she confess to me why she had become no longer welcome in their home. Madame Héger had come across Charlotte and her husband locked in an embrace within a sequestered garden bower. Outraged by what she had seen, Madame Héger had understandably commanded her husband to abandon seeing Charlotte or face a public denunciation of his infidelity. I know this revelation of Charlotte's wicked behaviour will upset and offend many and deeply lower her standing, but perhaps it is time that the world appreciates that it was her uncontrollable passion that subsequently fed into her writing and gave it its special magic. Without her all-consuming love for the professor, I think there would have been no portrayal of the intimate moods of young women for men like Rochester in *Jane Eyre* or Paul Emanuel in *Villette*. Her novels depict that a woman's strongest desire is to find a man whom she can call 'Master' and this stems entirely from her own response to Professor Héger.

Charlotte defended her actions to me by saying that she had no choice in the matter once her heart took over. I can do no better than to provide you with the following extract from one of her letters to me:

> At first I held him harsh and strange and his manner displeased me, but gradually I preferred him before all humanity. I saw his worth and goodness of heart. I was penetrated with his influence and I lived by his affection. He in turn ceased to see me just as a pupil. He put aside his faith and his marriage and he incited me to love him. He spurred me on by gesture, smile and half-word until he had gathered me near his heart. Before I knew what was happening, one day he held both my hands, then took me into his arms, and looked into my eyes with such a piercing love that I could not resist. He told me to take his love in the hope that one day I could share his life. How could I turn my back on such a hope? It is an imbecility, which I reject with contempt, for women like myself, who have neither fortune nor beauty, to make marriage the principal object of their wishes.

I was not prepared to condone her actions and reminded her that she had once written to me that what the French called *une grande passion* was just *une grande folie*. However, I let our friendship overcome my moral outrage.

Madame Héger did not insist on Charlotte's immediate departure because she understood that this might cause local gossip, which could damage the school's reputation. Instead she monitored her every move. Charlotte wrote to me how she never knew when the professor's wife might be observing her because of her silent shoes. By September such tactics had reduced Charlotte to a state of deep depression. In one of her letters she described to me how she so wished for death that she went on a kind of pilgrimage to a cemetery. Afterwards, she walked the narrow streets of the town until eventually she entered a Catholic church with a view to confessing her sins. She made her way into a box and knelt down. A little wooden door inside the grating opened and she saw the priest leaning his ear towards her. She told him she was a foreigner and a Protestant but he still let her make her confession. He wisely advised her to leave the pensionnat and so remove any further temptation to sinful thought. Her response was to say that it was impossible for her to leave the man she adored in the knowledge she would never see him again.

By letter I did all I could to persuade Charlotte to return to England. Our friend Mary Taylor added her weight to my arguments. Eventually we were successful and in October Charlotte told Madame Héger it was her intention to resign her teaching post and leave Brussels. This news was happily received. However, Professor Héger then intervened. He sent for Charlotte and, despite all the promises he had made to his wife, begged her to stay. Charlotte could not resist and acceded to his wish. Not surprisingly, a furious Madame Héger soon had this decision reversed. She gave out the news that a dire decline in Mr Brontë's eyesight was forcing Charlotte to have to return home at Christmas.

By this time financial pressures had led my widowed mother to move out of the Rydings to a smaller house in Birstall called Brookroyd and it was to this new home that I invited Charlotte in the March of 1844. On that occasion we talked much of her final hours at the pensionnat. So raw was her emotional state that I can still recall our conversation almost verbatim.

'As you know, Nell,' commenced Charlotte, 'it was expected that I should leave once I had bidden farewell to my pupils at the end of term. However, I tried to postpone my departure for as long as possible because I still clung to the faint chance that I might yet persuade Constantin to leave his wife. Each night I slept alone in a great empty dormitory surrounded by dark shadows and hoped he would come to see me. But he never did, and I do not know whether that stemmed from his own choice or whether his wife prevented him. Eventually the day came when Madame Héger would let me delay matters no longer and I had to leave. All in the household rose at the usual hour; all breakfasted as usual; all betook themselves to their normal routines, as if oblivious of my imminent departure. No one appeared to have a wish or a word or a prayer for me. My beloved was scarce a stone throw's away from me in another room yet I could not go to him. I wanted to see him, to remind him of what we had shared, to recall our former intimacies, but I could not. Indeed, had he walked past me, I would have had to suffer him to go by because Madame would else have intervened. Morning passed and afternoon came and I thought I would have to leave without seeing him. I thought all was over and I felt quite sick. Then a child brought me a note from him.'

'And what did it say?' I said, curiosity overcoming my embarrassment at the nature of what she was confiding.

'It said that he wanted to see me before I left and that he would come to the schoolroom at four o'clock. He asked me to be ready to speak with him at length, even though he knew our time together appeared to be over. You can imagine the turmoil this generated in my mind. I dared hope that I might yet acquire future bliss, and yet I also feared that his wife would somehow prevent him coming. And sadly my fear proved grounded in reality. When the appointed time arrived, there was no sign of him. At that moment all my life's hopes were torn out of my heart by the roots.'

Charlotte broke into floods of tears and I did my best to comfort her. Once her sobbing had eased, she continued her account, saying, 'A little before five Madame Héger summoned me to her room and, once we were together, she made sure we could not be overheard by closing not only the doors of her chamber but also drawing the shutters over the window. "He thinks you have already gone," she told me. "Gone?" I said. "How could he think I would leave without speaking to him, without saying goodbye?" "Because I told him that was the case, Miss Brontë." "Please let me see him before I go," I begged. "Is not my departure enough of a victory? Let me see him lest my heart break! I have accepted that you are his wife and that I must leave. All I want now is a cordial word from his lips, a gentle look from his eyes. That would comfort me in my future loneliness. The interview can be as short as you dictate."'

'But Charlotte, how could you expect a wife to heed such a request?'

'Because my love overrode all logic. Madame Héger shouted at me, "Foolish woman! How dare you ask for anything from my husband! Do you think I as his wife will permit that to happen? You are a foolish and wicked young woman and you should be deeply ashamed of your behaviour here. He is not only a married man, but also a father. Would you seek to take my husband from me and deprive our three children of a father in order to satisfy your wanton passion? Do you have no shame?" I had the courage to reply, "I am not ashamed of what has passed between us. I know what love is and believe that, if men and women are ashamed of the resulting passion, then there is nothing left in life that is right, noble, faithful, truthful or unselfish." To this she responded by saying, "There is nothing noble or truthful in your desire for a squalid little affair, Miss Brontë. I see nothing right in the way you have tried to selfishly turn my husband's affections from a faithful wife." Then she slapped me across the face in her fury and I saw beneath her mask she was quite heartless. Her blue eyes, usually so serene, flashed with anger.'

I could not help but side with Madame Héger's view of the unworthiness of Charlotte's behaviour, but to my shame I did not voice that. Instead I let Charlotte continue with her unedifying confession. She shook her head as if still recoiling from the blow and said defiantly, 'I retaliated by shouting back at her, "Let me alone! Keep your hand off me because in your touch there is a poisonous chill that paralyzes the heart and chills the blood." She snapped back at me, "It is your touch that has poisoned the happiness of this house. Let me make it quite clear. You will leave here without ever seeing my husband again. I shall watch his every movement and my spies will keep you under equal observation. Your pursuit of my husband is over. Now get out of my presence and as soon as possible get out of my house." I did as I was told, Nell, but I left behind my heart.'

Charlotte recommenced crying and I did all I could to comfort her, not only that day but throughout her visit. This seemed to make a difference, but when she travelled back to Haworth she soon returned to her depressed state. I visited her in June and again tried to raise her spirits. Emily also did what she could to comfort her sister, saying that they should revive the scheme of setting up a school in Haworth. She volunteered to run it if Charlotte undertook the teaching. I also undertook to promote the new venture among my circle of friends as best I could. For a time Charlotte spent hours planning its curriculum and designing advertisement cards that could be circulated by me. Sadly, these endeavours proved pointless for no parents responded to the publicity and eventually Charlotte wrote to me in October to desist my efforts. She said that no parents of any sense would ever see Haworth as a desirable location for their child's education.

I was aware that initially there had been some correspondence between Professor Héger and Charlotte, but that he had soon stopped writing. Charlotte drew comfort from his last letter for six months and then became desperate for him to write again. I told Charlotte she must prepare for the fact that not only might he never write again, but also that his wife might ensure that he never received any letter she chose to write to him. Charlotte wept, saying her life would be pointless if that happened. I know not whether my surmise was correct or whether the professor had put aside his feelings for Charlotte but she never heard from him again. Charlotte expressed her continuing love by having the few books he had given her specially rebound. At intervals she sent letters, including on one occasion arranging for Mary Taylor to personally hand him one because she was passing through Brussels.

By the spring of 1845 I was far less sympathetic to her continued grief. Her affair had made me fully realize for the first time just how much Charlotte was always driven by what suited her own interests. She had treated both her family and his family very badly in her determination to have the man she wanted. I even began to be suspicious that part of Charlotte's continued anguish did not stem from her continued passion for the professor but rather from her anger at having been out-manipulated and defeated by Madame Héger. I was not surprised a few years later to see her wreak her revenge on this poor woman by portraying her in *Villette* as the cruel, crafty and callous Madame Beck. I therefore determined to make one final attempt to stop Charlotte writing to Brussels. In the summer I invited her to help make alterations to my brother's vicarage in preparation for his forthcoming marriage. He had newly become a curate in Hathersage, a small village in Derbyshire. Charlotte joined me there in July and her three-week stay helped revive her spirits sufficiently for me to achieve success. I like to think that the reason she later took the name *Eyre* from one of the brasses in my brother's church for her novel *Jane Eyre* was to mark the importance of that stay and her decision to cease writing to her lost love.

Charlotte's use of me as a confidante over her unrequited passion undoubtedly drew us closer together, despite my reservations about her behaviour. This was because she now recognized that she needed me and over the next couple of years she did all she could to present herself to me in a more favourable light. She sent letter after letter stressing that her time was now entirely given over to serving the needs of her increasingly frail father and an increasingly dissolute brother. When Charlotte had returned to Haworth from Hathersage, she had found to her surprise that Branwell and Anne were back at home. This was because Branwell had been summarily dismissed for having had an affair with his employer's wife and Anne had felt no option but to resign her post in the circumstances. My feelings of sympathy for Charlotte were rekindled as she vividly portrayed the daily horrors of coping with Branwell's emotionally volatile state. She said that her life had become a living hell, not least because she had no time to develop her own gifts.

In fact the role of being a loving daughter and sister was not enough for her, even though she was pretending that was the case. There is a passage in her novel *Shirley* where the heroine says:

What am I to do to fill the interval of time which spreads before me and the grave? … I shall never marry … Other people solve it for them by saying: 'Your place is to do good to others, to be helpful whenever help is wanted' … Is this enough? Is it to live?

In secret Charlotte made writing her purpose for living. I am not saying that she did not help her father and brother but they were definitely not the priority, and, with typical selfishness, she demanded that her sisters should follow suit. It was agreed that no one would be told of this – not their brother or their father or me.

Charlotte used money the family could ill afford to secretly have a book of the sisters' poetry published in May 1846 under the pseudonyms of Currer, Ellis and Acton Bell. The name 'Bell' came from their father's new curate, the Reverend Arthur Bell Nicholls. Charlotte and Emily took the names 'Currer' and 'Ellis' from those of a local philanthropist and a well-known mill owner, while Anne used a name familiar to her from her time at Thorp Green Hall to become 'Acton'. The poetry book did not sell but this did not deter Charlotte. She persuaded Emily and Anne to join her in producing a trilogy of novels. Charlotte based her first attempt at a novel on her time in Brussels, calling it *The Professor*. When this proved unattractive to any publisher, she wrote the far more impressive *Jane Eyre*, which also drew from her affair with Héger. Charlotte bullied Anne into writing a new novel called *Agnes Grey* based on the latter's experience of being a governess, and knowing Emily's love for the moors, Charlotte suggested to her the idea for the story which became *Wuthering Heights*. Messrs Smith and Elder agreed to publish *Jane Eyre* in October 1847. My first intimation of what Charlotte had been doing was when she brought the proofs of that book to Brookroyd in the autumn.

I was upset that Charlotte had not told me earlier, but accepted her excuse – that she was desperate to hide any success from Branwell, who had totally gone to pieces. I promised not to let anyone know that Charlotte was the book's author and to hide from Emily and Anne that Charlotte had confided their secret to me. This was not an easy promise to fulfil because *Jane Eyre* proved an instant success with the public and the firm of T.C. Newby therefore published *Wuthering Heights* and *Agnes Grey* in the December, giving out that Ellis and Acton Bell were just alternative names for Currer Bell. Rumours soon began to circulate that Currer Bell was actually Charlotte – this was not surprising in view of the correspondence between her and the publishers that was passing through the local post office. When I warned Charlotte that her secret was getting out, she was not amused and demanded that I help deny her involvement. This was what she wrote to me on 3 May:

> I have given no one a right either to affirm, or hint, in the most distant manner, that I am 'publishing' – humbug! Whoever has said it – if anyone has, which I doubt – is no friend of mine. Though twenty books were ascribed to me, I should own none. I scout the idea entirely. Whoever after I have distinctly rejected the charge urges it upon me, will do an unkind and an ill-bred thing. The most profound obscurity is infinitely preferable to vulgar notoriety; and that notoriety I neither seek nor will have. If then any … should ask you what novel Miss Brontë has been 'publish-ing' – you can just say, with distinct firmness of which you are the

perfect mistress, when you choose, that you are authorized by Miss Brontë to say that she repels and disowns every accusation of the kind. You may add, if you please, that if anyone has her confidence, you believe you have, and she has made no drivelling confession to you on the subject.

I did as I was told, but the publication of Anne's second novel, *The Tenant of Wildfell Hall*, which appeared in July 1848, renewed the speculation.

Then a series of disasters struck. In the autumn I received a letter from Charlotte informing me that Branwell had died on 24 September. She had long been exasperated by the dissolute lifestyle that he had adopted, but that did not prevent her now mourning his loss. Unfortunately Emily caught a chill at his funeral and this led to what the doctor called 'galloping consumption'. To everyone's surprise it only took a couple of months to kill her. She died on 19 December, leaving Anne in particular inconsolable at her loss. When I heard that Anne had also been taken seriously ill, I travelled to Haworth to offer Charlotte my consolation and support. Little did I realize that my visit would uncover divisions within the Brontë family of which I had been totally unaware.

3

Suspicious Deaths

When I arrived at the parsonage in January 1849, Anne was far sicker than I had expected. Her father was insisting that she undergo a medical examination and a highly regarded lung specialist called Dr Teale came from Leeds whilst I was there. After he had examined Anne, he went to report his findings to her father, leaving her with Charlotte and me. As we waited to share in the outcome, Anne insisted on me helping her walk round the room. She appeared in capital spirits for an invalid, but that was Anne's way. She always made light of her sufferings. The doctor emerged but said nothing and made his departure. Then Mr Brontë made his appearance. He sat himself down on a couch and beckoned Anne to join him. 'My dear little Anne,' he began and then broke down. He did not have to say any more. We all immediately knew. The doctor had told him that Anne was dying and that there was nothing that could be done for her. The detail came later. She had consumption in both her lungs and they were deeply affected beyond any hope of remedy.

Anne, in typical fashion, appeared to take the news with great fortitude. It was not a question of us comforting her but of her consoling us. She kept her real feelings to herself, producing over the next month a long poem that none of us saw until after her death. In it alone she poured out her heart about the dreadful darkness that had closed in on her bewildered mind and prayed for resignation to her fate. I did not feel that my presence was helping the family come to terms with their grief and so I did not prolong my stay. However, before I left, I visited Anne in her room and we spoke alone. I had always found Anne reticent in speaking about herself, but when our conversation naturally turned onto the subject of Emily's recent death, she spoke far more openly than was her custom.

'Am I being selfish, Miss Nussey, to mourn my sister's loss when she is free from all suffering?'

'No, Anne, it is only natural,' I replied. 'We all miss her and you have more cause than any of us to grieve because she was always your constant companion.'

'Yes, she was. Emily wiped away my tears, held my hand whenever I was afraid, and made me laugh. She brought daily magic into my life so that I could see that which would otherwise have been hidden. I can recall as if it was yesterday how the sight of the fresh green grass of early spring would entrance her. She would sit on a dense clump of bilberries or walk along flower carpeted paths, breathing in the sweet scent of blue-bells and harebells, violets and primroses, or whatever else was in bloom. I can still see her enraptured by the call of plover or peewit or the wild dance of a spring-maddened hare, and hear her voice enabling me to share in her pleasure at the blue tints and the pale mists of the shadowy horizon or conveying her imaginings about the higher hills, wild, majestic and bleak, beyond the moor.'

I smiled at her reminiscences and she continued.

'Only when the weather was too wet or extreme did we play in the nursery with our toys. On those days, Miss Nussey, we dashed ourselves against the unseen walls that imprisoned us, like butterflies trapped in a jar, making no noise of protest, awaiting our precious release to the fields again. Part of my happiness amid the moors was that Emily and I could be whatever we chose to be – fugitive lovers, dethroned monarchs, wandering outlaws, intrepid explorers. Branwell and Charlotte used to encourage us to use our imagination to the full, populating the moor's emptiness with genii and giants and a host of mythical creatures. To me it seems only yesterday that Emily was joyously screaming and shouting as she pretended to be Charles II so she could scramble through our father's window to hide in the branches of the cherry tree. I cannot believe that she is dead. I prefer to remember her as she was then, all curls and smiles and constant motion, tall and gangly, limbs not yet fettered by the passing years.

'That is why, Miss Nussey, the skeleton form we buried in the cold earth may be the world's Emily, but it is not mine. The Emily that I knew and loved was never mere blood and bone but an airborne spirit that floated freely between the earth and the heavens, her vital imagination all awhirl and awash with wild fancies and fresh ideas, her fertile brain full of wondrous tales about uncharted oceans, towering cities, strange creatures, and heroic deeds, stories of imaginary lands that made Scherazade's tales seem shameful dross. I know in my heart that death cannot embrace Emily as she embraced life.'

'Cannot I persuade you to start calling me Ellen?' I interjected.

'I think Charlotte would disapprove. You are her friend and she would not wish to think I was stealing your affection away from her.'

'I think you are wrong. All that dominates Charlotte's thinking at present is helping you come to terms with Emily's sad loss.'

'Yes, Miss Nussey, I hear her invoke God's assistance that Father and I might find some comfort through her presence and support, but I do not find it helpful that she sees Emily's death as just a welcome relief from suffering. She talks only of how we must recognize that Emily's fever is quieted, her restlessness soothed, her hollow cough hushed forever. I watch her write letters to you and others expressing her sorrow at the loss of so dear a sister torn from us in the fullness of our love, a sister rooted up in the prime of her life and in the full promise of her powers. Yet I somehow feel the letters are not genuine and her grief no more than a façade.'

I was truly shocked by her words and protested that Anne should not speak so about Charlotte, but the normally reticent Anne would not be quietened.

'Miss Nussey, before I face my own death I wish to confide certain fears that I have. You see, I think it possible that my sister's death may not have been a natural one. I still cannot understand the speed with which Emily was struck down. She died after an illness that lasted only three weeks. All she had prior to that was a cold that she struggled to shake off. On the morning of 26 November – a day forever graven on my heart – she could not rise from her bed without doubling up because of a severe pain in her stomach. She was violently sick, not once but repeatedly, and, from then on, she could keep nothing down and suffered from chronic diarrhoea. I have never seen flesh drop off a person as rapidly as it did from Emily over the succeeding days till her death on 19 December.'

'But surely Emily was very ill long before those final three weeks? I received a letter from Charlotte just after Branwell's funeral and it spoke of how Emily had caught a terrible chill and was developing an obstinate cough. In subsequent letters she continued to voice her concern to me about Emily's failing health.'

'And you believe that?' she asked incredulously.

'I have no reason to disbelieve it,' I replied.

'Emily lived here in Haworth almost all her life! She walked the moors from childhood and frequently faced far worse than the damp breeze that blew on the day of my brother's funeral. You know as well as I do how much Emily loved the wildest of weathers. She relished the sting of lashing rain and those gales that literally take away one's breath. If storm and tempest could not harm my sister, how did that tame funereal wind? And, if she was so obviously ill, why did she not wish to see a doctor? And why did I do nothing?'

'Charlotte says that death came as an unrecognized stranger when step by step it sucked away Emily's life-force because you both were used to such good health.'

'What nonsense!' exclaimed Anne, her eyes flashing with indignation. 'We have been surrounded by disease and death all our lives! You only have to look out of the parsonage window and you can see almost daily some fresh display of earth in the graveyard, evidence that yet another inhabitant has joined that grim city of dead souls! Has she forgotten how we used to frighten each other as children with tales of the dying and the dead among its table-tombs and listing headstones? The truth is that, because of the putrid water supply and the slum housing, Haworth has a death rate that few can match. Half the children here do not even survive childhood. And why should either Emily or I think ourselves immune from danger when as young children we were left motherless, when we had to kiss the mouths of two of our sisters in their coffins, when our aunt screamed in agony for day after day before her spirit finally succumbed, when our father is a semi-blind shadow of the man that he once was, and when Branwell, dear, dear Branwell withered and died before our eyes?'

'So how do you explain why Emily would seek no medical attention until it was too late? Charlotte has told me how she pleaded in vain with her to see a doctor.'

'I know Charlotte has made out to you and others that Emily would take no medical treatment and that she had to stand by and witness her destroy herself. But what sister would accept such a state of affairs? Only the weakest and most ineffective – and yet Charlotte is the most determined of us all. You know as well as I that Charlotte has always achieved whatever task she has set for herself and that she has always manipulated all of us to do what she wants. We have been mere pawns in her hands. And yet Charlotte says to you that she could not make a very sick Emily go to a doctor for proper medical treatment! And you believe that!'

'How can I disbelieve my friend on such a matter?'

'The truth is, Miss Nussey, that whatever Charlotte might have been saying to you, I cannot recall her ever broaching that Emily should seek proper medical advice until the very end of November – and by that time she was seriously ill. All I remember prior to November is Charlotte one day saying that, because she was concerned about Emily's cold, she had written to a doctor called Epps and he had sent her some advice and medicine. Emily and I laughed at such pointless action on her part and at the doctor's naivety that he would prescribe anything without first seeing the patient. Needless to say, Emily did not take the potion that had been sent. I tell you Emily's death was not connected with the cold that she acquired after Branwell's funeral, even if Charlotte wants everyone to believe that.'

'It is in the nature of consumption that it can ebb and flow, Anne. You of all people have cause to understand that.'

'I do not recognize in my illness the symptoms that affected Emily. Even in those final three weeks she and I thought her illness would prove temporary. Indeed she did begin to show signs of recovery until the night of 18 December. Then she unexpectedly collapsed while going outside to feed Keeper, her beloved dog. That night her illness returned with renewed intensity and by the next morning her breathing was terribly laboured and she had not the strength to even comb her hair. She was so weak that, when she accidentally let the comb fall in the fire, she was unable to bend and retrieve it. With the same indomitable courage that she had always shown in life, she eventually got herself dressed – not without some assistance from me – and came downstairs. I stayed with her while she attempted to undertake some sewing, but Charlotte, despite Emily's condition, excused herself, saying she must write to you and others. It was I who said at midday that we should send for the doctor, not Charlotte. Does that not seem strange to you?'

'Not if her previous attempts to summon medical attention had been ignored.'

'But this was now an emergency. Poor Keeper refused to leave Emily's side, even when Dr Wheelhouse arrived. It was as if the poor creature already knew the outcome. The doctor ordered us to take Emily immediately upstairs but within an hour she was dead. Because of the intense suffering that she endured, there was no time even to exchange the briefest of words.'

Tears trickled down Anne's face as she relived that moment and I moved to comfort her. All the heartache in her soul sobbed, but gradually she composed herself and resumed her story.

'I can scarce recall anything about the next few days because I was so traumatized by what had happened. Charlotte took command and dealt with all the formalities – the obituary notices, the funeral cards and the arrangements for the burial service. I remember little of Emily's burial other than that Keeper accompanied us in the funeral procession and loyally followed his beloved mistress's coffin to the vault where she was buried. By the time I came back to my senses and began asking questions about what possible illness could have killed Emily so speedily, it was all decided. 'Galloping consumption' was the verdict. One that vindicated what Charlotte had been saying to people for weeks. However, I suspect that Charlotte stood over the doctor when he wrote the death certificate. I seek another cause for Emily's rapid demise.'

The strength of Anne's feeling shook me but I was reluctant to give any credence to her account of events. I thought her own illness had affected both her memory and her judgement. I therefore tried to present Anne with an alternative reason for the speed of Emily's decline and death. 'You know,' I said, 'that Emily was deeply depressed following Branwell's death and I am not surprised that she chose not to linger over passing from this world to the next.'

'My brother's death deeply depressed and demoralized us all but neither Charlotte nor I sought to replicate his tragedy by seeking self-destruction. Why should Emily? We still had each other and she was but thirty. She knew that she had much more that she could achieve in life. Tell me, Miss Nussey, do any of us choose the moment of our passing or does not that rest either with Almighty God or in the actions of a fellow human being – in this case, a sister!'

'Surely you are not implying that Charlotte had something to do with Emily's death?'

'I pray that she did not but I live with the fear that she might. You see, many years ago, I had good reason to believe that, when we were but young children, Charlotte may have poisoned our older sisters, Maria and Elizabeth. Because I was ill at the time, I put aside such thoughts as the product of my fevered brain, but now I am less certain. Was Emily, like Maria and Elizabeth all those years ago, poisoned? Did Charlotte deliberately encourage you and others to believe that she became ill immediately after Branwell's funeral simply in order to disguise her murder?'

'I am sure your grief at Emily's death is distorting your perspective, Anne. You are letting your imagination run away with you.'

'Then read these papers and judge for yourself about what happened to Maria and Elizabeth,' replied Anne. She handed across some pages that contained extracts clearly torn from her journal. 'I wrote this at the time when I was receiving my education from Charlotte,' she said. 'As you know, our father insisted she should become a teacher at her old school, Roe Head, in order that first Emily and then I should have a free education there. When Charlotte first returned there in 1835, it was Emily who accompanied her. However, it was not long before Emily became so dangerously ill that it was feared she might die unless she returned home. I therefore took her place in the October of that year. Read these pages and you will see how badly Charlotte treated me. If, having read them, you can tell me that my concerns are unfounded and that I wrongly malign Charlotte, I will be eternally grateful because at present living in this house with her is a constant torment to me. I only stay because I have nowhere else to go and because I fear to leave Father in her sole care.'

I took the papers and read them once I had returned to my home. They helped me understand Charlotte's frame of mind when she had written that letter of self-condemnation in December 1836. I provide what Anne wrote in its entirety because of the insight it gives into her view of Charlotte's character and the evidence it provided on her startling allegations:

December 1837, Roe Head

I have been in this place now for two years. When I first arrived it looked pretty enough and I had no expectation that this school would become my prison, no realization that in travelling the sixteen miles from Haworth I had transported myself from paradise to hell. Why should I? I knew from Emily that the school regime was not overly strict and when Miss Wooler greeted me I was left in no doubt of her kindness or her good intentions about my future education. I never thought that Charlotte would make my life here unendurable.

As I write this, I know I owe much, perhaps indeed my life, to the Reverend James La Trobe. A few days ago Miss Wooler sent for him to come from nearby Mirfield to attend me, fearing my life hung on a very slender thread following a severe attack of gastric flu. He leads a community of Moravians there, about a hundred in number. She was right in thinking that his kind nature might be exactly what my troubled spirit most required because his Christianity focuses more on pardon and peace than any sermons I have ever heard my father preach. His words about God's love for sinners brought me much comfort at a time when I was being encouraged by Charlotte to think that my sickness was a punishment sent by God and that I was destined for eternal damnation. He has assured me that I should not accept Charlotte's image of an unrelenting and vengeful God, who has cruelly predetermined our fate, but believe instead in a God of mercy, a God who offers forgiveness and love to all who repent – and I am repentant. It comforts me to know that Mr La Trobe believes that, if I were to die, it would be as a child who has been ransomed and redeemed.

It shocks me to write it down, but Mr La Trobe instructed Miss Wooler that she should prevent Charlotte from attending my bedside. He said her presence was detrimental to my recovery. And he is right. The truth is that all Charlotte's former love for me has turned to hate. She feels my education is the cause of her entombment here. Almost daily since we came here I have felt her resentment increase. I have lost count of how often she has said that all her hopes and ambitions have been reduced to ashes, consumed by the need to educate me. She detests having to earn her living in the very place where she was once a pupil herself. Had my own education not depended on her return here, she feels she might have persuaded our father to let her seek another and less onerous post. Sadly, the other girls have watched the mounting disfavour in which I am held and have been quick to recognize that the one way of winning Charlotte's favour is to ignore me. That has also contributed to my unhappiness.

I can only write this because I have been much better since Mr La Trobe's advice took effect and Charlotte has been kept away from me. I have become stronger not just spiritually but also, strangely to say, physically. I am no longer thought likely to die and my convalescence has given me much time to reflect on my deep unhappiness here. Looking back, I can only describe the whole of my time here as an ever-increasing nightmare. No wonder I hark back to my former freedom on the moors at Haworth with such heartfelt longing. What did it matter to me and Emily then that our home contained no curtains or carpets or ornaments or that our garden was adorned only with a few weeds and stunted fruit trees? The never-ceasing roar of the wild wind on the moor used to make our hearts beat exultingly and our souls rejoice! We had nature's beauty to please the eye and excite the senses with an ever-changing kaleidoscope of seasonal colour – the smoke-blue harebells, the bright yellow buttercups, the rich red poppies, the purple and cream clover, the plum of heather. And on quiet sunny days, when the sky was at its brightest blue and the light clouds drifted by in ever-rolling procession, we would listen with joy to the call of linnet or lark or catch the matchless melody of the nightingale as it rose above the far-away, gentle bleating of the lambs or the occasional barking of a distant sheepdog.

Sadly I have no time for such imaginings now. Reality holds sway and crushes my spirit. What I now appreciate is that our love for the moor grew in part because none of us had strong reason to love our father. He gave us little of his time beyond what duty demanded. Even now, on our infrequent visits home, he chooses not to eat with us except for the breakfast that follows our daily family prayers. I wish he loved us more because then he would not demand that Charlotte and I should stay here, but his domain was ever his study and never the nursery. I am old enough now to realize that is why he willingly handed over our early upbringing to our Aunt Elizabeth. Charlotte says she has acted only from a sense of duty, but I think she is wrong. Aunt loves us all more than Father, even if she does sometimes hark on too much about hell and damnation.

In my innocence when I first came here I tried to please by working hard, but the award of a prize for good conduct at the end of my first term served only to annoy Charlotte, who felt it would only justify our staying at the school. It also upset poor Emily when I showed it to her at Christmas. She felt that I was gaining an education beyond hers. It was with a heavy heart that I returned here in January of last year and with good cause. Far from showing me any sisterly favours, Charlotte avoided my presence as much as she dared and she subjected me to a coldness that far exceeded her indifferent manner to the other girls. If ever she spoke to me, it was merely to say how much she felt she was being exploited as payment for my education. Charlotte has always been oblivious of anyone's state of mind but her own, and she gave no thought to my feelings. I think that I survived only by counting the days till my next holiday home in July.

Last autumn was even more unbearable. On one occasion I tried to explain to Charlotte how much I required some evidence of her love if I was to survive at the school. She replied by saying that I knew nothing of the evil thoughts with which she continually battled and that, if I knew what was really in her heart, I would despise her and not wish for her company. She told me how she mourned being tied to a school desk when outside her window the year was revolving in its richest glow. Unfortunately, before I could sympathize, her tongue became more waspish. She said that she was wasting her time at the school because we were all just fat-headed oafs. It was only our asinine stupidity that prevented us seeing how much she loathed us. Then she ordered me out of her presence, saying I was like a vampire bat, sucking dry her very life-blood.

I will not dwell on my renewed sufferings when we returned to school this spring but what undoubtedly made matters worse was a letter which Charlotte received in March. Branwell had encouraged her to send some of her verse to Robert Southey, the Poet Laureate, with a request that he judge its worth. Southey's response was devastating. He said that writing poetry was acceptable as a hobby for a woman but no more and that while her writing showed she had the capacity to write verse it was not of a quality to win her any distinction. He told her that she should abandon any hope of becoming famous lest it led to having what he called 'a distempered frame of mind'. Charlotte was so upset by his letter that for once she sought my presence, seeking my consolation for his cruel reply. I comforted her as best I could, but I could not deter her from immediately penning a highly emotional reply, in which she vowed never to be ambitious again to see her name in print and to undertake only the role expected of women. I felt the full consequences of that vow because it seemed to kindle all her latent Calvinism. One evening she told me that she was so destined for damnation that it mattered not what future crimes she committed.

I increasingly sought solace in solitary occupations. I spent the time when I was not studying either in sketching and painting or in playing the piano. Once Miss Wooler heard me singing a song and, though my voice is weak, she praised me, saying I must be happy to sing so. She had no idea how wrong she was. Unfortunately I saw little of Miss Wooler because she increasingly left Charlotte to run the school entirely. I missed her teaching and her knack of keeping in check the silly nonsenses to which young girls are prone. This is not a gift that Charlotte possesses. I now know that she was also turning down invitations for us to spend some weekends visiting family friends. I think she feared she would not be able to disguise from them her mounting hatred of me or that I might inadvertently betray her. She informed them that she could not leave her tutees because that would be a dereliction of duty yet she neglected all of us constantly, retreating into personal reveries that had nothing to do with our care. I could scare believe this was the same sister who, when she taught Emily and I at home, opened our ears to music, our eyes to art, and our minds to literature.

When we heard that my godmother, Mrs Franks, had unexpectedly died this September, it reduced Charlotte to tears because she had pinned her remaining hopes of ever escaping this place on Mrs Franks finding her an alternative position. I tried to comfort her and, in response, Charlotte begged forgiveness that she could neither draw pleasure from my company any more nor impart any pleasure to me. She described her life as a walking nightmare. It made me feel very guilty that I am the cause of such unhappiness in my sister.

When I was taken ill Charlotte rejoiced in my sickness because she saw my possible death as an escape route for her from Roe Head. She told our father that I had developed a hacking cough and laboured breath due to the damp and unhealthy air at the school. This greatly upset Miss Wooler and I am not surprised because that is not true. Is it the product of a diseased mind that I should fear Charlotte may have had a hand in my illness? I know she believes that she is one of the damned and those who are damned see no reason why not to embark on acts of wickedness. I am sure that I can recall one evening seeing Charlotte placing some powder into the hot milk that lay by my bedside. On her face was such a cruel and evil look that it was as if I could see the inner demon in her eyes. Was this just a nightmare or did it really happen? If I were to say anything to my father, he would think me mad. And yet did not Emily before me become direly ill under Charlotte's care? I can still vividly recall her shockingly white face and attenuated form when she came home. At the time her illness was attributed to excessive homesickness – that at least was Charlotte's take on events – but now I have my doubts. Did Charlotte also make her ill?

Now I am recovering I dread what will happen when Charlotte is once again permitted to see me! How can a sister have become so hard and unloving? I can only hope that I remain frail enough to warrant my father keeping me home. In the tumult of my worst imaginings I have begun to hearken back to those tragic earlier illnesses of my two oldest sisters, Maria and Elizabeth. I was but a mere child of three or four when my father determined to educate them by sending them to a school at Cowan Bridge. I know my father and one of my godmothers visited the school and found everything to their liking and I am told my sisters were happy there – though whether that is true I have no way of knowing. Our father lives in his own world and little understands our feelings. I am sure he has told people that Charlotte and I are very happy at Miss Wooler's school. What I do know is that when Charlotte was sent to join her sisters at Cowan Bridge, she hated it and shortly afterwards Maria and Elizabeth became seriously ill. Maria was brought home in the February of 1825 but developed consumption and never recovered, dying in the May. Elizabeth was brought home with Charlotte that same month and she died in the June.

It is shocking to write this – but did Charlotte have a hand in their initial illness? Though my brain tells me a young girl of eight could not possibly have the means to destroy her sisters, I recognize Charlotte's intelligence has always been beyond her years and my heart has good reason to fear the darkness that lies deep in her heart. If Maria and Elizabeth's enjoyment of the school meant she had to stay in a place she disliked, I can see Charlotte acting against them, perhaps only intending to make them ill. My father says almost thirty of the girls at the school were taken ill and died. If Charlotte were in any way responsible for what happened, she would be a mass murderer! Could it possibly be these untimely deaths that lie behind Charlotte's belief in her own ultimate damnation?

I begin to fear that Charlotte in her unhappiness is turning to laudanum to relieve her mind. Where will this all end? What am I to do? I must cease these wild conjectures before they drive me insane.

I must confess that I did not read the pages from Anne's journal with an unbiased mind. In my mind I had already concluded that Anne must have seriously underestimated the extent of her sister's illness and that her accusations were no more than a way of seeking to absolve her guilt by attributing Emily's untimely death to something that Charlotte had done. For that reason I quickly dismissed what the journal contained about possible earlier poisonings. This did not prevent me being taken aback by the extent of Charlotte's harsh treatment of Anne, but, after reflection, I attributed this to her state of depression and so forgave her. I recalled how, when Charlotte was teaching at the school, I had often invited her to visit me because Roe Head was within walking distance of my home, but she had seldom taken up the offer because she felt that she was fit company for no one. I therefore wrote to Anne and did my best to convince her that she was wrong and that it was only her illness and her grief that lay behind her painful imaginings. Had I known what I was to uncover in 1854 I would have written differently.

4

A Scarborough Farewell

A nne made no reply to my letter. My knowledge of the progress of her illness therefore became entirely dependent on Charlotte's letters. She informed me that Anne was spending her time either in bed or sitting in what had been Emily's chair. She tried to pass the time by reading but some days she was so weak that she could not focus either her eyes or her mind on the task. The only medicine she had been prescribed was cod-liver oil and carbonate of iron, but this seemed to have little effect other than to make her feel sick and unable to eat. Yet in coping with her illness, Anne was so patient and placid, so calm and serene, that she seemed to be holding the terrible disease at bay.

What surprised me was that Charlotte insisted on Anne staying in unhealthy Haworth. It seemed to me the worst possible environment for someone with consumption and I repeatedly urged that she should be taken to somewhere else where she could breathe a cleaner air. Charlotte kept replying that Anne's doctor was insistent that she should not be moved. I said the family ought to seek a second opinion and offered to take personal responsibility for Anne's welfare should she be permitted to travel. I said I was willing either to have her stay at Brookroyd or to take her to some coastal town such as Scarborough. I indicated that the only time I could not undertake to do this was during May when my mother was expecting visitors, but I thought that no problem because the weather in that month was undesirably variable to risk the venture then.

Charlotte repeated that the doctor could see only danger in moving her sister and said Anne was resigned to the fact that she had become far too emaciated and weak to travel. Imagine, therefore, my surprise when shortly afterwards I received a letter from Anne dated 5 April saying that she felt it was vital she moved to a better climate in line with medical advice. Here is part of that letter, which I have still in my possession:

[If I could go with you] I know you would be kind and helpful as anyone could possibly be, and I hope that I should not be very troublesome. It would be as a companion and not as a nurse that I should wish for your company otherwise I would not venture to ask it. The doctors say that change of air or removal to a better climate would hardly ever fail of success in consumptive cases if the remedy were taken in time, but the reason why there are so many disappointments is that it is generally deferred until it is too late. Now I would not commit this error, and, to say the truth, though I suffer much less from pain and fever than I did when you were with us, I am decidedly weaker and very much thinner. My cough still troubles me a good deal, especially in the night, and, what seems worse than all, I am subject to great shortness of breath on going up stairs or any slight exertion. Under these circumstances I think there is no time to be lost.

I have no horror of death. If I thought it inevitable, I think I could quietly resign myself to the prospect, in the hope that you, dear Miss Nussey, would give as much of your company as you possibly could to Charlotte and be a sister to her in my stead. But I wish it would please God to spare me not only for Papa's and Charlotte's sakes, but because I long to do some good for the world before I leave it. I have had many schemes in my head for future practise – humble and limited indeed – but still I should not like them to come to nothing, and myself to have lived to so little purpose. But God's will be done.

Armed with the contents of this letter, I contacted Charlotte and this time she reluctantly agreed that both she and I would take Anne to Scarborough. Anne knew exactly where she wanted to stay – in Wood's Lodgings on St Nicholas Cliff, which overlooks the South Bay. She had stayed there when acting as governess to the Robinsons and had happy memories of the place. Charlotte tried to persuade us that it might be preferable to take up residence with our former headmistress, Miss

Wooler, who owned a house in Scarborough and where we could be more private at less expense. However, Anne was adamant she wanted Wood's Lodgings and, having recently inherited some money, saw no reason to worry about the potential cost.

Despite having agreed, Charlotte found reason after reason to delay our departure, whilst saying she longed for the day when Anne would be able to have some sea air. It was Anne, frail as she was, who in the end made Charlotte concede defeat and fix a date. I agreed that I would meet up with them in Leeds and that we would then visit York before proceeding to Scarborough. This was because Anne said she had a desire to see its Minster. However, I waited for them in vain at the station in Leeds. They did not turn up. I spent a sleepless night and then headed for Haworth the next morning. Charlotte said that Anne had been too ill the previous day to travel. At one level this did not surprise me because it looked to me as though Anne was clearly dying, so skeletal was her frame. Nevertheless, she was obviously delighted to see me and said to Charlotte that my arrival now meant there could be no more delays in leaving the parsonage.

The weather was very good and so we set off that very day. I was surprised at how much Anne brightened once Haworth was no longer in sight. When we reached York we took up residence at the George Hotel. Charlotte had told me for months that Anne was barely eating anything, yet that night she had dinner with us and, though she did not consume very much, clearly enjoyed it. She reminisced about how she and Emily had visited the city in happier days. Though Anne had to rely on being transported by chair, we not only visited the beautiful York Minster but also went shopping and spent some money on bonnets. All in all, I felt that within the space of twenty-four hours Anne had staged a remarkable recovery. The next day we took the train to Scarborough and Anne spent the whole time looking out of the window, taking pleasure in the bright sunshine and pointing out interesting features in the landscape. She was overjoyed to see the flower-filled fields after the bleakness of Haworth and, of course, once we neared our destination, the sea.

Wood's Lodgings turned out to be a large house, four storey high, with facilities for fourteen sets of lodgings and with extra accommodation available in cottages in its grounds. I could see immediately why

Anne desired to stay there because all its rooms had wonderful views over the cliffs of Scarborough and the sea. We had a lovely evening and again Anne seemed to eat more than Charlotte expected. This did not prevent Charlotte trying the next day to persuade Anne that she should rest in bed. Anne refused and not only announced she wanted to go to the Bath House but insisted that she wanted to walk there and back. A compromise was reached. She was carried there and she walked back, a distance of about 500 yards. The unaccustomed exertion took its toll and she collapsed once she had reached the garden gate but, refusing our aid, she got to her feet again and entered the hotel. In the afternoon she made us agree to her having a ride across the beach in a donkey-carriage and when she saw the driver maltreat the poor creature, she not only lectured him on the importance of being kind to animals but also then insisted on driving the carriage herself.

Charlotte was furious, saying that Anne was being irresponsible, and for a time she stalked off. Anne took the opportunity of her absence to talk with me once again about matters that she said she did not want her sister to hear.

'I love this place, Miss Nussey, because it is here that I knew my happiest time.'

'I would love to hear you speak of it, Anne, but only if you wish to share the memories.'

'You know I am not one to talk about myself, but I think I would like someone to know. I cannot speak to Charlotte. She would disapprove.'

'Surely you misjudge your sister,' I replied.

Anne made no comment but her silence indicated she thought otherwise. She finally commented, 'Charlotte has always had very set ideas on what I should do.'

'Only because she loves you deeply, Anne.'

'You say that yet she has permitted the damp air of Haworth to daily advance my illness. I should have come here sooner. But none of us have ever truly been able to escape doing what Charlotte desired. I fear she only let me talk of coming here once she was sure my disease was sufficiently advanced so recovery was impossible. She was worried that others might begin to doubt her motives in keeping me at home if there was not even an attempt to let me have some clean, invigorating air. Even then she blocked the journey until you turned up at the parsonage and more or less forced her to bring me here.'

'I am sure you are wrong,' I protested. 'Charlotte has always thought only of what is best for your health.'

'So she would have you and I believe, and you know Charlotte well enough, Miss Nussey, to recognize she always thinks she knows best.'

'You make her sound unreasonably harsh.'

'You read the extracts from my journal. It is just the way Charlotte is made and I have learnt to accept that, though it has sometimes cost me dear.' She turned and looked out over the golden sands as if she wanted to burn their image permanently in her mind. 'Let us change the subject because I would not have you think that I am ungrateful for her attentions.'

'Why were you so happy here?'

'It has always been my secret but if God does call me, I think perhaps I would like someone to know there was a different Anne to the one they knew. One who loved and was loved.'

'I would be honoured to be that person, Anne, if you are willing to trust me.'

She gave no reply. Time seemed to stand still as Anne sat watching the waves fall upon the shore. I thought she had withdrawn into herself and I would hear no more, but I was wrong. With her face turned away from me, almost as if she needed to pretend she was alone, Anne suddenly but calmly started her confession, saying, 'In December 1839 I returned home to Haworth for Christmas after many unhappy months working away in my first employment as a governess at Mirfield. I was surprised to discover the extent to which my normally reticent sisters had admitted a stranger into our close family circle. This was our father's curate of six months' standing, the Rev. William Weightman. You met him, Miss Nussey.'

'I recall him well,' I said, conscious that I had never associated Anne with having any romantic attachment to him – it was only Charlotte and I who had flirted with him.

'I was sitting in my chair reading when he entered the room and I saw him for the first time,' continued Anne. 'It was love at first sight as far as I was concerned, though none knew it. If a woman is smitten by a man there are usually obvious signs – a blushing cheek, a foolish obsession with smiling, a tendency to gaze too long upon the beloved. I am more difficult to read. We exchanged no more than the usual pleasantries made when two people first meet and there was no blush on my cheek, no lustrous sparkle in my eye, no tremor in my voice, But, Miss Nussey, I can assure you my heart beat full and fast. Of course I had no hope that my feelings might be reciprocated. I looked at myself in the mirror and saw that, though there might be intellect in my forehead and expression in my eyes, there was no beauty in my features. I also feared my unamiable reserve and foolish diffidence would make me appear to be cold, dull, awkward and even ill-tempered. Imagine then my amazement when within a week I discovered that this fair angel was also a little attracted to me. Most men look only at outward form, but he was prepared to look at the person within. Does that not bear witness to the fact his fine outward appearance was matched by an inward beauty?'

'Yes, he was a fine man and had not his match among the clergy for twenty miles around.'

'I soon grew to understand, Miss Nussey, that his real worth lay not in his charm, great though that was, but in his Christian thoughtfulness and kindness. Many a parishioner benefited from his assistance, given without fuss and without publicity. He was no hell-fire preacher out to damn everyone for their unworthiness, but one who truly understood Christ's message of forgiveness and compassion for all, even the worst of sinners. He never put on that air of superiority which so disfigures many clergymen. His was a gospel in which I could rejoice because it was evident in his daily living.'

I smiled. Whilst what Anne said was true, I appreciated that a woman of her sensibility would be the first to want to present her lover as a man of worth and not just beauty. I also wondered whether Anne had been sufficiently worldly to understand that her father's curate was the sort of man who would fain persuade every woman under thirty that he is desperately in love with her! It was typical of his nature that, when he discovered that none of us girls had ever received a Valentine card, he sent one to each of us! Charlotte had said the poor man should never have become a parson because he was far too romantic.

'Much though my heart continued to jump every time we met, I knew in my mind there was no possible future for us as a couple,' continued Anne. 'Our relationship seemed destined to be pointless. I had no financial means to enable me to justify remaining at home and Charlotte was most insistent that I should work. At the end of March I left to take up a new post as governess at Thorp Green Hall. Life seemed unendurable – and then my employers brought me here and I saw the sea for the first time. And my spirit, which had been so downcast, soared as if it was back on the moors. It was as if I saw the world through the eyes of God. Each succeeding wave seemed to bring with it healing to my soul and each sea breeze carried me aloft as if I had angel wings. I enjoyed with equal rapture both the bright sunshine and the storm clouds. My lifestyle was still as before but it no longer was master of my spirit. And when we returned to the Hall I coped with the sorrows generated by its prison walls by recalling, as best I could, my time here. I suspect my faults were much as before but I had a greater wisdom and self-possession.'

We sat for a long time in companiable silence till finally I summoned up the courage to ask, 'And so what of your feelings for Mr Weightman?'

She turned to face me and said, 'I thought I had suppressed them. But then I returned home for Christmas and I knew I had not. He was still much in our house, though the relationship between him and Charlotte, once so positive, had become obviously strained to the extent that Emily sometimes acted as mediator. I think I might have confided my feelings to Emily had not she and Charlotte been so taken up with the excitement of planning their visit to Brussels. I acted as if he meant nothing to me, but he sought me out at every opportunity when I was not in the company of my sisters. To my delight I realized his interest in me had changed to love. Even when we were in church he would try to catch my eye. When Charlotte noticed this, she made a great point of telling me how fickle he was and saying that she must invite you, Miss Nussey, back to Haworth so he could fall desperately in love with you again. I made out that I was indifferent to his charms. My prayers, my tears, my wishes, my fears and my hopes were witnessed only by myself and heaven.'

'Why then did you return to Thorp Green Hall? Surely your chance of entering into a more open relationship would have been eased by the departure of your sisters for Brussels?' I asked.

'Charlotte was insistent I should return before they left. She said I was not fit enough to run the household for our father and it would be better that she found a good servant to do the work. I did as I was bid and I never saw William again. As you know, he died that autumn from having caught cholera from some of the poor he was visiting. He was only twenty-six. I had not even been told that he was ill.'

A tear ran down her cheek but she did not seek to brush it away. My heart went out to her. I do not know whether he truly loved her or whether he was indeed just flirting with her as he had flirted with us all, but I doubted not that poor Anne, whom we had all judged to be so passionless and controlled, had desperately loved him. All I could inadequately say was, 'I am sorry that none of us appreciated your true feelings, Anne. Surely there is no greater love than that a person lay down his life for others.'

'It is hard to square such an event with a God of justice and mercy, Miss Nussey, and I had no one to whom I could open my heart. Sometimes I think it was only the subsequent visits of the Robinson family to this place that kept me from breaking down. Here on the sea-kissed sands of Scarborough I could somehow once again feel close to William's free-ranging spirit. My duties were such that I could usually only come onto the sands very early in the morning, long before breakfast, but I welcomed that – nothing else stirring, no living creature visible besides myself and the soaring seagulls. It meant my footsteps were the first to press the firm, unbroken sands because the previous night's flowing tide had obliterated the deepest marks of yesterday and left it exquisitely smooth, except where the subsiding water had left behind it traces of dimpled pools and little running streams. I would take pleasure in the purity and freshness of the air and walk along the shore, forgetting all my cares, feeling as if I had wings to my feet. I felt as if I could go at least forty miles without fatigue. There was usually enough wind to keep the whole sea in extra motion and make the waves come bounding to the shore, foaming and sparkling. I cannot express how much the deep clear azure of the sky and the sea refreshed and delighted and reinvigorated me. Here I could forget my painful life.'

'I now fully understand, Anne, why you were so keen to come here.'

'And I want to die here, Miss Nussey. I think perhaps I might have drawn sufficient strength to live a little longer but today I saw the panic in Charlotte's eyes when she saw some of my vitality return. It made me realize that I cannot escape. I fear she will somehow ensure our return home so my decline can recommence. I will not let that happen. For the first and last time in my life I will deny Charlotte what she wants – I will not die at Haworth. I will die here.'

'These are false imaginings. I know Charlotte loves you.'

'I do not doubt that in her own way Charlotte has always loved us, especially Branwell, but Charlotte's love is of a strange kind that defies logic. Believe me, since I received your response to reading those extracts from my journal I have tried hard to put aside my suspicions, but they keep returning. I could possibly put aside my conjectures about the deaths of my sisters Maria and Elizabeth all those years ago if only I was not so sure that Charlotte had a hand in making first Emily and then me ill at Roe Head. More importantly, I am even more certain that Charlotte had a hand in the illness that swept Emily away, even though there is not a day that passes without signs that she grieves for her loss. I even begin to fear that she may also have had a hand in Branwell's unexpected death, much though she loved him.'

'What possibly can have led you to such a conclusion?' I said, amazed by this new accusation.

'I have asked myself time and time again why Charlotte grieves yet wants me dead. All I can surmise is that she realizes I am suspicious about Emily's death. Did she decide she had to get rid of Emily because my sister had become equally suspicious about Branwell's sudden death?'

I know not what I would have said or Anne replied because at that point Charlotte returned and we both went silent. Anne never referred to our conversation again. I still gave no credence to her wild fancies about Charlotte being a murderer but I had no doubt that Anne was correct in thinking that Charlotte's insistence on her going away to Thorp Green Hall had been a deliberate, cruel move to separate her from Mr Weightman. As I indicated earlier in this narrative, Charlotte at one time had wanted him for herself and she had been cross with me when she suspected I might have feelings for him. When I recalled all the many letters in which Charlotte talked to me over the years about 'poor Anne' and how unfortunate it was that she had to stay a governess, I saw now the hypocrisy that lay behind them.

Charlotte's mood was a very dark one as we returned to our lodgings. As soon as Anne went to rest, Charlotte turned on me and asked whether I wanted to let Anne kill herself. She said she wished she had never let her sister leave Haworth. I tried to defend myself, saying that as far as I could see Anne's health was improving now that she was away from the damp parsonage. As if to back my cause, Anne reappeared and insisted on going out again after tea. She said she wanted to walk across the Spa Bridge that spanned the valley between St Nicholas Cliff and the South Cliff. It is, of course, the bridge that appears in *Agnes Grey* as the setting for Mr Weston's proposal of marriage to Agnes. I feel I can only do justice to our subsequent walk by quoting from Anne's novel: 'I shall never forget that glorious summer evening and always remember with delight that steep hill, and the edge of the precipice where we stood watching the splendid sunset mirrored in the restless waters at our feet.'

The next day being a Sunday, Anne wanted us to go to church, but Charlotte refused to take her. She said Anne would get too emotional and it would not be good for her. After the scolding I had received the day before, I dared not take Anne's part. For most of that day Anne was confined to our lodgings. In the evening Charlotte and I walked along the beach whilst Anne was left to sit watching us from a chair. When we returned to our lodgings the day closed in with the most glorious sunset ever witnessed. The castle on the cliff stood in proud glory gilded by the rays of the declining sun. The distant ships glittered like burnished gold and the little boats, which were nearer the beach, heaved on the ebbing tide, as if inviting occupants. The view was grand beyond description. Anne was drawn in an easy chair to the window to enjoy the scene with us. Her face became illuminated almost as much as the glorious scene she gazed upon. Little was said, and it was plain to me that her thoughts were driven by the imposing view before her to the region of unfading glory.

'I would like to die here,' she whispered to me.

The next day – 28 May – Anne was very unwell. She could not walk unaided and she could not eat anything. She asked to be allowed to sit quietly by the window so she could look again at the sea. At lunchtime she asked us to call a doctor. This we did. Anne's only concern seemed to be whether Charlotte would insist on taking her back to Haworth. She was pleased when the doctor told her sister that travel was out of the question. 'There is only one journey your sister is now going to make,' he said.

Anne insisted that we should let her stay in her chair by the window. I am sure that if Charlotte had been there alone, she would have denied this request and forced her sister to go to bed, but, in my company, she acceded. The doctor returned two or three times and was amazed by Anne's tranquillity of spirit and her settled longing to be gone. Though she was just twenty-nine years old, she was serenely resigned to her life coming to an end. I have only to shut my eyes and I can hear again her weak voice whispering to me, 'I thank you for your kindness, Miss Nussey, but do not mourn for me. There is little for which to grieve. I have done nothing of much purpose with my life and those I loved most have all gone. My poor brother, my dearest sister, and the one man with whom I might have found some happiness. My greatest hope is that we will soon be reunited again. I have had enough of this life such as it is and I am content to lay down the burden.'

There was no thought of seeking assistance to prolong her life, no expression of dread. I saved my tears for later. Only Charlotte wept. Anne, despite all that she had confided to me, somehow found the strength to try and comfort her, even though there seemed to be no ounce of vitality left in her wasted frame. She told Charlotte she was happy to be passing from earth into heaven. This did nothing to curtail her sister's tears. Anne gestured feebly for Charlotte to come closer to her. Charlotte leant over her and Anne whispered into her ear, 'It is life not death that needs courage. Take courage, Charlotte, take courage.' It was the last words she spoke. A slight tremble of her frame was all that marked the passage from this world to the next.

To my surprise Charlotte was insistent that Anne be buried as quickly as possible. She said this would prevent their seventy-three-year-old father from having to undertake the difficult journey to attend the funeral. The burial service therefore took place just two days later at Christ Church in Vernon Road, just a street away from the hotel, and she was buried in St Mary's churchyard. Only Charlotte and I attended. The doctor volunteered to join us but Charlotte declined his offer. I thought it a fitting resting place for a creature who had loved the great open spaces because it overlooks the sea and the surrounding green headlands. I knew poor Anne had not had many of her life's wishes come true, but at least in death she fulfilled one of her hopes – that her body should come to rest in Scarborough and not Haworth.

After I had returned to my home, Charlotte wrote to me the most anguished letter about returning to a parsonage now devoid of her brother and both her sisters. Here is an extract from it:

> I left Papa soon and went into the dining room. I shut the door. I tried to be glad that I had come home. I have always been glad before, except once and even then I was cheered, but this time joy was not to be the sensation. I felt that the house was all silent, the rooms were all empty. I remembered where the three were laid, in what dark narrow dwellings ... I do not know how life will pass. Solitude may be cheered and made endurable beyond what I believe. The great trial is when evening closes and night approaches. At that hour we used to assemble in the dining room – we used to talk. Now I sit by myself and necessarily I am silent. I cannot help thinking of their last days, remembering their sufferings and what they said and did and how they looked in mortal affliction – perhaps this will become less poignant in time.

I wept at my friend's lonely existence and, reading that letter, you will understand why I continued to give no credence to Anne's conjectures about Charlotte. I did not ask the questions that I should have asked. Why had Charlotte kept Anne for so long in the unhealthy air of Haworth? Was there a reason why Charlotte wanted her to die sooner rather than later? Was Anne right in surmising that Charlotte wanted her dead because she was suspicious of the circumstances surrounding Emily's death? Why had Anne's initial regaining of strength in Scarborough so speedily collapsed? Was it that we had allowed her to overtax herself or was there something more sinister – perhaps a dose of poison – behind her rapid death? Had Charlotte similarly killed Emily because she was suspicious about Branwell's death? And, if so, what on earth had led Charlotte to destroy the brother she had once so adored?

5

Cathy's Story

For a number of years Charlotte had been telling me how she was resigned to remaining a perpetual spinster, but the isolation that she felt after the deaths of her brother and sisters changed her mind, especially as her father had never been good company even at the best of times. Her thoughts turned increasingly to finding a marriage partner. However, she was not so desperate that she was prepared to accept the overtures of her father's Irish curate, Mr Nicholls. He had loved Charlotte ever since his arrival in Haworth in 1845, although she had consistently given him no encouragement and treated him only with cold civility. Her distaste for Mr Nicholls was shared by me. He was not a handsome man, even though he had a commanding height and a strong-looking face. His eyes were too small and his curtain-fringe of a beard focused attention on his unsmiling mouth. Moreover, he was very narrow-minded and, in matters of faith, a man who would brook no disagreement from what he held to be true. I thought him unpleasantly taciturn. Charlotte deserved a better partner than him.

Just after the Christmas of 1849 I went to stay with Charlotte for three weeks and it was obvious to me that her heart inclined towards Mr George Smith, the handsome and intelligent editor who had published her novel *Shirley* six months after Anne's death. He was desperate for her to produce another book and so he had entered into a very regular correspondence with her. I sensed that she was misinterpreting this as being evidence that he loved her. Charlotte said I was being unromantic. She was delighted when he invited her to stay at his mother's residence in London in the summer of 1850. For a month he wined and dined and entertained her and he introduced her to the rich and famous, including the great writer William Thackeray. Charlotte visited me at the end of June and informed me that 'George' had invited her to join him in a trip to Edinburgh and the Highlands. I told her that it would be most inappropriate for her to spend so much time with a single man and that she should refuse. After two days of arguments she agreed only to go to Edinburgh.

She was not to see him again until May 1851 when, once again, he invited her to London. From my perspective, his motive was clear. Charlotte could not find the inspiration to write. Her mind kept casting back to the suffering last days of those she had lost. The fact that everyone now knew she was Currer Bell did not help because it brought her unwelcome visitors, curious to meet her. He wanted to raise her spirits in the hope this would bear literary fruit. However, I could see Charlotte hoped for more. She insisted that I should help her purchase the best possible clothes and her manner became increasingly agitated. Imagine her disappointment, therefore, when this time she was entertained in London largely by Mr Smith's mother. The rest of that year saw Charlotte sink into an ever deeper depression and that Christmas the death of Emily's dog, Keeper, seemed to strike her like a hammer blow. She begged me to come to Haworth, saying that she feared she might otherwise die of the same disease that had killed her sisters. I went and did what I could to cheer her up.

Encouraged by me, Charlotte began to re-work her first novel, *The Professor* into what eventually became *Villette*. It was finished in November 1852 but during that time I had to steer her through one state of depression after another. By then even Charlotte could see that her dream of becoming the wife of her editor was unlikely to come to fruition and this may have been why, in December, Mr Nicholls seized his opportunity to formally ask for her hand in marriage. Charlotte wrote to me describing how he had proposed and I can do no better than to quote from her letter:

Shaking from head to foot, looking deadly pale, speaking low, vehemently yet with difficulty, he made me for the first time feel what it costs a man to declare affection where he doubts response. The spectacle of one ordinarily so statue-like thus trembling, stirred and overcome gave me a kind of strange shock. He spoke of sufferings he had borne for months, of sufferings he could endure no longer, and craved leave for some hope … That he cared something for me – and wanted me to care for him – I have long suspected, but I did not know the degree or strength of his feelings.

Her father encouraged her to reject his offer because he, like me, viewed him as an inappropriate choice. Charlotte surrendered to our joint wisdom and declined his proposal, but I could sense that her relations with him had nevertheless undergone a profound change. I think rejection by Mr Smith had put Mr Nicholls' passion for her in a new light.

It was Charlotte's increasing obsession with whether or not she should have said no to Mr Nicholls' offer that led indirectly to me uncovering the deep and hidden evil buried within her family's history. In the spring of 1853 I received a letter from a family saying that they had discovered an old chest belonging to a Nelly Dean whilst cleaning out the attic of the house that they had recently acquired. As far as they could tell, it contained nothing of value but they wondered whether I might like to pass on its contents to the Brontë family. Nelly Dean was, of course, the name of the household servant in Emily's novel *Wuthering Heights*. Like everyone else, I had assumed she was entirely a product of Emily's imagination so the letter intrigued me, but when I spoke to Charlotte about the matter, she was not interested. She refused even to discuss how she and Emily had devised the story contained in the novel. It appeared to her a complication not worthy of her attention at a time when she was entirely focused on the need to find a husband.

I asked her to let me at least take a look at what was in the chest. She acceded and I arranged for it to be brought to my home. Although I was curious, I assumed it likely that I would find nothing of any worth, so it was something of a shock when I discovered that one of the old cloths at the bottom of the trunk contained a sheaf of old papers roughly tied together. On opening these I saw they were covered with a spidery handwriting and signed 'Cathy Linton'. I began reading the papers and suddenly realized that in my hands I held a manuscript containing what purported to be a true version of what had happened at Wuthering Heights. I read the whole account avidly. Although it had a number of similarities to Emily's novel, there were some hugely significant differences. Those differences were to set me off on an investigation that was to shatter my perception of Charlotte and the rest of the Brontë family and make me revisit Anne's allegations. Here is Cathy's story:

Thrushcross Grange
March 1784

To my unborn child
I fear in giving you life I may die and I know that should that happen, Nelly Dean will undoubtedly spread false stories about Heathcliff and me. I therefore write this account in the hope that you will not think ill of me or believe for one moment that I have loved anyone other than your father.

My father, Hareton Earnshaw, counted himself a Methodist, much to my mother's outrage because she had a horror of religious enthusiasm. His Methodism stemmed from the influence of the Reverend William Grimshaw. It may sound blasphemous but many men and women round here used to regard this minister as if he was the Lord Jesus himself. Few dared to miss his services and even the toughest of men would jump out of the window of a public house rather than face his wrath. In 1767 a business matter took my father to Liverpool, a city he visited very rarely. Whilst there he agreed to join some local Methodists in offering some clothes and food to the desperate poor amid the city's squalid slums. In the course of that evening he saw such terrible sights that he would never describe them to me. Those that know little of the Methodists are sometimes surprised at the eager and joyful way they will enter places that most people would avoid like the plague. They should not be. For them every human being is a child of God and therefore worthy of their compassion and love.

My father ended up entering a particularly loathsome basement that acted as a home for several families, even though sewage-filled waters repeatedly flooded it. There he saw a woman who looked like a living corpse and her skeletal-shaped child, whose stomach was cruelly extended with hunger. The boy was but six years old yet had the appearance of an old man. The woman had done all she could to keep her son alive and was now so weak that she could not even attempt to eat the food that my father proffered, but the boy ate what he was given like a wild animal. Kneeling in the putrid water, my father prayed over the dying woman. She responded by making her confession, seeking our Saviour's blessing, and entrusting her son to my father's care. I suspect many a lesser man would have left her child behind, but my father felt that God had called him to rescue the poor creature. And so, to my mother's surprise, when my father returned home, he drew from under his greatcoat the ragged, dirty and cruelly emaciated black-haired boy and announced that it was his intention to adopt him and name him Heathcliff after an earlier son who had died.

I was just two years old and my memory of that evening is therefore slight. However, I know from my brother Hindley, who was six years my senior, that our mother immediately objected to this new addition to our family. She said our father had no right to bring such a dark-skinned gypsy brat into the house. I am ashamed to say I spat at Heathcliff and that Hindley swore to hate him forever. My brother kept his vow but I gradually took Heathcliff to my heart because I loved my father and was prepared to love what he loved. Yet Heathcliff showed no response to any affection. The brutality of his early life appeared to have robbed him of all natural feeling. Nevertheless, when Heathcliff became ill, my father insisted my mother should nurse him day and night. She caught the same disease. He recovered but she did not. Before she died, she summoned Hindley to her side and confided in him that she believed his father had done things no Christian should and that Heathcliff was his bastard child, born from an illicit affair in Liverpool with a woman from Penzance. Whether this was true or not – and I do not believe it was – it made Hindley hate Heathcliff even more and he put the blame for our mother's untimely death entirely on the cuckoo that had entered our family nest.

Hindley took to striking him whenever our father was out of the house. Hardened by years of neglect, Heathcliff bore the many blows without shedding a tear, but my father was furious when he found out what was happening. He took the decision to send Hindley away. Publicly it was said that this was done to ensure he received the best possible education, but everyone knew it was really to protect Heathcliff. Our servant Nelly Dean, with whom we had grown up, was furious because Hindley had always been her favourite. Over the next couple of years Heathcliff and I spent more and more time together, and both Nelly and our oldest servant, Joe, complained regularly to my father that he was letting Heathcliff corrupt me. They said that from morning to night I did nothing but try their patience by countless acts of mischief. My father became increasingly agitated and eventually was taken seriously ill. He was constantly vomiting and his once ruddy complexion turned a pallid and sickly white. The doctor came regularly but could find no remedy. One evening when I went to bid him good night, I found him lifeless.

I mourned my father deeply and I was upset that Heathcliff showed no emotion over his death. When Hindley returned for the funeral, I hardly recognized him so much had he grown in the three years since his expulsion. He had become quite the gentleman, though I sensed an innate cruelty in his look that did not bode well. He brought home with him a newly acquired attractive wife called Frances. Her background was kept a secret from us. I could not gauge my brother's real feelings for her because sometimes he seemed besotted with her and at other times he treated her with contempt. Only later did I come to know that his mood changed according to whether or not Nelly Dean was present in the room.

Hindley quickly made himself master of the house and he reduced Heathcliff to the standing of a farm labourer. When I objected, he treated me as no more than a servant. The only person who defended me was Nelly Dean. She had been dumbfounded when Hindley had arrived with a wife in tow and she made little disguise of her contempt for her new mistress. I found consolation for my frequent banishment from the house in being able to spend more time playing with Heathcliff in the fields. Having the attention of a very attractive sixteen-year-old boy when you are but twelve is very flattering but, with hindsight, I recognize this was undesirable. I dread to think how much I might have fallen in character had not an injury intervened to end our unfettered association.

In the October of 1777 I foolishly agreed to join Heathcliff in a night-time exploration of the grounds of nearby Thrushcross Grange. I blush with shame now to think of such inappropriate behaviour and I was rightfully punished when, in trying to peep in at the windows of the house, I was savaged by a guard dog. As a consequence I was carried indoors and thus introduced for the first time to the very different and fashionable world of the Lintons. The family was not entirely unknown to me because I had seen its members at church, but I had never had occasion to speak with any one of them. Mrs Linton ordered the servants to tend to my wound and, seeing my filthy condition, bathe me, while Mr Linton dispatched Heathcliff back to Wuthering Heights to inform my brother of my injury. Dressed in borrowed clothes that were far finer than anything I had ever possessed, I was immediately befriended by their daughter Isabella. She was a year younger than me but far advanced in terms of behaviour. She could not have been kinder and her handsome brother Edgar was no less welcoming.

I stayed at Thrushcross Grange five weeks till my ankle was fully recovered and in that short time my life was utterly transformed. Outwardly I abandoned my rags for a grand plaid silk frock, white trousers and shiny shoes. Inwardly I changed from someone content to wander the moors to one keen to remain in polite society. On my return home I greeted Heathcliff warmly because I still valued our previous friendship, but I soon made clear to him that our earlier free association should end. I had come to accept that he was, in the words of the Lintons, a 'naughty swearing boy' and not worthy of being my companion. Heathcliff made an effort to improve his appearance and dress but his black-browed visage, surly manners and foul language did not compare favourably with Edgar Linton's fine features, graceful etiquette and entertaining conversation.

Hindley encouraged me to visit the Lintons whenever I wished. Heathcliff thus found himself truly alone for the first time since he had joined our family and, not surprisingly, he cursed the day he had taken me to Thrushcross Grange. He turned for comfort to my sister-in-law and she seemed to welcome that, though never, of course, when her husband was around. The following summer Frances gave birth to a son and he was named Hareton after his grandfather. Nelly tended mother and child, but this did not prevent Frances being seized with such violent vomiting that, within a couple of days, she died. Over the next few weeks I have never heard a man so curse God as did my brother. Despite the fact that Hindley had often mistreated her, he now appeared to be devastated and yet strangely he took no interest in his infant son. Nelly did all she could to comfort him, leaving me to care for Hareton. Increasingly my brother took to drinking heavily. This made him violent and I tried to avoid him when he was at his alcohol-induced worst.

One day he came home so drunk that I hid in a cupboard, clutching Hareton, then not yet aged two, to my breast. I prayed the child would not cry and so betray our presence. For a while all I could hear was Hindley's swearing once he entered the room, but then I heard Nelly's voice. She told him in no uncertain terms that his behaviour was a disgrace. I could not see what was happening, but his words and her scream left me in no doubt of his response. He had placed a carving knife to her throat. I should have gone to her rescue had not fear rooted me to the spot. Fortunately, I heard Nelly break free and the knife drop to the floor. It was then I heard a conversation that I wish I had not.

'I cannot believe you are the man I have loved since we were children together,' said Nelly. 'How can you have sunk so low! Do you not recall the life we used to have before your wretched wife entered the scene? Why mourn her passing when you can once again have me? What was her weak love compared to mine! Did you and I not vow to be eternally one long before your father sent you away? Did I not give to you freely what no man should have until a marriage has taken place? It was only because you promised me faithfully that you would return to make me your wife that I stayed in this hellhole. And when the months passed and still your father refused to permit your return, who do you think it was that ensured his untimely demise? I poisoned him day by day so that you could return and inherit his property.'

I almost fainted with the horror of what Nelly had disclosed and even my poor brother's befuddled mind grasped the hideous enormity of what she had said. I could not make out what he muttered, but Nelly continued remorselessly, 'And what was my reward? It was the shock of discovering that you had married another. You had given me no warning, no word. Can you even begin to imagine my horror when you turned up with a bride, smiling at me as if I was just a servant, as if there had never been anything between us?'

'I told you, Nelly, I had no choice in the matter,' replied my brother. 'My father arranged the marriage. I had to obey him or face penury. It is you that I truly love.'

'It was because I foolishly believed you loved me that I administered to your wife the same poison that killed your father,' muttered Nelly in reply.

My brother's sobbing became even more uncontrolled at this revelation. Whatever he might have said to Nelly, and despite his infidelity, I suspected that he had chosen his wife and that my father had not demanded the marriage. Nelly continued speaking, unmoved by his obvious anguish. 'It was only once she was dead and I saw your grief that I knew I had been deluded. I have been no more to you than an occasional fancy. Look at you! The bottle holds more attraction to you than I do. I have killed two people for your sake and this is my reward. To have a knife held at my throat!'

'I do not drink, Nelly, because I mourn my wife. I drink because I fear that I may not be Hareton's father. I see more of Heathcliff's appearance in the child than mine own! That bastard destroyed my mother and turned my father against me. Now I fear that he has also cuckolded me!'

'It would not surprise me if he had,' sneered Nelly. 'Heathcliff is twice the man you are. I now think it would have been better for me if I had attached myself to him from the start. I'm sure your father would have blessed our marriage and given me part of your inheritance.' I heard my brother beg her to be quiet, but this only incensed her further. 'Look at me, you pathetic sot! I know you will not even have the courage to denounce what I have done.' I heard her slap his face with all her might. 'And if you did dare, I would deny everything and attribute your accusations to a brain confused by too much gin.'

She hit him again and then left him. It seemed an age before my broken brother summoned the strength to also exit the room. Only then did I leave my hiding place. I had no confidence that anyone would believe me if I said what had happened. My father's death was far too removed for me to prove foul play and too many women die after childbirth to make my sister-in-law's death appear an unusual occurrence. Nelly would deny my allegations and I feared that Hindley would not support me. Would he really wish to admit to having seduced Nelly and to having made her his mistress? And, if he admitted her guilt, would not others assume that he had encouraged her to get rid of our father and his wife? And, as to the accusation that Heathcliff might have seduced Frances and be Hareton's father, what evidence did I have? Surely that belief just stemmed from Hindley's obsessive hatred of Heathcliff?

I was rescued from the dilemma of what to do by Edgar Linton. He offered to marry me in the January of 1780. I did not want to risk losing him by telling him of my brother's sinfulness and so I decided to say nothing to anyone. Nelly tried to dissuade me from the marriage, presumably because she knew it pleased Hindley and she wanted to further upset him by engineering its failure. She tried to persuade me that my first love was for Heathcliff, saying that he was twice the man compared to Edgar Linton and that only his lowly station prevented me seeing that. According to her, our souls were made for each other, whereas Linton's and mine were as different as a moonbeam from lightning or frost from a fire. To this nonsense I responded by saying I had no intention of degrading myself by marrying Heathcliff. I assured her that Edgar had no equal in my sight and that I loved the ground under his feet and the air over his head and every word he uttered.

Nevertheless, I asked Hindley if I could take Heathcliff as a servant to Thrushcross Grange once I was married. I did this because I feared what my brother might eventually do to him, but Hindley's response was to accuse me of intending to cuckold Edgar – in this I detected Nelly's influence. When I foolishly persisted with my request, Hindley waited until I was away for a few days at Thrushcross Grange and, in my absence, summoned Heathcliff and ordered him to leave and never return. When I heard what had happened, I asked Edgar to send out a search party but it could find no trace of where Heathcliff had gone. I confess part of me was relieved.

I married Edgar on 16 May 1781 and after a joyous honeymoon we returned to take up residence at Thrushcross Grange. Imagine my horror when, on going upstairs to my room, I was greeted by Nelly Dean. Without consulting me – for he wished it to be a surprise – my husband had secretly appointed her to be my maid-servant, believing this would please me. I would have stormed downstairs and denounced her had she not made it clear that she would accuse my brother of the murder of our father and of his wife if I tried to get rid of her. I surrendered to this blackmail and accepted her appointment. I paid a high price for this decision. Not only did I have to put up with Nelly's smirking and hateful presence, but also, unbeknown to me, she insidiously began making my husband believe that I had married him only for his wealth and position and that I had always loved Heathcliff. His manner to me became gradually cooler – to my great distress, for I knew not its cause.

The discovery that I was pregnant in the autumn of 1782 temporarily changed all that. Edgar rejoiced in his forthcoming fatherhood and Heathcliff's continued absence made it difficult for Nelly to find reasons for still linking his name with mine. Unfortunately our happiness proved short-lived. One day in January 1783, just as Edgar and I were about to have our tea, a servant announced the arrival of a Mr Heathcliff Earnshaw to see us. Edgar wanted to refuse him entry to the house but I foolishly said that I could not turn away my half-brother. And so, after a gap of almost three years, I met Heathcliff again. The last time I had seen him he was just a dirty uncouth ploughboy. Now he appeared looking like the handsomest of gentlemen – upright in body, intelligent in face, dignified in manner. I could not believe the transformation. He looked at me with undisguised admiration, much to the understandable annoyance of my husband. I was stupid enough not to register the significance of this and to take delight in seeing how much Heathcliff had bettered himself. In that moment I unwittingly rekindled all your father's latent jealousy.

'It is wonderful to see you again, Catherine,' said Heathcliff. 'I have always remembered your affection for me with much gratitude. I knew that you were always genuinely sorry for the way that your brother treated me and I am still eternally grateful for that, even though our paths have separated. I've fought through many bitter battles since I last heard your voice and I want you to know the memory of you alone sustained me and enabled me to persevere in my attempts to better myself.'

Edgar interrupted this flattering speech, making it clear that he felt the visit was ill-timed. Heathcliff said that he would return at a more convenient moment. To our surprise he announced he was staying at Wuthering Heights. I had retained very little contact with my brother since my marriage and I wrongly assumed Heathcliff must have sought and achieved their reconciliation. It was left to Nelly to disillusion me. She took delight in telling me in the privacy of my bedroom that my drunken brother had stupidly gambled with Heathcliff and was now so far in his debt that he had no option but to let him take over the family home. If I had possessed more sense I would have recognized that Heathcliff was now not only the master of my former home but also becoming the master of Nelly's heart.

Nevertheless, I continued to welcome Heathcliff to Thrushcross over the next few weeks, ignoring Edgar's dislike of him. Had I been less solicitous about upholding Heathcliff's character, I might have seen earlier that my pretty and vivacious sister-in-law, Isabella, was falling in love with him. It was Edgar who first realized. He told her in no uncertain terms that he would not tolerate her marrying a nameless man and that Heathcliff was at heart a brute. I belatedly did all I could to ensure that Isabella should cease seeing him by putting a stop to Heathcliff's visits. If truth be told, I was also now beginning to have my own doubts about his character because Nelly was informing me with delight of the extent to which he was manipulating my unfortunate brother, robbing him of his remaining wealth.

I foolishly arranged for Heathcliff to see Isabella and me when Edgar was away on business. I hoped to persuade him to leave her alone, but the meeting got out of hand when Isabella said that the only thing that prevented Heathcliff loving her was his love for me and he concurred. He said that he had always loved only me and that he had no desire to marry Isabella because her mawkish, waxen face reminded him constantly of my husband. For the first time I realized that Heathcliff did not just feel friendly affection for me and I wondered how I could have been so blind for so long! No wonder Edgar had been unhappy about my willingness to meet my half-brother! I told Heathcliff in the strongest possible terms that I loved only my husband and ordered him to leave. He obeyed but not before threatening to pursue Isabella out of sheer devilment. He told me in words I shall never forget: 'What is it to you? I have a right to kiss her, if she chooses, and you have no right to object. I'm not your husband: you needn't be jealous of me!'

The next day I decided to go to Wuthering Heights in the hope of persuading Heathcliff that his love for me was pointless and that he should leave. To travel to the house was not a wise action for a pregnant woman and when Edgar discovered my absence and heard where I had gone, it is not surprising that he followed me. Furious, he demanded Heathcliff depart from our region, saying that his presence was a moral poison and that there was no way he would ever permit him to be entertained again at Thrushcross Grange. Unfortunately, his anger was equally directed at me because he wrongly assumed that it was love for Heathcliff that had led to my action. I told Edgar I had only been defending him and Isabella and that, if he truly loved me, he should not think any evil of my actions. Edgar then lashed out a blow at Heathcliff. Despite my condition, I intervened to prevent what would have proved a most unequal fight. My husband was not versed in any fighting skills.

When we returned home, Edgar refused to listen to my protestations of innocence and said many bitter things. I retired exhausted to my room and in deep distress. Later that evening he came to see me but his manner was icily cold. 'Stay in your room, Catherine,' he said. 'I am come neither to wrangle nor to be reconciled; but I wish just to learn whether you intend to continue your intimacy with this man. Will you give up Heathcliff or give up me?' 'Oh for mercy's sake,' I interrupted, 'let us hear no more of it! The sight of your chillness towards me makes my blood boil. Your veins appear to be full of frost and ice water. Don't you see how you are destroying me?' He stormed out and locked himself in his study for three days. During that time, I stayed in my room, partly because of the state of my health and partly because I had no desire to see Isabella, whom I blamed for turning my husband against me. Only Nelly saw the intensity of my despair and I am sure she took a quiet delight in it.

I could not see how to undo the harm that my unwise actions had created. In my despair and sickness I stopped eating. As time passed the knowledge of my innocence made me increasingly angry at Edgar. How could he believe me capable of loving another? On the third day of my isolation I confided my feelings to Nelly, momentarily forgetting that she was no real friend of mine. She gave me little comfort but expressed deep concern that I would lose my child if I continued not to take sustenance. She must have feared for my health and the impact that might have on her position in the house because she reported to Edgar that he needed to see me. When he came he was taken aback by my haggard appearance and he voiced his anger to Nelly that she had not told him earlier of the deterioration in my condition.

'You encouraged me to harass her,' he said, 'and look at what this has achieved. Months of sickness could not have wrought such an evil change!'

'The mistress is always headstrong and domineering,' replied Nelly, refusing to be put down. 'Her condition is a product of her waywardness.'

'The next time you say anything against your mistress, you shall quit my service,' said Edgar, shocked by her rudeness.

'You'd rather hear nothing then when Mr Heathcliff comes courting every time that you are away?'

'How dare you! Get out!'

Nelly swept out of the room and I flung myself into Edgar's arms, reasserting my innocence. This time I had the joy of knowing he believed me. We agreed it was vital we talk with Isabella and make sure she understood both my position and the undesirability of her attempting to see Heathcliff. Our happiness proved short-lived when a servant informed us that for the past three days Isabella had been using my absence to secretly meet Heathcliff and that she had now eloped with him. That night neither of us closed our eyes, so anxious were we for her. I wanted Edgar to pursue them but he was reluctant to leave me until he was sure that the doctor had assessed my condition. He told me he felt she had gone of her own accord and it would be pointless to try and intervene. He said that henceforward he had no sister.

The strains of these events proved too much for me in my pregnant condition. I fell ill with a brain fever and it was thought I might die. Your father nursed me day and night and I think it was only his love that enabled me to survive. However, I remained frail, able to move from room to room only by leaning heavily on his arm. And it was in this condition that I had to receive Nelly Dean when she arrived uninvited with the news that Isabella was now living at Wuthering Heights. We had not seen her since our altercation. She said that she had gone back to seek service with Hindley but found the house in an uproar. Heathcliff had reverted to his former brute-like status and was making a misery of Isabella's life. She had sent Nelly to say that she begged her brother's forgiveness for disobeying him and attaching herself to such a monster. I urged Edgar to forgive his sister but he was adamant he would not go to see her. He told Nelly, 'Return to Wuthering Heights and say to my sister that I am not angry and I have nothing to forgive, but that it is out of the question that I should go to see her. I can have no communication with anyone connected to Heathcliff Earnshaw.'

Nelly returned the next day. Edgar was out but I stupidly agreed to see her alone. She inserted into my hand a letter, saying that it was vital I should read it. I thought it came from Isabella and was horrified when, upon breaking its seal, I saw it was written in Heathcliff's hand. I immediately tried to return it unread to her, but Nelly declined to receive it. Moving to the door that opened onto our garden, she opened it and, to my dismay, Heathcliff entered the room. In a stride or two, he was at my side and had grasped me in his arms. Imagine my predicament. I was too frail to either cast him aside or leave the room unaided. Nelly had also taken care to remove the bell by which I could summon assistance.

I am ashamed to say that Heathcliff bestowed kisses upon me, despite my protestations. He voiced all the anguish of his heart: 'Oh, Cathy! Oh, my life how can I bear it? I had no idea you had been so ill! I wish I could hold you till we were both dead. You and Edgar have broken my heart. Why did you betray me and behave so cruelly? What right had you to leave me? For the poor fancy you felt for Linton? Nothing that God or Satan could inflict – no misery or degradation – could have parted us, but you, of your own will, did it.' I urged him to see sense, saying, 'Heathcliff, listen to me. I would have liked us to be friends. I have never wished to torment you. But I love only Edgar. Can you not let me live in peace? Do you want to kill me and my unborn child?' To this he replied, 'I could as soon forget you as my existence! You lie to say that I might kill you. Is it not enough for your infernal selfishness that while you are happy and at peace I writhe in the torments of hell?'

I tried to leave the room but he easily restrained me. My agitated heart beat wildly and I feared that I was about to die. I turned to Nelly for assistance but my pleas fell on deaf ears until she saw through the window that Edgar was returning. She then urged

Heathcliff to leave me before he was discovered. I fainted away and, when I regained my senses, I found myself back in my bed.

Since then I have spent the day writing this account and I am pleased it is finished because already I begin to feel the onset of labour, though it is before the time expected. Dr Wroughton has already been summoned and I know he will do all that he can. I end this document as I began it. If I die and you, my child, survive, know that I have always loved your father and that my last breath will be a blessing on his head. Whatever others may say, I never saw Heathcliff as any other than a friend. And that friendship has cost me most dear.

Your loving mother
Cathy Linton

6

The Cornish Connection

Cathy's account swept away the entire basis of *Wuthering Heights* by recounting that Cathy truly loved Edgar Linton and not Heathcliff. Her version made Edgar appear a far more worthy figure, exposed Nelly as a manipulative and murdering monster, and stripped Heathcliff of all the romance that had made him so memorable a literary figure. I felt the manuscript had the ring of authenticity but I could not begin to think why Nelly should have preserved it, given its contents. Surely it would have been in her interests to destroy such evidence of her heinous activities?

I did not take any immediate action because this was a difficult time for both Charlotte and me. I was upset because my mother had been unwell for some time and I feared that I would shortly become home-less. I therefore agreed to take up the offer of distant relations who lived in Suffolk to undertake an experimental visit with them in May. I assumed that, if the outcome of my visit were satisfactory, they would in a sense adopt me. Unfortunately it transpired that they only wanted me as an unpaid servant and so I ended up fleeing their house. In Charlotte's case, she was upset that Mr Nicholls had announced that he was resigning as her father's curate and therefore leaving Haworth. This was because her father had treated him very harshly for having had the temerity to propose to her. She wrote to me of how on his last day she had initially thought it best not to see him, but then relented when she caught sight of him standing for the last time outside her house:

Remembering his long grief I took courage and went out trembling and miserable. I found him leaning against the garden door in a paroxysm of anguish, sobbing as women never sob. Of course I went straight to him. Very few words were interchanged and those few barely articulate ... Poor fellow! He wanted such hope and such encouragement as I could not give him. Still I trust he must know now that I am not cruelly blind and indifferent to his constancy and grief ... However, he is gone – gone – and there's an end to it.

If I had been in a calmer frame of mind, my reply to her letter might have been more politic, but, as it was, I wrote back saying that she should, like me, resolve herself to spinsterhood and that Mr Nicholls was not worth a moment's thought. In the same letter I told her about Cathy's letter, thinking it would give her something else to think about. Charlotte was incensed by my insensitivity to Mr Nicholls' position. She told me to destroy Cathy's letter and to count myself no more her friend. What was worse, she wrote to mutual friends saying that I hated the thought of her finding a husband when I could not. This cruel and undeserved lie caused me much pain and all correspondence between us ceased. I locked away Cathy's account, unable to decide what I should do with a document whose accuracy I could not verify.

It was not until the autumn of 1853 that, annoyed by Charlotte's continuing silence, I decided to undertake some investigative work on Cathy's letter. The obvious starting point was to see if I could make contact with the doctor mentioned in her account. My initial enquiries quickly uncovered that there had been a doctor called Wroughton but that he had died many years ago and his son was working as a doctor in Leeds. I decided that I should visit this man on the chance that his father might have spoken to him about Wuthering Heights. Dr John Wroughton proved to be a fine-looking man, smartly dressed, dark haired and very clean cut, and it was not long before I appreciated that here was a man of real integrity. Unfortunately, it soon became obvious that he knew absolutely nothing of the matter that I was seeking to investigate. His father had died many years earlier and he had never spoken to his son about the Lintons. I feared therefore that my journey had been wasted.

However, my initial dismay was fortunately soon dispelled because Dr Wroughton then informed me that he held in his possession some of the journals that his father had written. These he took down from a shelf in his study and he permitted me to see if I could find anything of value. Fortunately the volume for 1783 was intact and my laboured efforts to decipher the at times difficult handwriting proved worthwhile. With Dr Wroughton's permission, I transcribed the following extracts, which date between March and June of that year. You will see that the passages raised an entirely new and totally unexpected issue:

20 March 1783

Today I attended Mrs Linton again. Her pregnancy is going well. Having given her a close examination, I suspect she may be expecting twins, but I have not told her lest I am mistaken. This family deserves what happiness it can have because we all know the terrible fate that has befallen Mr Linton's poor sister. All that I hear of the behaviour of Heathcliff Earnshaw since he took over that farmhouse from his half-brother Hindley is to his detriment. The man is a monster!

4 April 1783

I was summoned to deal with an emergency at Thrushcross Grange today. Mrs Linton went into labour four weeks early. I have been telling her to be careful and the foolish woman has over-exerted herself. The whole house appeared in uproar. I gather that Heathcliff Earnshaw had earlier forced himself into the house. What is wrong with that man! Poor Edgar Linton was distraught with anxiety.

I needed help and summoned a woman called Nelly Dean to assist me. Mr Linton objected but I overrode him, saying I needed a woman with nursing experience and it was no time to let petty differences endanger a mother. I was right in my judgement because Nelly proved a most able assistant. I am not sure that I would have succeeded in bringing both the babies into this world without her skilful help. Even so the two girls were puny little things and I feared neither of them would survive. I handed them both over to Nelly with strict instructions as to how she should care for them whilst I gave my undivided attention to Mrs Linton.

For the next couple of hours I did all I could but it was to no avail. Poor Mrs Linton died without ever gaining consciousness. I sat with my head in my hands and wept. How can life be so cruel to one so lovely! She was not yet twenty years old! Even as I mourned, Nelly returned with the news that one of the baby girls had sadly died, though the remaining baby was clinging to life. She suggested that we spare Mr Linton the pain of another death and let him think there had only been one child born. She said she would dispose of the dead child so none would ever know of its existence. Overwrought at the loss of the mother I nodded my agreement without really thinking of the consequences. At the time it seemed an act of kindness. Now I am sure that what I did was very, very wrong. How could I as a Christian give no thought to the fact that the baby deserved a proper Christian burial with her mother? What right had I to deny Edgar Linton knowing the truth? I hope God may forgive me.

What makes this matter even worse is that I cannot now tell the truth. It would destroy my reputation! What on earth possessed me! I should never have listened to Nelly Dean, however well-meaning her suggestion. All I can now do is pray daily for the soul of the poor lost child.

12 April 1783

Am I going mad? One of my patients told me he had seen Heathcliff Earnshaw and Nelly Dean entering a hired carriage with a tiny babe wrapped in swaddling clothes. Has that woman deceived me? Did both twins survive? Why did I not ask to see the lifeless child? Has she now given one of Cathy's daughters to Heathcliff? What possible purpose would that serve and surely she could not be that deceitful and cruel? I keep saying to myself the bundle was probably something else. That is what I told my informant and she fortunately has believed me. She has assured me that she will not tell others of what she thought she saw.

5 May 1783

I continue to sleep badly. I cannot get out of my head my concern over what I allowed to happen at Thrushcross Grange. I have made guarded enquiries and, as far as I can tell, Heathcliff and Nelly Dean have gone south to Penzance in Cornwall. Why should they go so far away?

14 June 1783

Heathcliff Earnshaw is back! I must go and see him.

16 June 1783

Today I went to Wuthering Heights. Heathcliff agreed to see me. I asked him about the child. He declined to answer my questions, but the very fact he has not denied the existence of the child makes me believe he has indeed taken it. But to where and for what purpose? The man is insane. What am I to do? I am powerless. Even if I risk my reputation and now inform Mr Linton, I have not a shred of proof the child ever existed. Though it grieves me to the heart, I must therefore force myself to stop thinking about what I have let happen or I will go mad.

After reading these extracts, I was convinced that Cathy's account was a truthful one, but like the doctor, I could not imagine what bizarre motive had lain behind the actions of Nelly Dean and Heathcliff in abducting a baby. I assumed the journey to Penzance was linked to its disposal, possibly to some relative of Heathcliff if there was any truth in the tale that his mother originated from Cornwall. In reflecting on that possibility, it suddenly occurred to me that Charlotte's mother had come from Penzance. Unlikely as it seemed, was there a possible connection between Heathcliff Earnshaw and the Brontë family? Travelling as far as Cornwall on what was likely to be a wild goose-chase seemed a very unattractive proposition unless I had more to go on. I began dredging my memory to recall all that I had been told about the past history of Charlotte's parents, in case that provided me with any clues.

It soon dawned on me that Charlotte had talked to me far more about her father than her mother. She had been proud of the way that he had achieved so much from very humble origins. Born one of ten children in a poor farming family in the tiny village of Drumballyroney in County Down, Patrick Brunty (as he was then known) had studied as best he could from the limited resources at his disposal and become a teacher in the village school. The local vicar had encouraged him to seek ordination and, having taught him the classical knowledge that was required for entry to university, obtained a free place for him at St John's College in Cambridge. Charlotte's father had then become one of the university's top students and had changed his name to Brontë in order to symbolize his determination to place behind him the poverty of Ireland once and for all. At the age of thirty, he had successfully obtained ordination in the Church of England. I suspect a more career-minded man would have ensured that he took up a parish in London, where his abilities would have more easily come to the attention of those who matter in issues of ecclesiastical preferment. However, Mr Brontë had chosen instead to link himself with the despised evangelical wing of the Church and to accept a position in the industrial heartland of England. He had first taken a curacy in the tiny Shropshire town of Wellington, and then moved to Yorkshire, eventually ending up as Vicar of Haworth.

All I knew about Maria Branwell, Charlotte's mother, was that she had come up from Penzance in 1812 to help an aunt run the domestic side of a new Methodist school called Woodhouse Grove at Apperley Bridge. Her uncle, John Fennell, had been appointed as its first headmaster. There she had met Patrick Brontë and, after a whirlwind romance, married him. She was twenty-nine and he was thirty-five at the time, but this did not prevent them having six children before Maria's agonizing death from cancer in September 1821. Charlotte had often told me how her father had personally tended his wife every night throughout her illness. Because my conflict with Charlotte prevented me asking her more questions about her mother, I opted to try and visit Woodhouse Grove School. I gathered that its governor, a Methodist minister called William Lord, had been at the school for a number of years and it was my hope that he might have talked with many who knew both Maria Branwell and Patrick Brontë. I therefore wrote seeking an interview, stating that I was undertaking some research into Charlotte Brontë's parents for a possible forthcoming biography of the authoress. He replied saying that he was very willing to share what limited knowledge he had, but I had to bear in mind he could only provide information that was second-hand.

Thus on a very cold but sunny morning in January 1854, I found myself on the train that runs between Leeds and Bradford. Mr Lord had informed me that the station at Apperley Bridge was situated not more than forty or fifty yards away from the entrance to his school; I would not have ventured forth without such reassurance because of the heavy snow that had fallen. One of the school servants was awaiting my arrival as the train pulled into the tiny platform. He was armed with a pair of heel spikes which he attached to my shoes. Together we slowly ascended from the deep cutting in which the railway station was set and I soon found myself facing a park-like entrance. The snow hid its carriage-drive but, as we walked along, the high ground that was covered with beech trees gave way on my right to a beautiful open view across the vale of Apperley. It made me stop in admiration. I could see in the distance the meandering River Aire and beyond that snow-covered hills sparkling in the sunlight. The crisp air was invigorating and I wondered whether I should take that as a sign my forthcoming meeting would prove an auspicious one.

The winding nature of the drive meant it was only towards the end of our walk that the school came into sight. I knew Woodhouse Grove served the educational needs of the sons of the Methodist clergy and, given the relative poverty of that movement, I was not expecting much. I was therefore very surprised to see before me a very impressive building with an imposing stone façade that was made even more beautiful by the snow that surrounded it. It was only afterwards explained to me that this magnificent mansion, which had yet to be officially opened, was not the building that Patrick Brontë and Maria Branwell had known. It owed its existence entirely to the new railway upon which I had arrived. Apparently the Methodists had been paid compensation for the line passing through their estate and they had used this money to fund extensive improvements, including creating the school's new and very attractive south-facing frontage and building new wings to both east and west.

Such was the extent of the new work that I found it hard to imagine what the place had been like when Maria Branwell first crossed its threshold. From what I could gather, the original main building had simply been an old manor house that was not much suited to educational use. The servant who had accompanied me led me into an impressive library where Mr Lord was waiting. He rose to greet me and we exchanged initial pleasantries. I was struck with the fact he was a 'big' man in every sense of the word, large in girth, rugged in appearance, and domineering in manner. His close-cropped hair was white and his facial features were firmly set and strongly marked, with an austerity that only occasionally relaxed into a genial smile and sparkling eye. Though his voice was sweetly toned, his manner betrayed he had an inner steeliness to him. My escort had informed me that the governor was in the process of successfully engineering the removal of the school's long-serving headmaster, with whom he had fallen out. I suspected that he was not a man who liked anyone disagreeing with him.

'I am afraid, Miss Nussey, that you find us in a state of upheaval at present,' he said, 'and not just because the work on this building is only just nearing completion. We are also in the process of acquiring a new headmaster. I have my eye on a man called Dr Sharpe.'

'In the circumstances, sir, I am very appreciative of the fact you are prepared to give me some of your valuable time.'

'I am very happy to tell you what I have heard, though I suspect that it will be far less than you desire. I hope you will not view your journey here as a waste of time.'

'I can assure you, sir,' I replied, 'that anything you can tell me will be appreciated, however little.'

'Well, let me start at the beginning,' he said. 'When Woodhouse Grove opened in January 1812 it had only nine pupils but within less than a year it had sixty. I have spoken with some of them and they all speak highly of Mr Fennell. There is no doubt he regarded this school as a house specially created to serve God's purposes, a place where the young could be prepared not only for this world but also for the one to come. He prayed that God might help him nurse the lambs of his flock and he took great pleasure in hearing children pray and speak of the work of God on their hearts. His wife acted as the school's housekeeper but I am told she was not very good in this role. Even with the help of her daughter, Jane, she found the task of feeding, clothing and organizing the boys very onerous and, as a consequence, Maria Branwell was sent for. Apart from the family connection, she was well known to Mr Fennell because he had been once her teacher in Penzance. She arrived in June 1812 just in time to meet Mr Brontë, who had taken on the role of school inspector.'

'Pardon me for interrupting, but I do not understand how Mr Brontë came to be associated with a Methodist school?' I interjected.

'That is easy to explain, Miss Nussey. When Mr Brontë was first ordained he accepted a curacy working in the Shropshire town of Wellington, which is near to the immense coal and iron works of Ironbridge and Coalbrookdale. He witnessed the impressive work of the Methodists in that region and made friends with a number of them, including Mr Fennell, who at that time was master of a day school in Wellington. In 1809 Mr Brontë moved to this region as a curate in Dewsbury, which also had a flourishing Methodist society, and then, in 1811, he became curate in nearby Hartshead cum Clifton. It was natural for Mr Fennell to renew their acquaintance and seek his help. It was agreed Mr Brontë would inspect the quality of the classics teaching and he did a good job on that.'

'Why do you think Maria Branwell was so attracted to Mr Brontë?'

'From the reports I have heard, Maria was neither pretty nor young. She was quite short in stature and very plain in looks, but what she lacked in appearance she made up for in money. Her parents had recently died and left her possessed of a small income of her own. She doubtless hoped this wealth might attract a suitor and I think there is no doubt that she set herself to capture Mr Brontë as a husband – and, of course, she succeeded. He thought her intelligent, pious and witty. Their courtship took place at a time when there was massive opposition to the introduction of machinery into the factories around here, but the presence of rioting mobs did not prevent him walking the dozen or so miles from Hartshead to here, and then back again, almost every day so he could see her. I have heard it said that Maria Branwell began to nickname him "her saucy Pat", but I find that hard to believe as she was a former pupil of Mr Fennell and he always inculcated that women should be grave and serious in manner and speech.'

'I think, Reverend Lord, there are very few romances that take place without some conversation of that kind.'

He smiled in response. 'Perhaps you are right, Miss Nussey. And love was certainly in the air because their romance was not the only one taking place here. Mr Brontë's closest friend from his time at Wellington, William Morgan, had become the curate of the Reverend Crosse in Bradford and he was simultaneously courting Mr Fennell's daughter, Jane. Both couples were married in a double wedding at the end of December.'

'And did they keep any connection with this place?'

'No, because Mr Fennell ceased to be headmaster of Woodhouse Grove. He was deeply unhappy by the decision of the 1812 Methodist Conference to separate itself from the Church of England. After much soul-searching, he announced it was his intention to seek ordination in the Church of England and, as a consequence, he was promptly dismissed from his post. He and his wife moved to Bradford and he encouraged both Mr Brontë and Mr Morgan to undertake evangelical work there. In 1815 Mr Brontë agreed to become perpetual curate of the Old Bell Chapel in Thornton, which is about four miles from Bradford. It offered him a rent-free parsonage to live in and an opportunity to mix with some more genteel society.'

'So why did the family move to the far more isolated Haworth?'

'Quite simply because the size of his family demanded Mr Brontë should seek a more lucrative post. The parsonage was not large enough for his growing family. Moreover, by 1820 working in Bradford had lost much of its appeal and Haworth offered a fresh challenge. It is a busy place with many needs to be met, and although you describe it as isolated it is only a dozen miles away from Bradford, Halifax and Burnley. It also brought the family close to Halifax, where Mr Fennell had moved to become a vicar. As you are probably aware, the two men kept in very close touch until Mr Fennell died in 1841.'

'Do you think Mrs Brontë liked living here in Yorkshire?'

'Yorkshire is a bleak place compared to the area in which she grew up and living surrounded by moorland can be overbearing. I do not need to tell you that there is always a cold wind here. I think almost certainly she missed her hometown and the far warmer climate of Cornwall, but she had no choice but to stay once she was married.'

'And do you think she and her husband were happily married?'

'Who knows what lies at the heart of any marriage other than the couple themselves?'

'There are often signs that outsiders can see.'

'I am not one to listen to gossip, Miss Nussey.'

I feared that I might have offended him. 'No,' I said, 'but I am sure you have your own considered view on the matter. You strike me as a man of insight.'

He appreciated the compliment but still hesitated before saying, 'For what it is worth, I suspect that Mrs Brontë found the atmosphere in her home oppressive. She had been attracted to her husband like a moth to a flame, but she found her lively nature was soon scorched. Mr Brontë was a dedicated and conscientious minister but he was a difficult man and I can personally vouch for the fact that on the one occasion we met I found his behaviour at times quite strange. I have no doubt he could be affable and considerate and generous – and I am sure all those quali-ties were at the fore when he courted Maria Branwell. However, I am equally certain that, when he chose, he could be domineering, stubborn and self-centred. I suspect it was those less happy aspects of his character that became increasingly apparent once they were married.'

'What makes you think that?'

'Tales abound that when he was angry he would repeatedly fire his gun or set fire to the house rugs or even saw off the backs of chairs. It is said that on one occasion he objected to a dress that Mrs Brontë had bought and he took a pair of scissors to it, hacking off its sleeves. Although I refuse to give credence to such malicious nonsense, I suspect they have a basis in truth. There is no doubt that he had a flaming temper and that, when roused, he was capable of behaving very unpleas-antly to those around him.'

'From my own experience of Mr Brontë, I do not think his temper is his only problem. I have seen the way he often seeks seclusion in his study rather than spend time with his family.'

'Men of God have to spend much time in study and prayer, Miss Nussey. You should not forget that. But I suspect you are right in thinking he liked the silence of his own company.'

In my imagination I envisaged what all this meant. Mr Brontë might have shown a more sociable side when he was courting Maria Branwell, but then, like many a man who has gained what he wanted, he reverted to his true nature. 'And what is your impression of how Mrs Brontë coped with such behaviour from her husband?' I asked.

'She turned for affection to her children and she loved to socialize. Her father had been a successful merchant and I gather his house was always full of people. At Thornton I know Mrs Brontë became especially friendly with Miss Elizabeth Firth of Kipping House. I suspect she unburdened herself to her more than any other, even though Miss Firth was young enough to be her daughter. And then, of course, there was her older sister, Elizabeth, who sometimes stayed with the family. As you know, she was very supportive to Mr Brontë and the children after Maria's death.'

'Yes, I knew her very well,' I said, recalling in my mind a picture of the dour Elizabeth Branwell when I first met her. 'I wish now that I had taken the opportunity to talk with her more about her upbringing in Cornwall. All I can recall is how strongly she felt that she had taken a step down the social ladder in abandoning her contacts in Penzance for the primitive society of Haworth.'

'I think that is not surprising. Mrs Fennell used to tell people here with pride what a prosperous tea merchant Thomas Branwell had been.'

'And was such pride justified?'

'Pride is never justified, Miss Nussey, but in this case it was not without foundation. I have studied what I can about the Branwells. Mr Branwell was a prosperous merchant who imported luxury goods and stored them in cellars that he owned at the quayside before selling them on, some wholesale and some in his own shop in a place aptly named Market Square. Trade was good because Penzance is a regular port of call for ships going to and from London, Bristol and Plymouth. However, this was not the only source of his wealth. He also owned property in and around the town, including a mansion called Tremenheere House and a hostelry called the Golden Lion Inn. To supply the latter he also ran his own brewery. What is more, he had made a good marriage by selecting as his wife Miss Anne Carne, the daughter of a silversmith. Her family was sufficiently wealthy to be partners in a bank called Oxnam, Batten & Co. that was opened in Chapel Street. Both the Branwell family and the Carne family worshipped in St Mary's Chapel, which was their local parish church, but they also belonged to the very strong Wesleyan Methodist community in Penzance. I believe Mr and Mrs Branwell took their young children to hear the great John Wesley himself on more than one occasion.'

'You know far more than I would have expected about them,' I said.

'Methodists speak a lot about each other and our clergy travel the country. It is not difficult to discover information if you seek it. Since the publication of Miss Brontë's *Jane Eyre*, I have taken an interest in the family because of their connection with the school, limited though it was.'

'I am sorry to have interrupted you. Please continue.'

'I have almost told you all that I know. The Branwells set up home in Chapel Street and Mrs Branwell gave birth to eleven children, though three of those did not survive infancy. Thomas Branwell died in 1808 and his wife in 1809. Maria's uncle, Mr Richard Branwell, took over her father's house and business and became her guardian. Unfortunately further tragedy then struck in the winter of 1811. His son was drowned at sea, and that broke the father's heart. He never recovered from his loss and died in 1812. I can understand why Maria Branwell was keen to find herself a husband when she joined her aunt here at Woodhouse Grove.'

'You have been most helpful, sir, but are you sure there is not something else you can tell me about the family in Cornwall at that time? Any story or tale that is told, even if you cannot vouch for its authenticity?'

Mr Lord looked at me, clearly weighing up whether he should say more or not. Then he answered, 'Having met you, I judge you to be a woman of good sense and propriety and I am convinced that your interest in the Brontë family is both genuine and well-meaning. For that reason, Miss Nussey, I will confide to you what I have hidden from all others. A few years ago I received a manuscript from a Methodist preacher called William Clowes, who served in Cornwall for a time in the 1820s. Apparently he was preaching in a place called Redruth and his words so moved a man called John Reynolds that he chose to make a written confession of his sins. It proved a shocking tale, not just because it told of grave criminal acts he had committed but also because it alleged that the Branwell family were involved in smuggling and ship-wrecking. Clowes told me that he would have questioned Mr Reynolds about what he had written but unfortunately the man disappeared shortly after handing over his account. Two days later his body was discovered. His throat had been cut. Clowes surmised that one of his former companions had judged him to be a danger and that he silenced the poor unfortunate man.'

'May I see this manuscript?'

'You can have it. I have long struggled with what to do with it. Parts of it read as if it is a true account but I believe it cannot be so because it alleges that the Branwells were punished for their sinfulness by having a man called Heathcliff Earnshaw foist on them a child. I cannot for the life of me work out how something written in 1825 can contain a character that was invented by Emily Brontë twenty years later!'

'Tell me about the child,' I urged.

'Read it and you will see. If, like me, you judge what it contains false, burn it. That is probably what William Clowes or I should have done long ago.'

I could not disguise my surprise at this sudden turn of events, but I was quick to express my gratitude at the confidence he showed in my judgement. I took the proffered manuscript and shortly afterwards took my leave. If outwardly I had kept my composure, inwardly my mind was in turmoil. I had gleaned much background information from my visit but clearly in my hands I held a document that promised far more. Once I was safely back home, I read the papers written by the murdered Cornishman. Afterwards I falsely conveyed to Mr Lord that I had destroyed the manuscript, thinking he might otherwise request its return. He seemed greatly relieved because I think he had regretted his impulsive act in handing it over to me. However, I did not destroy it. Indeed I have the manuscript on my desk now as I write this. In its pages I found the unholy link between the real Heathcliff and the Brontë family.

7

Recollections of a Cornish Wrecker

Dear Mr Clowes,

Hearing you preach today reminded me of that day so long ago when as a young man I stood listening to the great John Wesley. You have the same air of authority that he had. How I wish that I had listened to him and given my life to God! My life would then have followed a happier path.

Today you preached of forgiveness, but for years I have known that all the oceans of the world cannot wash clean my bloodstained hands. I say this because I joined on one night with those who, for the sake of wealth, murdered the innocent. We valued brandy, tea and tobacco more than the souls of our fellow men. With my own hand I killed a man and I stood by while my comrades in sin bludgeoned others with club and stone. How can God forgive such a crime? In my nightmares I see our victims' long-dead, seaweed-surrounded faces, pale and white. I see the horror of their absent eyes, consumed by the fish. I see how wave and rock have torn their bodies to ribbons and, although I thrust my fingers in my ears, I hear the sound of their suffering. Their spilt blood calls out to God for justice and not for mercy.

But let me begin at the beginning. My name is John Reynolds and I was born here in Redruth, but my whole life has been involved with the sea. I was only twenty-three and in the prime of my life when I became an excise officer in Penzance. Then I was an upright and God-fearing young man, but my early hopes of promotion and earning a decent salary soon expired and with them my integrity. Once I paid my expenses, I found I was only earning thirty-two pounds a year, or one shilling and ninepence farthing a day. For that scanty pittance it was expected not only that I should always be sober and diligent but also that I should risk life and limb in preventing or detecting frauds against the revenue business. Believe me, my life was truly wretched. I was removed from all my natural friends and relations and I scraped a solitary existence because 'tis impossible to support a family on so meagre a wage. I wish the pay had been enough to set me above temptation and to make it worthwhile to remain honest, but it was not and a tender conscience is easily overcome by the sharpness of want. Ask many a destitute woman who turns to whoredom.

I asked myself why should I stay honest when all around me were not? Forty years ago most of the people were involved at some level or other in smuggling and not just those who sailed the seas, but also merchants and farmers, miners and labourers, innkeepers and shopkeepers, even the clergy. They simply called it 'free trade'. In Penzance the Oxnams, the Branwells and the Carnes presented to the world a face of respectability, attending church regularly, but that did not prevent those families making much of their money by paying farm labourers to carry smuggled goods inland and by providing horses to transport them further afield. It was an accepted part of running your business. What could I do in the face of this? I had no force at my command and, if I tried to prevent the trade, I risked being killed because no Cornish jury would find guilty those who chose to remove me. It was safer and easier to cast in my lot with men like John Carter, the self-styled 'King of Prussia'. In return for ensuring he faced no hassle, I was amply rewarded. Carter was a rough man but he was good to those who played fair with him.

My descent into further sin can be traced to the spring of 1782 when I first met a young man called Heathcliff Earnshaw, who had newly arrived in Penzance. The previous year charges had been brought against the Mousehole officials for accepting bribes and I think the authorities foolishly assumed that by bringing in a non-local there was a greater chance of preventing future deals between excise officers and the local populace. Earnshaw was then in his early twenties and he had just newly become an excise officer. He had a strange way of speaking and he told me that he was from Yorkshire, but that his mother was Cornish. He said that his step-brother had driven him out of the family home after their father's death and he had joined the excise in Liverpool as an alternative to hard labour. I know it sounds strange that a man so little experienced should be appointed, but few are turned down because hardly any wish to become an excise officer. The decision to send him to work in Penzance had come as a surprise, but he was determined to seize what opportunities this offered, legal and illegal.

We soon struck up a friendship and it did not take long for him to also join the payroll of one of the smuggling groups. He took service with Mr Thomas Branwell, who imported most of his tea illegally. Some of the smuggled tea was sold in his shop in Market Square and some was passed on to personal contacts and other local shopkeepers, but most was secretly stored in the cellars that he owned at the quayside. From thence it was taken by his agents up-country to the small village of Stockwell on the outskirts of London. Like many tea merchants, he had his own warehouse there and from this the tea was sold direct to various teahouses in the city. Mr Branwell argued that he was doing his fellow man a service by providing tea at less than half the cost of the East India Company. Heathcliff laughed at this attempt to justify smuggling. As far as he was concerned, the only motive was to make money and he felt Mr Branwell should honestly own up to that.

It was not long before Heathcliff began putting pressure on his new master to take up an even more profitable activity – that of deliberately wrecking ships for plunder. I know some think that wrecking ships was then a commonplace activity but I can assure you this was not the case. Though hundreds happily involved themselves in smuggling, few if any were prepared to engage in drawing ships onto the rocks for plunder. Most Cornish people live so close to the sea that they know of many a relative or friend who has drowned in stormy waters. Such an experience does not lead you to wish to doom innocent people to a similar fate, whatever riches you might acquire from the process. What is true is that

95

when wrecks happen – and that is not an uncommon occurrence on our storm-dashed coastline – people see no reason why they should not benefit and therefore they flock to the shore to seize whatever they can from the wreckage. Heathcliff had witnessed this happen and, coming as he did from up-country, wrongly concluded that the people caused such disasters.

Mr Branwell was at first utterly contemptuous. He made clear that he would never deliberately wreck a ship because he had no desire to meet his maker with the blood of innocents on his conscience. Heathcliff merely laughed at this, saying it was the first time that he had heard the godforsaken scum who sail in ships referred to as innocents. I backed up Mr Branwell, saying that those who wrecked ships were doing the devil's work and that the sea claimed enough lives without us desiring to add to their number. Heathcliff damned our consciences and urged us to recognize that it would only take a couple of good wrecks to make us very rich men. He said that we should seize the moment because it would be only a matter of time before His Majesty's government took more effective steps to patrol our coastline in such a way as to end any profit from smuggling. Mr Branwell responded by saying that Heathcliff could do what he wanted but he must accept that all dealing between them would come to an end if he embarked on such a damnable activity as wrecking.

This declaration did not go unchallenged. Heathcliff muttered that it would not be difficult in his position to turn informant on those who engaged in smuggling. However, when he faced Mr Branwell's fury, he asked to be forgiven for his ill-tempered words and attributed them to his deep desire to have enough money to return to his home in Yorkshire. The topic of wrecking was postponed until the day when rumours began that the government was going to slash the high taxes on tea. Mr Branwell knew such a move would sweep away his business virtually overnight and Heathcliff seized the opportunity to reopen talk of obtaining money by wrecking. In a fit of depression, Mr Branwell reluctantly agreed to assist him. He salved his conscience by saying to himself that he was only lending Heathcliff money and providing him with some smuggling contacts in return for a future payment and that how Heathcliff chose to 'invest' the money was his decision.

Heathcliff then persuaded me to assist him because I had far greater local knowledge than him. I do not seek to justify my decision but I think my participation in smuggling made participating in another criminal activity seem less immoral and so helped me crush my conscience. I felt I could not return to living just on the meagre income of an excise officer. I will not bore you with all the details of how Heathcliff and I planned to wreck our first ship. It was easy enough for me to identify a good spot from which we could lead a ship onto the rocks by placing a misleading light. I knew enough also to point out which men he should approach to join us. The latter was important because I knew most would not countenance such an evil act. The contacts provided by Mr Branwell made disposing of what we would acquire by our actions seem a very easy process.

The events of the stormy night on which the actual wrecking took place are deeply engraved on my mind. As we made our way to the chosen cove, dark angry clouds scurried across the sky and there was a salty tang to the air from the wind-whipped waves that crashed relentlessly on the black rocks below us. As we hurried on, the heavy onslaught of heavy, driving rain seemed to drive away the merriment that our earlier drinking had induced and our party fell silent. The bare cliff side offered no shelter for man nor beast and we were all sodden by the time we reached our destination. From the beach most of us waited for the tide, peering into the semi-darkness with an intense watchfulness. After a while the rain eased and it was replaced with a mist that blocked out everything but the sound of the sea breaking upon the shore and crashing upon the rocks. Occasionally the mist would temporarily lift and then the line of breakers would show thin and white against the surrounding darkness.

I know not what time passed but eventually I saw a small white light come to life on the clifftop to our left. This was our weapon, the means by which we hoped to draw a passing ship into our clutches. I looked at the flickering flame and tried not to think of the ship beyond the breakers and its crew, seeking a symbol of hope amid the turbulent seas, and yet falsely turning to our light for guidance. Suddenly one of our men came rushing down to us, scattering small stones in his descent. From the clifftops he had seen through a gap in the mist a large ship headed for us. We knew then it was only a matter of time before it struck the awaiting rocks. Heathcliff ordered everyone to spread out in a thin line along the shore. Before long we could make out the lights of the ship. They were rising and falling with the waves and drawing ever nearer. Only then did the full enormity of what I was engaged in strike home. I bitterly regretted my decision to join in such an unholy crime. I wanted to shout out and warn the sailors of their danger, but I feared the men we had hired would kill me for such an act of treachery.

Silent I therefore watched as the unsuspecting ship struck the rocks and there was the sound of splintering wood and voices crying in alarm. The mist lifted sufficiently for me to see its masts and yards snapping as if they were no more than threads. Its rigging tumbled into the sea, trapping many of the crew like some monstrous spider's web. I watched helpless as some of those on board the ill-fated vessel drowned in the stormy sea. However, others began to make their way to the shore, despite all the raging tempest that surrounded them. Our men moved to stop them, wading out into the sea. I followed suit, feeling the stones beneath my feet move as they followed the powerful drag of the sea. I saw to my left a woman reach where Heathcliff was standing. She was obviously both terrified and exhausted and she struggled to keep her footage, not least because she held to her breast a young infant child. Heathcliff made a gesture as if he was offering her assistance and she, poor wretch, thrust out her child into his arms, thinking first of its safety. He seized the child but then, to my horror, he swung it so its head was shattered against a nearby rock. Then he took a short weighted club from his belt and struck the distraught and traumatized woman. She collapsed into the foaming water and he hit her twice more before holding her head under the waves till she struggled no more.

I turned from this horrible sight only to find a man emerging from the water before me. I sensed from the shocked look on his face that this might be the woman's husband, the child's father. With a savage oath he moved to attack me and, in defence, I struck at him with the knife in my hand. My blade ripped his stomach and even in the gloom I could see the water darken as his blood flowed from the gaping wound I had inflicted. I trembled at what I had done for I had never injured a man like this before. Seeing me hesitate over what to do next, Heathcliff moved rapidly to my side and slit the poor man's neck from ear to ear in order to finish the task I had started. Whilst he was doing this, I could hear the cries of the other survivors as our fellow wreckers slaughtered them one by one. I cried out that I had never given my assent to such butchery and that we were committing a crime that would stink to highest heaven. Then I vomited, my stomach sick at the sights I had seen.

Heathcliff told me not to be a fool and think of the wealth that the night's work would bring. Had I really expected that the sea would do all our dirty work for us? Did I not realize that our safety depended upon there being no witnesses? Did I want to be hung on a gibbet? I made my way back to the beach, screaming that I wanted no blood money. Heathcliff followed me, cursing my stupidity and saying he would happily take my share of the profits. Then he moved off to begin directing the salvaging from the wreck. He ran up and down the beach like a man demented, urging how best to seize the sodden wreckage that was beginning to come ashore on the incoming tide. I watched as the spoils were dragged ashore by those prepared to wade waist-deep into the breakers. Time passed and the tide began to turn. The corpses of those who had been aboard the ship were stripped of any possessions worth having and then the bodies were returned to the sea for burial. I could not help but feel that our shrouded wagons, which we had brought to receive the looted goods, might better have served as hearses. Instead they groaned under the weight of our ill-gotten gains.

Heathcliff told us it was time we left once the gloom of night began to give way to the grey of dawn. I did as he bid but that night our friendship came to an end. I regretted bitterly the day his path had ever crossed mine. Needless to say, I took no money from the success of the venture. Nor did Mr Branwell when I described to him what had taken place. Fearful that we might betray him, even though that would have cost us dearly, Heathcliff took all the profit from the wreck and headed almost immediately back to Yorkshire. He had heard that his half-sister had married and he told me that he intended to set himself up as a farmer, so he could live near to her again. This appeared an honourable move, but there was something in his face, some wild look in his eyes, that made me question whether he was telling me the entire truth. There was something about his half-sister's marriage that clearly upset him. Were I her husband, I questioned whether I would want to have as my neighbour someone as ruthlessly cruel as Heathcliff Earnshaw.

Mr Branwell and I thought we would never see that devil again, but that proved not to be the case. One day in April 1783 I saw Heathcliff emerging from the house of his former employer. On his face was a look of such demonic joy that I shuddered. I confess that I hurriedly entered a shop so that he would not see me. I watched as he headed off up the street and then, re-entering the street, I knocked at Mr Branwell's door. He opened it. All the colour was drained from his face and he looked like a man who had seen the devil himself. He bade me enter in a grief-stricken voice. I asked what Heathcliff had wanted and was told that he had demanded the Branwells should bring up his child as if it was their own. He said that if they refused he would turn king's evidence and inform the authorities of their involvement in shipwrecking.

This seemed to me incredible. How could the man expect anyone to take his hellish brat? It was doubtless the offspring of some lustful dalliance. How was the sudden arrival of a child to be explained? Then I saw Mrs Branwell in the corner of the room, clutching to her breast a red-stained bundle. She was rigidly silent with shock. Her husband's voice cracked with emotion as he sobbed how Heathcliff had murdered their newborn infant with his knife before they could intervene. Never have I seen a man with such haunted eyes as he turned to me and added how Heathcliff had told them to expect the replacement that afternoon. I know not what other men would have done in this situation, but Mr Branwell took the murder of his daughter as God's punishment on his sinful decision to provide Heathcliff with the means to wreck the ship. He therefore secretly buried his child and commanded his wife to take Heathcliff's child as her own. This was to be their life-long penance for his sinfulness. He vowed to bring her up in such a way that she would never share her true father's nature. He said he would make sure she was a truly God-fearing child.

I alone therefore of all those living in Penzance know that Maria Branwell is actually the daughter of Heathcliff Earnshaw. No one has ever guessed her hellish origin. To my astonishment and their great credit neither Mr or Mrs Branwell ever showed any hostility to the child that had replaced their own daughter. Maria had there-fore every reason to believe she was a full member of their family. If anything, she was a favoured child and I watched her grow up to be a fine young woman under their influence and that of the Methodists, with whom the family was increasingly bound up. I hope that their kindness to Maria will count on that day when we are all called to account for our lives. Maybe Mr Branwell has earned forgiveness for his participation in Heathcliff's evil scheme. I know I have not.

The only cloud that hung over the merchant was that he feared one day Heathcliff would return to reclaim his child. He made me vow to look after Maria should that day ever happen and he not be alive to protect her. However, not long after the death of him and his wife, Maria was summoned to Yorkshire. I feared to see her go to the county from which her real father had come, but there was nothing I could do without betraying the family secret. I therefore remained silent and Maria left. I never saw her again. I can only hope that Heathcliff played no part in her life.

As for me, I never married or had family. I have lived the years since the events I describe in continual penitence. If I had truly listened to the voice of Christ I would never have become a party to Heathcliff's foul scheme! How I wish I could give my life to God now, but I find it hard to believe he can offer me forgiveness. It has come to me that perhaps I need to confess publicly not only what I write in this document but all the other crimes in which I have engaged over the years. However, I know there are still some alive who would fear to be named in such revelations and I must first speak with them. Should they silence me, then maybe God will still take pity on my unworthy soul.

Pray for me and those I have wronged,

John Reynolds

I was shocked at the document's revelation that Cathy's missing child was Maria Branwell but I doubted not for a moment that Reynolds' confession was a true one, not least because it explained how Heathcliff had been able to return to Yorkshire as a wealthy man. However, it left many unanswered questions. What had possessed Heathcliff to go back to Cornwall with the stolen daughter of Cathy and pass the child off as his own? Why had he forced Thomas Branwell to take care of her as if she were his own flesh and blood? Was there some conscious aim being pursued or were his actions the product of mounting insanity? And why had his child been so graciously accepted by the merchant and his wife after Heathcliff had murdered their own daughter? Could it truly be explained entirely as an act of penitence on Thomas Branwell's part? Did Maria Branwell ever discover her true ancestry? Were Emily or Charlotte aware of their mother's real identity? Had at some stage Heathcliff made himself known to Maria and was that why she came to Yorkshire in 1812?

The only information I had of what might have happened next was in Emily's novel, *Wuthering Heights*. I did not know why Charlotte had given her the idea of writing this nor did I know precisely what she had told her. The book contained no reference to Cathy's second child, but I re-read it in the hope it might provide some clue that I could pursue. The first thing that struck me was the extent to which the book contrasts Heathcliff's love for Cathy with his hatred for poor Isabella Linton. He physically and verbally abuses her until a knife wound finally acts as the catalyst to make her flee to London and there she gives birth to his son, whom she names Linton. After her departure Hindley Earnshaw dies from over-drinking and his son, Hareton, is therefore left alone to face

Heathcliff's brutal maltreatment. Despite this, he grows up at Wuthering Heights worshipping his uncle, who increasingly becomes a recluse because of his continuing grief at Cathy's death.

All this part of the novel gave me food for thought. By my reckoning the real Linton must have been born sometime in 1785 and I thought that I might be able to find records of the precise date if I investigated. Hindley's death would probably have been in 1786, but I found it hard to believe that a young man of just twenty-seven would perish so quickly from drinking too much. Surely his death would have been far more protracted? I wondered whether in reality Heathcliff and Nelly had found a means of ending the poor man's life so they could fully access his estate. I noted that in the novel Nelly organized Hindley's rapid burial. Was this to avoid anyone questioning the manner of his death? I also speculated about why Hareton should have worshipped a man who treated him so cruelly. Was this because he believed that Heathcliff had seduced his mother and that he was therefore Heathcliff's son? Sons will bear much from a father that they would not suffer from another.

To my frustration the events of the next twelve years were then passed over in *Wuthering Heights*. Emily's novel resumes its story with Isabella's death and the decision of Edgar Linton to bring back his nephew, Linton. By my reckoning this must have been in 1798. Cathy's daughter, Catherine, then aged fourteen, warmly welcomes her young cousin. Unfortunately Heathcliff, out of sheer spite, insists on reclaiming the thirteen-year-old Linton and makes him his prisoner in the farmhouse. Edgar does not tell Catherine where Linton has gone because he is so anxious to keep her away from any contact with Heathcliff. However, about two years later, Catherine uncovers what has happened. Whilst walking on the moor with Nelly Dean, she accidentally comes across Hareton, who introduces himself as her cousin. Then by another chance she subsequently meets Heathcliff, who uses all his charm to convince her that the quarrel between him and her father is unwarranted. She agrees to write in secret to Linton, whom she is told misses her badly. Heathcliff knows that he can have no better revenge on Edgar Linton than to make Catherine's life miserable. He threatens to uncover her duplicity to her father by revealing she has been secretly writing to Linton unless she visits his farmhouse. Once she starts doing that,

Heathcliff makes Linton court her – an easy task because Linton is frail and weak-minded and totally under his control. Catherine is overwhelmed with pity for her sickly cousin and Heathcliff persuades the naive girl to think that her feelings are a product of love. He eventually forces her to marry Linton by saying her cousin will die unless she does. The news of the ill-fated marriage proves fatal to Edgar Linton and when the frail Linton also dies, Catherine is left as a prisoner with Heathcliff and Hareton.

I found all of this very unconvincing. For a start I could not accept Emily's account of how Catherine accidentally met first Hareton and then, much later, Heathcliff, whilst walking on the moors. Was Heathcliff a man who left things to chance? Did it not make more sense if Nelly had deliberately engineered both these meetings? But, if so, why was there such a long delay in this happening? The implication in the novel is that they did not meet until 1800 yet Wuthering Heights and Thrushcross Grange were not so very far apart. If I accepted that Emily was right and that Heathcliff did not see Catherine Linton until she was a young woman, then his first meeting with her must have come as a shock. He would have seen a Catherine who was fair of face, and graceful, and lively in manner – a Cathy reborn at least in outward appearance. In the novel his response is to exert all his charm to captivate her, though he hates her for being the cause of her mother's death, and such is his success that Edgar Linton cannot persuade his daughter that the man whom she has met is truly diabolical in character. However, I could not believe that the real Catherine would have been so easily duped as to put a stranger before her father.

Question after question sprang to my mind about the inherent flaws in Emily's version of events. Why should Catherine commit the worse crime of going to Wuthering Heights rather than admit writing a few innocent letters? What possibly could she have found attractive in the almost effeminate Linton? Could she really have been forced to marry him? Surely the deaths of both Linton and Edgar were too convenient to be natural? Was it possible that Heathcliff and Nelly Dean had poisoned them? What I did not dismiss in the novel's account was that Heathcliff hated Catherine. What I had uncovered gave me a strong reason as to why that might have been. He knew of Cathy's other child, Maria, and he intended one day to reclaim her. She, not Catherine, was Cathy's true heir in his mind. He obviously saw Catherine more as the daughter of his enemy, Edgar Linton, than the child of the woman he loved. But, if that was the case, then why had Heathcliff never summoned Maria back from Cornwall? Or had he?

I realized that it is the sheer power of Emily's prose that has made her readers accept all the inherent flaws in her story, including those in the novel's unforgettable but highly melodramatic climax. After Edgar Linton's death, Thrushcross Grange is rented out to a Mr Lockwood, who witnesses Heathcliff's final dramatic descent into madness as he is haunted by the ghost of Cathy. Heathcliff engages in an all-night vigil, standing at the window of Cathy's former bedroom, totally without any regard for the stormy weather that rages around him. Nelly finds his soaked lifeless body in the morning:

> Mr Heathcliff was there – laid on his back. His eyes met mine so keen and fierce, I started; and then he seemed to smile. I could not think him dead: but his face and throat were washed with rain; the bedclothes dripped, and he was perfectly still.... I hasped the window; I combed his black long hair from his forehead; I tried to close his eyes: to extinguish, if possible, that frightful, life-like gaze of exultation ...They would not shut: they seemed to sneer at my attempts: and his parted lips and sharp white teeth sneered too!

Dramatic stuff indeed, but why this sudden remorse? And surely a strong man like Heathcliff would not have died from sitting all night by an open window? What follows in Emily's account is even more unbelievable. The book ends with the marriage of Catherine to Hareton! Surely, after all that had happened to her, Catherine would not have married this illiterate and boorish cousin of her own volition?

Though fifty years had passed by since these events, I knew I must somehow uncover what had really happened. I decided that my best option was to see if I could discover whether Mr Lockwood was a real person because, if by some remote chance he was still alive, he might be able to tell me what was true and what was false in Emily's novel. The only clue I had to follow up was that Mr Lockwood had leased

Thrushcross Grange so that became my starting point. I knew the mansion had long ago changed its name but I sent a letter to its current residents, requesting a meeting and explaining my long connection with the Brontë family and my desire to know more about the house and its previous occupiers. I received in reply a courteous letter from a Mr Opie saying that it would be his and his wife's pleasure to entertain me, but that I must not expect them to be very knowledgeable about the property because they had only recently taken over its lease. His profession of ignorance did not augur well but, nevertheless, I took up his kind offer. The meeting was to provide far more information than I could possibly have dreamed of and totally destroy Emily's version of events.

8

The Thrushcross Grange Letters

It was early in the February of 1854 that I made my way to Mr Opie's home. As I travelled along the two-mile drive that stretches from its entrance gates to the mansion, I realized just how much the place was like Emily's description of Thrushcross Grange. Mr and Mrs Opie were awaiting my arrival and they proved to be really kind and generous hosts. He was a distinguished-looking brown-haired man in his mid-forties, tall, straight-backed and slim. He had obviously dressed smartly for my benefit but he looked rather uncomfortable in his suit. I fancied therefore he was a man who loved the outdoors more than polite society. However, he was charming in manner. There was no trace of affectation about him. His blue eyes had a kind look and his smile a natural warmth, and his face, which was slightly ruddy in complexion, showed few wrinkles beyond some laughter lines.

His wife had a more nervous manner on first acquaintance, but once she was at her ease with me she proved very affable and most kind. Her voice was viola-like and had an almost siren quality to it. In her youth I suspected she must have been quite a beauty, and age had been kind to her. She was still quite lithe and there was no trace of that matronly weight that so often comes with middle age. Her dark hair was unmarked by grey and her oval face, delicate-coloured skin, straight nose and grey-blue eyes were still very striking. So too was her attire. She was wearing the most sublime butterfly-blue silk gown into which had been sewn some peacock feathers, which shimmered in the sunlight.

Once the initial pleasantries were over, they delighted at seeing my genuine interest in their home, so Mr Opie insisted on escorting me round both the mansion and its garden, though it was far too early in the year to judge the beauty of the latter. He was clearly a man who enjoyed beautiful things, whether their glory sprang from the natural order or was shaped by human hand. His wife was able not only to name most of the plants and how they would flower as we strolled together outside but also to tell me whence they came. The interplay between the couple left me in no doubt that theirs was a very happy marriage, based on mutual interests and mutual respect.

They next gave me a tour of the inside of the mansion. Mrs Opie delighted in showing me some of the more interesting paintings and sculptures that adorned its gracious silk-lined rooms. When we entered the library, Mr Opie handed me a book. He said that prior to my arrival he had searched the shelves to find anything about the house and found only this one hand-kept business journal, which contained information about the leasing of the property. Within it was Mr Lockwood's name. He showed me the entry and it recorded that his tenancy had begun in 1802 and ended in 1803. The mansion's name had been changed shortly afterwards. I was bitterly disappointed that there was no mention of where Mr Lockwood had gone and no reference at all to either Catherine Linton or Hareton Earnshaw. Emily's novel, of course, ends with them taking up a new life at Thrushcross Grange.

Mr Opie saw my obvious disappointment at reaching a dead end and he immediately tried to comfort me by saying there might be other leads to follow. I thought he was just being kind, but then he pointed to an old walnut bureau in the corner of the room and said that there were masses of old papers relating to the house in its drawers. He had possessed neither the time nor the inclination to sort through them, but he was willing to let me see if I could find anything. I immediately assented and he summoned their housekeeper and told her to give me whatever support I required in my search.

Over the next couple of hours I found nothing that bore any relation to my quest. All I acquired were sore eyes from trying to decipher the poor handwriting that covered most of the documents that I was examining. I had almost given up hope when I turned my attention to a small bundle of letters that were contained within an envelope. To my intense excitement, these consisted of three letters written by Edgar Linton to Catherine and no less than six written by Catherine and addressed to a friend called Lucy Wright. Collectively these nine letters provided an account of events after Isabella Linton's death that was just as melodramatic as Emily's novel but far removed from her version of events. Some of my speculation proved accurate but in my wildest dreams I would never have imagined the cruelty borne by the poor unfortunate Catherine Linton.

Mr and Mrs Opie rejoiced in my successful find and were content to let me transcribe the letters before I left. In the pages that follow you can read at first hand what befell Catherine Linton – how her father deceived her, how her nurse betrayed her, how her lover proved false to her and, above all, how Heathcliff aimed to destroy her. You can also discover the reason that lay behind his abduction of Cathy's other child and therefore the full extent of his irrational villainy.

*

Edgar Linton to his daughter Catherine 7 February 1798

My dearest child,
I am safely come to London and I am now at your aunt's house. I was deeply shocked to see how near to death is Isabella. She has grown so thin and looks so old that I can scarce recognize her as my younger sister. The doctor says there is no hope of her surviving for more than a couple of weeks at most. I will do all I can to comfort her and make her passage from this life seem a welcome release. Your cousin Linton is a fine young man and I am sure you will like him when I bring him home. He is not as physically strong as I would wish, but I trust the fresh air at Thrushcross will do wonders for him. The constant smog of London does little to help someone who has a weak chest. Now, with you as his nurse, he will doubtless thrive!
    Your loving father

Catherine Linton to her friend Lucy Wright 11 February 1798

Dear Lucy,
Father has been called to London because his widowed sister is dying and so I am left here all alone except, of course, for Nelly.

She tells me that it is likely Father will bring back my cousin Linton, who is just six months younger than me. I am sure it will be delightful to have him as a playfellow.

Normally, as you know, I am never allowed to go beyond the confines of Thrushcross but yesterday Nelly encouraged me in my father's absence to go for a walk with her across the moors to Penistone Crags. I was surprised because she normally only does whatever my father wants and it is his expressed wish that I should never roam the moors. However, the thought of such unaccustomed freedom made me readily assent. It was a beautiful clear morning as we set off and Nelly insisted on taking with us a small bag that contained something to eat and drink so that we could have our lunch outside, even though it is so early in the year. We had walked about four miles or so and were almost at the Crags when she insisted we seek some water to refresh ourselves and led me to a nearby farmhouse. There we were greeted by a youth, who was clumsy in manner and shy in speech. He was a handsome young man to look at, but this was offset by his shoddy dress, which looked like that of a servant. It showed all the signs of the kind of manual labour in which no gentleman would engage. Imagine my surprise therefore when he hesitatingly introduced himself as Hareton Earnshaw and called himself my cousin. He told me he was the son of my mother's brother, who was now deceased, and that he lived under the care of his uncle, Heathcliff, who farmed nearby.

The name of Heathcliff Earnshaw was not unknown to me because my father has long banned me from having any contact with this neighbouring farmer. That his nephew might be my cousin was a most intriguing development! I confess that at first I found Hareton's manner rather coarse but, after we had exchanged more words, he appeared to me to be a good if rather simple-minded young man. He was very anxious that I should promise to see him again. I felt that I ought to decline, but Nelly encouraged me to think otherwise. She said that I should not let my father's prejudice put me off seeing my newfound cousin again. According to her, my father's hostility arose because of an unnecessary quarrel between the two families at the time of my mother's death. She said that my father's grief had distorted his judgement. At one point he had even threatened to dismiss her, but her role in tending to my birth had made him reconsider. I whispered to her that I had heard others say Mr Earnshaw was a cruel and hard man, who deliberately avoided his neighbours' company. Nelly replied that the poor maligned farmer only avoided company for the sake of Hareton, who was ill-equipped to deal with polite society because he was slightly retarded and unable to read or write.

In the light of Nelly's comments, I gave Hareton my word that I would see him again. If I have two cousins, should not poor Hareton be just as much worthy of our attention as Linton? However today I am fearful about what Father will say if he hears of all this! Nelly says he will be angry and so I must keep the meeting and any future ones a secret. I know now not what to think!

Please send me your thoughts about what I should do.

Your fondest friend, Catherine

Edgar Linton to his daughter Catherine 14 February 1798

My dearest child,

Your aunt died yesterday and I am pleased to say peacefully. Her life has not been an easy one. Over the past few days I have learned just how evilly she was treated by her devil of a husband. Had I known what I know now I would have had the man horse-whipped. I bitterly regret that I did not offer my sister more aid all those years ago. My only defence is her marriage occurred shortly before that dark time when I lost your mother, who was the light of my life. My world was plunged into such an abyss of darkness that what was happening to my sister did not even enter my consciousness. Only gradually did your love draw me back to life and by then my sister Isabella was settled in London without her husband to trouble her. I have vowed to repay my earlier neglect by promising to provide for her son as if he were my own. I hope that your cousin Linton and I will be with you soon, but you must be

patient because there are many issues to resolve here before we can
return.

Your loving father

Catherine Linton to her friend Lucy Wright 12 March 1798

Dearest Lucy,

A week ago my father returned home from London and he brought
with him my cousin Linton. He is charming and quite good-
looking but he is very pale and it is obvious his health is not good.
The journey from London had clearly exhausted him. I insisted he
should rest on our sofa and I placed a footstool next to it so I could
sit and talk with him. I heard Father say to Nelly that he was sure
Linton's health would improve, not least because my company
would instil fresh spirit into him.

We soon agreed that it would be best if my cousin had an early
night. I said I would also retire for the night. Just after we had gone
upstairs there was a harsh knocking at the front door. I crept out of
my room and listened to what was happening. The man at the door
announced himself to be a servant of Heathcliff Earnshaw and he
told Father that his master wanted his son Linton sent immediately
to Wuthering Heights. You can imagine how my mind reeled at the
news that Hareton's uncle was also Linton's father! I had been
brought up to believe that my aunt's husband was long since dead.
My father replied to the messenger that Mr Earnshaw had shown
no interest in his son until now and that, as far as he was concerned,
the request stemmed not from love but from sheer devilment. He
then added he had no intention of getting Linton out of bed but he
would bring the boy over the following morning. The servant tried
to insist that his master's command be instantly met but my father
cast him out of the house.

I slept very fitfully that night, troubled by the way I had been
deceived, and that may explain why I was disturbed by the sound of
my father moving around the house in the early hours of the
morning. I made my way downstairs and, hearing the sound of
voices in the library, crept to its door. My father was talking with

Nelly Dean, telling her that she must take Linton immediately to Wuthering Heights before I was awake. He said that he now realized that he could have no influence over his nephew's destiny and that from thenceforward he must treat him as one dead. He did not want me to know that he had lied about the continued existence of Linton's father and so it was important that I should not know where my cousin had gone. Poor Linton was crying, saying he had no desire to leave Thrushcross and go to live with a man who had so cruelly treated his mother. Nelly tried to persuade him that the fresh air at Wuthering Heights would be good for his health and that he would enjoy having the company of his cousin Hareton, a boy near to him in age, but Linton remained adamant that he did not wish to leave.

I was tempted to enter the room and support my cousin, but I feared to expose that I knew my father's deceit. In the end I ran back upstairs and threw myself sobbing on my bed. When I came down again in time for breakfast, Linton was gone. My father told me that he had not realized how frail my cousin was and that he had therefore made immediate arrangements for him to go to a place where he could improve his health and that I would not be seeing him again for some time. I hid my knowledge of the real truth but, even so, I know that these events have made my father more determined than ever to keep me under lock and key at Thrushcross. I think my chances of ever seeing Hareton or Linton again are very slim. What must Heathcliff Earnshaw be like as a man to instil such loathing in my father? Or were Nelly's earlier words right and, in this matter, is my father needlessly damning his brother-in-law's character?

My mind is in such a whirl that I know not what to do. Think of me, dearest Lucy, and pray that this unhappy situation in which I find myself may be resolved.

From your loving friend, Catherine

Catherine Linton to her friend Lucy Wright 5 April 1800

Dear Lucy,

It is over two years since I last wrote to you. Your failure to reply understandably upset me. However, I am putting aside my hurt and writing to you again now because you and I were once so close and I must tell someone that I am in contact with my cousins. I can scarce believe it because I had given up all hope of our ever meeting again!

As you know, my father has never been able to bring himself to truly celebrate my birthday because it also marks the anniversary of my mother's death. This year – as usual – he locked himself away in his study. Nelly asked me if I would like to mark my sixteenth birthday by having a day with her on the moors because it was such a beautiful day. She said she knew my father would not grant his permission but the outing could be our little secret. I readily assented and promised not to get her into trouble by telling him about our venturing out.

It was such a joy to be free in the sweet morning sunshine. We crossed over various hills till we reached near Penistone Crags. Nelly said she needed a rest but urged me to continue on ahead over the brow of a hill. This I did, recalling how I must be very near the place where we had met Hareton Earnshaw two years before. Suddenly two men approached from the other side of the hill. It was almost as if they had been waiting for me. The younger of the two I immediately recognized as Hareton and the older introduced himself as Mr Heathcliff Earnshaw. After all these years I was face to face with the man my father so loathed. Yet he appeared charm itself and, when Nelly made her appearance, he urged her to bring me for refreshments to Wuthering Heights. He said his son Linton would be especially delighted to see us because he had often talked of wanting to see his cousin again. Only my father's prohibition had prevented him visiting Thrushcross.

I did not know what to say. My brain told me that my father must have good reason for hating this man, yet my heart urged me to seize this opportunity of seeing Linton again. In the end curiosity won the day and I said I would accompany them. Nelly made only a token protest, saying she was not convinced my father would approve. I felt in reality she was as keen as I was to go to the house. When we reached Wuthering Heights, Linton was awaiting us. He had grown much taller and, though not as well built as

Hareton, he looked every bit as fit. His sunburned face and sparkling eyes were a far cry from the pale boy I had last seen. I know it sounds mad but my heart went out to him so much that I felt I knew there and then that my cousin was the person I should like to marry!

Linton's father could not have been more solicitous of our welfare and we were entertained to a very fine meal. It was almost as if the family had been expecting us. Only Hareton seemed unhappy about what was happening. Mr Earnshaw noticed this and apologized to me. He told Hareton it was time that he behaved more like a gentleman and less like a sullen labourer. Eventually our conversation inevitably turned to the animosity that existed between Mr Earnshaw and my father. He said that it was unfortunate but my father had taken a prejudice against him, believing him to be of insufficient good birth to warrant marrying his sister. This prejudice had become an obsession when my mother had died because for totally irrational reasons my father had blamed him for her death. In the conflict that had resulted, my father had poisoned his sister's mind to such an extent that she had left her husband to live in London. To my surprise, Nelly confirmed the truth of this.

We moved on to happier topics and I was downcast when Nelly insisted it was time we should return home. She said even my grief-stricken father might notice we were not at home if our visit was any more prolonged. Mr Earnshaw said that I was welcome to visit his house at any time and Linton urged me to come frequently. I promised I would, though as yet I did not know how I might persuade my father to let me do that. We said our goodbyes and set off walking back towards Thrushcross.

After we had gone some distance, we realized that we could hear someone was running to catch us. It was Hareton, looking wild-eyed and distraught. He grasped my hand and urged me not to be taken in. He said my father had every right to think Heathcliff was a monster. Nelly tried to silence him but he ignored her. He told me that I should not be deceived and that his uncle had only one aim and that was to get control of Thrushcross Grange by ensuring that I, as the heiress to the entire estate, married Linton. I blushed (not least because marriage to the handsome Linton already seemed to me a desirable outcome) but Nelly was furious. She insisted Hareton should leave us at once. She said she would have words with Mr Earnshaw if he dared repeat such nonsense ever again. At hearing this, the young man looked terrified and fled. For a while, we resumed our journey in an uncomfortable silence. However, as we drew near Thrushcross, Nelly urged me to totally ignore Hareton's wild and unfounded statements. She said the poor boy was half-mad and illiterate, a colossal and ungrateful dunce, whom any man less kind than Mr Earnshaw would long since have had locked away.

When we got back my father was waiting for us. We had been away too long for even him not to notice our absence. He was very angry that Nelly had taken me out on the moors and even angrier when I told him I had seen Mr Earnshaw and my cousins, Hareton and Linton. He said that Heathcliff Earnshaw was an inhuman devil who had destroyed my mother and my aunt and he made me promise never to go to Wuthering Heights again. Seeing my Father would brook no objection, I said I would do as he said and retreated into my room in tears. But I confess to you Lucy that I am not going to let my father make me forget my cousins. Nelly has already told me she will be the secret means of sending letters between Linton and me, providing I do not let Father know.

Please write to me.

Your loving friend, Catherine

Catherine Linton to her friend Lucy Wright 12 July 1800

Dear Lucy,

Why do you still not write to me? My situation has become desperate. Today my father discovered the letters that Linton has been writing to me! I foolishly had kept them wrapped in a handkerchief in the drawer of my desk, and he, having become suspicious, searched and found them. In the later letters Linton declares his love for me and it is obvious from their content that I have expressed my love for him. My father said he had no intention of anyone else reading what he described as 'this bundle of trash' and he insisted I watch as he threw each letter one by one into the fire to burn. I sobbed and cried and even tried once to snatch a letter from the flames, but this only made my father angrier. Once he had finished burning them all, he raked the very ashes so that not even a blackened fragment might survive.

I refused to tell my father who had been carrying our letters. He then forced me to sit at my desk and write the following words:

> Master Heathcliff is requested to send no more notes to Miss Linton, as she will not receive them.

He told me he would see this letter was safely delivered to Wuthering Heights and, if I tried to send another via any messenger, I could rest assured that messenger would be uncovered and punished most severely.

Please give me your advice, Lucy. What am I to do? Even Nelly has said she now dare not risk taking any letter from me to Linton. She agreed to post my letter to you but she says my father is suspicious of her and that he is keeping her movements under close watch so she can do no more.

Your loving but distraught friend, Catherine

Catherine Linton to her friend Lucy Wright 3 November 1800

Dear Lucy,

I still have had no letter from you. I begin to fear that maybe my letters have not reached you or that my father has somehow seized your replies. But I write again because there is no one else in whom I can confide. You are my only hope.

For over three months I have been virtually a prisoner at Thrushcross. However, this changed a week ago when my father became very ill with a heavy cold that settled on his lungs. As a consequence, I was able to regain a temporary freedom from his watchful eye. Nelly managed to get a message to Wuthering Heights and six days ago I climbed across the wall that bounds our estate in the hope that Linton would be awaiting me. To my dismay it was his father who was there. Mr Earnshaw told me that his son had made himself ill again over my prolonged silence and that, unless I came to see him at Wuthering Heights, he was sure he would die. I hesitated to risk being absent for too long a time lest my father become suspicious, but, knowing I could count on Nelly's support, I agreed to go there the following day.

The next day I made my way to the farmhouse near Penistone Crags. Mr Earnshaw seized my hand in gratitude and led me to Linton's room. His son was in a chair and wrapped in blankets. He looked as if he had a fever and he could scarce speak without coughing so much that I feared he might that instant die. He told me that he was glad I had come because the letter that I had last written had broken his heart. He begged me to marry him and never leave him again. When I said my father would never permit this, he collapsed to the floor as if I had pushed him a step nearer to his grave. He would not be comforted until I promised to return the next day.

I kept my word and this time found Linton slightly stronger. Mr Earnshaw blessed me, saying I was bringing his son back to life. Linton and I planned where we would go and what we would do when I was free from my father's control and that day we exchanged our first kiss. What joy there was in that moment! Needless to say, I promised to return again the following day. That night I dreamt of my sweet, darling cousin and of the day when we would be man and wife, but my third visit proved less happy. As I was nearing the farmhouse Hareton appeared and grabbed my arm forcefully. I confess I was scared as I looked into his scowling face. He proceeded to call me a fool. He said Linton was a worthless weakling who was only pretending to love me because he feared what Heathcliff would do to him if he did not. I slapped his face and, as he let go of me, ran towards the farmhouse. I think he would have followed but at that juncture Mr Earnshaw appeared at its door.

Once inside I shook with the shock of what had happened. Mr Earnshaw apologized profusely and said I had to understand that Hareton was consumed with jealousy. I vowed that I would marry Linton whether or not my father approved. But I fear that promise will not be fulfilled because, when I returned home, my father had risen from his sickbed. Hareton had betrayed us!

Lucy, for the last two days I have been more a prisoner than ever before. Was ever a daughter so cruelly treated by a once loving father? I fear that Linton will think I have deserted him and that he will lose the will to live.

Please help your loving friend, Catherine

Edgar Linton to his daughter Catherine 12 March 1801

My dearest Catherine,

For many years I have wished that I could lie beneath the green mound of earth that marks your mother's grave, but now I fear death is coming and who will protect you when I am no more? I know not what mysterious illness has struck me in recent weeks and Nelly's nursing seems only to make my condition worse. It deeply pains me that you who were once always by my side now avoid me. I know you think me heartless but I ask you to think back to happier days before the cursed Mr Earnshaw poisoned our relationship.

Linton has written to me saying that he is more my nephew than Mr Earnshaw's son and that, for the sake of your happiness, I should forgive any faults that make him unworthy of your love. I see in this letter the hand of his wicked father, but despite my continued fears, I feel I must respond positively. I realize I can no longer persevere in making you sad in the few months I have still to live. Our separation is a worse agony than any of the pain I suffer from my illness. I have therefore decided to grant my permission for Linton and you to meet regularly here at Thrushcross over the summer months. All I ask is that you use those meetings to make sure he is not just acting as his father's pawn and that you never agree to go to Wuthering Heights. If, after the summer, you remain convinced that Linton loves you, I will give your wedding my blessing before I die.

Your most loving father

Catherine Linton to her friend Lucy Wright 8 August 1801

Dearest Lucy,

You probably will think it strange to receive this letter from me after years of silence. In fact I have written to you but I have only just discovered that my nurse has never sent my letters. I therefore send this by my cousin Hareton's hand in the hope it will be the first to reach you. I need your urgent help because I am being held a prisoner at the farmhouse known as Wuthering Heights by Mr Heathcliff Earnshaw whilst my father lies dying at Thrushcross.

Let me explain what otherwise may sound madness. Three years ago I discovered I had two cousins, Hareton, the son of my mother's brother, and Linton, the son of my father's sister. I thought that I loved Linton and we hoped to marry but my father opposed this. In March, my father, relenting to my misguided wishes, gave permission for Linton to visit me each Thursday at Thrushcross. Far from making me happy, his visits made me increasingly realize that I had made a mistake in thinking I loved him. I was disappointed at the lack of interest he showed in anything I said and his inability to contribute in any way to my entertainment. More and more he appeared to me to be a handsome but peevish child rather than a loving and manly suitor and he frequently gave way to a listless apathy that I found irritating. Only when my nurse, Nelly Dean, was in the room did he show any sign of courting me and I now know that was because he feared she might report his ineptitude as a lover to his father, Mr Earnshaw.

Three days ago I had my worst ever meeting with Linton. I was not well disposed to give him my time because my father was seriously ill and I grudged every moment that took me away from being seated at his side. Linton greeted me with an animation that seemed to spring more from fear than joy. I told him that I would rather forego his visit on this occasion and spend the time with my father, who was suffering much. He pleaded not to be disgraced in the eyes of his father by being sent away before his allotted time. I angrily replied that he should not reduce himself to the state of an abject reptile. This only served to convulse him with terror. He got on his knees and begged me not to be angry with him for being a worthless, cowardly wretch. He said that his father would kill him unless I fixed a date for our marriage. Looking into his eyes I saw beyond any doubt that there was no love for me in his heart, only dread of his father.

Once Linton had gone, I confided my feelings about Linton to Nelly, who had witnessed his pathetic behaviour with mounting anger. I said I was determined to break off my relationship with him when he next visited Thrushcross. Hearing this, she said that the matter should not be postponed a week and that I should go to Wuthering Heights the next day. In that way I could have the whole matter immediately resolved and inform my father. She felt sure that he would welcome the news and that it might even bring about his recovery. Her words stirred up in me a hope of my father surviving his illness that I had thought dead but, nevertheless, I resisted her advice at first because I did not wish to leave my father unattended for so long. Moreover, when my father had granted permission for Linton to visit me, he had made me promise never to go on my own to Mr Earnshaw's home. However, Nelly made me alter my mind. She said she would give my father a sedative so that he would not worry about our absence, and that she would accompany me to ensure my safety.

Oh, how I regret my decision to go to Wuthering Heights! Once Nelly and I had crossed its threshold and made clear the purpose of our visit, Mr Earnshaw locked the door behind us. He said that he would not let us go till we had taken some tea with him and Linton. I replied that I had no intention of remaining within their house because I wanted to get back to my father as quickly as I could. He laughed and when I tried to grab the key from him he pushed me to the floor. I quickly rose and, seizing his hand, tried to make him release the key by biting his fingers. He called me a bitch and struck me repeatedly with his other hand till my head reeled and I had no option but to desist.

Linton urged me not to cross his father and to do as I was bid. I rushed weeping into the arms of Nelly, begging her protection. To my horror she brushed me away, calling me a stupid fool. Mr Earnshaw laughed at this and went over to Nelly, putting his arm round her waist. Only then did I realize the enormity of my folly. It was clear she was Mr Earnshaw's all-too-willing assistant. In my terror I turned to Linton for support, but he simply said that he and I had no choice but to marry as his father demanded. Mr Earnshaw told me that he would keep me prisoner whilst Nelly returned to Thrushcross and informed my father that I had eloped with Linton. If I remained obstinate in rejecting his son, then he would instruct Nelly to make sure my father died and died painfully.

I begged the monster to explain what we had done as a family to deserve such treatment. His face blackened and he snarled that my father had taken from him the one woman he had ever loved and that my birth had caused her death. He had plenty of reason therefore to curse both of us, just as he had every reason to hate Linton, who was the unwanted offspring of his marriage to my Aunt Isabella. I replied that I still could not see what he hoped to gain by making me marry Linton. His response chilled me to the bone. He said that he could foresee that both Linton and I were shortly to die and that he would then become the undisputed owner of Thrushcross. Then he could marry his intended bride.

I looked towards Nelly and he laughed at my mistake. I shall never forget his next words. He said that he was not going to marry Nelly, fond of her though he was. His future bride was going to be the sister that neither my father nor I knew about – a child who had been secretly snatched from my dying mother and taken to Cornwall. There she had grown up untainted by contact with her father or with me. He said with total conviction that, by marrying my sister, he would finally get to marry his Cathy. Believe me, Lucy, he is not just an evil and wicked man. He is utterly and completely insane!

122

So far I have refused to marry Linton, though my heart bleeds at the thought of my father's distress at my absence. My one hope rests with my cousin Hareton. He is a poor simpleton in many respects, having been brutalized from his childhood and denied all education, and he fears Mr Earnshaw for good reason, but he alone in this household seems to care what happens to me. At great risk to himself he has brought the means of me writing this letter and he has promised to ensure it reaches you. My life is in his and your hands. Please, Lucy, tell the authorities of my plight so that I may be rescued from this terrible place and restored to my father.

Your most desperate friend, Catherine

9

Walter Hodges

I was deeply moved by reading poor Catherine's pleas for help, not least because it seemed certain that Hareton had been prevented from delivering her final letter. I could not see how else it could have ended up with the others. I presumed that they had all been collected together by Nelly Dean because it was she who had never sent the letters to Lucy Wright and who would have been able to access Edgar Linton's correspondence with Catherine. What I could not understand was why Nelly had not destroyed these letters. Had she taken some strange delight in being able to read the torment that she had helped inflict? I was sure no normal woman would have aided and abetted Heathcliff Earnshaw's crazed behaviour in the way that she had. Or was the explanation simpler? Was it possible that Nelly had not been able to read? If so, she might have had no idea of the contents of what she kept. That might also help explain why she had retained Cathy's manuscript, though I could not fathom how that ended up in her home whilst Catherine's letters had remained at Thrushcross.

Reading the letters left me more determined than ever to discover what had happened to Catherine Linton, but unfortunately my investigative journeys across Yorkshire in the harsh weather of January and early February led to me catching a severe chill. For a time it was feared my life might be in jeopardy. News of this reached Charlotte and, towards the end of February, she broke her silence to write to me, wishing me a speedy recovery. I gratefully received this olive branch and our regular correspondence was soon after resumed. However, neither she nor I broached the subject of what I had found in Nelly Dean's trunk. Charlotte wrongly thought that I had long since destroyed it in line with her original wishes and I had no desire to disillusion her.

Our renewed correspondence made me realize just how much Charlotte was viewing Mr Nicholls as a serious potential husband. After leaving her father's employ he had taken up a curate's position in the village of Kirk Smeaton, near Pontefract, but he had not lost hope of making Charlotte his wife. In July 1853 he had secretly gone to stay with the Rev. Joseph Brett Grant, the incumbent of Oxenhope, which is but a few miles from Haworth, so that he could contact her without her father knowing. The two men had long been friends because of their shared interest in education. Mr Grant was the schoolmaster of the Free Grammar School and Mr Nicholls was a prominent supporter of the National Schools Society. Once contacted, Charlotte had agreed to enter into a secret correspondence. The announcement of Mr George Smith in November that he was marrying another undoubtedly had removed the one thing that had still held Charlotte back from committing herself to Mr Nicholls – her hope of a more distinguished husband.

Charlotte told me how in December she had gone to her father and confessed how she and his former curate had been writing to each other for six months. She then demanded he give permission for them to meet. With bad grace he had conceded to her request and, in January, Mr Nicholls had spent ten days staying with Mr Grant so he could easily travel to Haworth and see her as her official suitor. The fact that I had no wish to risk damaging our renewed friendship did not prevent me voicing my unchanged opinion that Mr Nicholls was unworthy of a woman of her talents. For that reason Charlotte stopped informing me of the progression of their relationship and I chose not to enquire. This was the situation until the end of March when Charlotte mistakenly put a letter to Mr Nicholls in an envelope addressed to me and a letter to me in an envelope addressed to him. This revealed that although I had received no invitation to visit her at the parsonage at Easter, he had. Embarrassed by what I had inadvertently discovered, Charlotte belatedly invited me also, saying that Mr Nicholls would be staying at Mr Grant's. I thought it safer to decline.

The outcome of Mr Nicholls' visit was relayed to me in a letter dated 11 April. Charlotte told me that her father had assented not only to their engagement but also to Mr Nicholls becoming his curate again. She said she recognized that, in my eyes, her fiancé lacked talent and congeniality, but she felt this was more than made up for by his high principles, his conscientiousness and his affectionate regard for her. For that reason she trusted that she would love him as a husband. She said their marriage was likely to take place in July. What could I say? I still thought she would regret her decision. How could a woman who had written so powerfully of the passionate love of Jane Eyre and Caroline Helstone and Lucy Snowe resign herself to a marriage of convenience? Had she not years ago rejected my brother as a suitor on those very grounds and my brother had been a far better man than Mr Nicholls.

Given my desire not to cause her further pain or disrupt our renewed friendship, I am not sure what my next step would have been had I not received, a week earlier, a letter from Mr Opie. He had been delighted with the success of my visit and given considerable thought to the matter of how I might follow up what I had found. His letter suggested that I should consider examining the parish records because they would supply details of any births, marriages and deaths. I had thanked him profusely while inwardly cursing my own stupidity in not thinking of that idea for myself. My dilemma had been to see the records without alerting Charlotte's suspicions until I discovered quite by chance that there was a copy in the new church of St Mary the Virgin, which had been built at Oxenhope in 1849. Armed with the news provided by Charlotte, I wrote to Mr Grant saying how pleased I was that his friend was to marry Charlotte and that I would love to see his church because I had heard much about it. As I had hoped, he replied, inviting me to come to the two hamlets that comprise Oxenhope whenever I liked. I instantly accepted this offer, confident that I would be able to engineer a look at the parish records during my visit.

I knew that I would be a rare tourist because few ever make their way through the marshy land that surrounds Near Oxenhope (so-called because it is near Haworth) or Far Oxenhope. There is nothing picturesque for them to see because for centuries neither hamlet has acquired any prosperity from the many surrounding hill farms. I chose not to travel by the turnpike road but by the older paved road that is aptly named the 'Long Causeway'. I refused to let the dour and rather depressing nature of the hamlets affect me because it was one of those beautiful days in late April when you finally feel the dark and grey sombre hues of winter are giving way to the happier tints of spring, when you can see the fields and hills are turning a warmer green. Beneath an almost cloudless sky, I ignored as best I could the ugly slum buildings built to house the workforce for the textile mills and took pleasure instead in the blackthorn bushes that were dappled with white blossom, the hawthorns that were splashed with the first vibrant green of the coming leaf, and the occasional horse-chestnut tree that was proudly displaying its swollen and ready-to-burst sticky buds. All around I could hear birdsong – the raucous cawing of rooks and the deep hollow bass sound of wood pigeons intermingled with the more delicate chirping of sparrows and the call of the first finch and, high above my head, a spiralling lark. Hopeful that my mission would prove fruitful, I could not help my heart singing with theirs.

My mood was only dampened when I arrived at the vicarage and was greeted warmly but rather officiously by Mr Grant. He was a man of middling age and rather pompous authority who seemed to delight in trite conversation – a rather worthy companion, I thought, for Mr Nicholls! Looking at his red turned-up nose, which bore all the signs of a fondness for drink, I could not help but wonder whether he was more influenced by spirits than the Holy Spirit. I found it disconcerting that in almost everything he said he found a way of condemning his parishioners. He repeatedly told me that all those born and bred in Yorkshire lacked manners and respect for their betters and he constantly bemoaned the lack of any civilized society in Oxenhope. He said his church was the only building of elegance and style in the entire valley and that it had been created only because for three years he had almost single-handedly raised the money to build it. This I knew to be true because I had heard from Charlotte that he would not leave a person alone until he or she had made a contribution. She had nicknamed him 'the champion beggar' and made him the basis for the Rev. Joseph Donne in her novel *Shirley*, just as she had used Mr Nicholls as the model for another clergyman in that same book. I knew Mr Nicholls had laughed at his caricature but I doubted that Mr Grant had.

I cannot say the new church was a building that pleased my eye because it was built in an old-fashioned Norman style. Its tower was terribly squat and its windows were unattractively small and plain. I suspected that Mr Grant had built the church and vicarage more to satisfy his own needs than to meet those of his parishioners. He took pride in the fact the church could seat over 400 people, even though, from what I gathered elsewhere, his preaching did little to fill it! This did not prevent him describing to me in nauseating detail the latest sermon he had given from the pulpit that dominated the right-hand side of the nave. Not surprisingly, my mind easily wandered and I began imagining what scene I might like to see engraved in the glass of the round window which acted as the main feature behind the altar. Fortunately, before he could notice my inattention, one of his parishioners came into the church seeking advice. He was going to rudely turn the man away but I insisted he should attend to his needs.

I volunteered to retire into the vestry whilst they concluded their business and this gave me the opportunity to fulfil the real purpose of my visit. I quickly found the copy of the parish records among a few other books that sat on a shelf. You can imagine the trepidation with which I turned page after page, scanning its columns and looking for any entry in the name of either Linton or Earnshaw. To my delight I first found the entry for the wedding of Edgar Linton and Cathy Earnshaw and next put my finger on the burial of Cathy and subsequent baptism of her daughter. There was, of course, no reference to her other child, the one taken to Cornwall and baptized there as Maria Branwell. Then I found three entries that totally astounded me – the burials of Catherine, Hareton and Linton all on the same day, 12 August 1801. Against all three was listed 'death by fire'. Turning the page I found listed the burial of Edgar Linton just a couple of weeks later. The cause was listed as heart failure. There was no happy ending as depicted in *Wuthering Heights*, only an appalling tragedy. I knew Nelly Dean had not died till years later and it seemed likely that, in the absence of his name in the register, Heathcliff must also have survived.

Hearing Mr Grant returning, I hurriedly returned the book to its shelf and, despite the deep shock I had experienced, resumed listening to his interminable account about his work. After some twenty minutes of excruciatingly dull conversation, I tentatively asked him whether any of his parishioners had had anything to do with Wuthering Heights or Thrushcross Grange in years gone by. To my surprise he replied in the affirmative, saying, 'Yes, there were a few but they are all long dead, except for an old man called Walter Hodges, who in his youth was a stable boy. He is now old and frail and in his seventies, but he has a keen memory and an even keener love of talking about the past. He has often tried to speak with me about the fire that destroyed Wuthering Heights over forty years ago, but to be honest I've not chosen to hear the tale in its entirety. I have better things to do with my time.'

'Where does this man reside?' I asked, trying to hide my intense excitement.

'He lives in a tiny ramshackle cottage just as you head out of Near Oxenhope towards Haworth. You cannot miss it because it looks more like a cowshed than a house but it's been his home for many a year. Not that he will stay there much longer. He is already reliant on charity and I am in discussion with the authorities to have him moved for his own good to the nearest workhouse. I can assure you that a lady like you has nothing to gain by talking to a wretched man like him.'

'I'm sure you are right,' I replied, and proceeded to draw our meeting to a close as rapidly as courtesy permitted. I thanked him for showing me his church, made a number of compliments about his work that pleased him but made me feel ashamed at my untruthfulness, and then took my leave.

Needless to say, I headed straight to find the small cottage in which Walter Hodges lived. I felt it was just possible that this old man might have the answers to what exactly had happened all those years ago. I easily identified his house and, to my delight, Hodges was outside it, trying to do some work in what remained of what had once doubtless been a fine vegetable plot but was now largely neglected. He returned my greeting as if I was some long-lost daughter. I suspect that my arrival was a welcome relief in what was probably a rather lonely existence. He was a tall, well-built man with the large hands that one associates with those who have worked manually all their lives, but his back was now terribly bent and his grizzled white head and deeply lined face bore all the traces not just of age but of a hard life. Nevertheless, his blue eyes had a kindly twinkle that indicated he had a warm heart, even if his voice was gruff and unrefined.

I told him the reason for my visit and he beckoned me to enter his home, cautioning me to bow my head and avoid the heavy beam that crossed the low ceiling. The room I entered would have been oppressively dark if he had not kept the door open because the narrow dirty panes of the small window admitted little light. The room was shockingly bare. Its grimy walls contained not a single picture frame and its uneven and damp stone floor was only partially covered with a carpet, which had long since lost not only its colour but also most of its threads. The furniture comprised just a large but very aged and badly scarred oak table and two of the commonest horsehair chairs. He invited me to sit down and I obliged, though part of me feared what dirt might transfer to my dress. He sat in the other chair with his back to a partition that partially obscured some worm-eaten wooden steps. These I assumed led up to his bedroom. The partition had once been whitewashed but was now grey with age and spotted with unidentifiable dirt. As far as I could tell, the only other room was a tiny kitchen that could be glimpsed through an open doorway.

I think my face indicated my disgust because he commented, 'Aye, miss, it's not now a place of which one can be proud but it's far better than the workhouse to which most are condemned in their old age. At least here I am still my own master and I can potter a little in my garden and still produce a few vegetables. I wish I could still do the odd job but the truth is I cannot work anymore. My strength is all but gone and my eyesight is now so poor that it can no longer guide my hands.'

I felt embarrassed and muttered something about how difficult it must be for him to manage on his own. To this he replied, 'I cannot complain. I'm now in my seventy-eighth year and, if truth be told, I've lived too long – long enough to see every member of my family gone, most to their last home. One of my two sons enlisted in the army and I've heard naught of him since. The other perished from a fever ten years ago. My three daughters all married but two died in childbirth and the other left with her husband to live in York so I have not known the love of any grandchildren. My wife died just over twelve months ago and I had to watch her body go into a nameless grave.'

'I'm sorry to hear of your loss,' I said.

'Thank you, miss, but I still daily give thanks for the life I have lived and the people I have loved.'

'And did you love any connected to the Linton and Earnshaw families?' I asked, not wishing to prolong my visit beyond what was necessary.

He looked surprised but answered, 'Not love, miss, but I liked the young Hareton Earnshaw well enough. There was not a touch of evil in the lad even though he worked for the devil himself. By rights he should have inherited his father's farm, but instead he was treated like a labourer. Nay, worse than a labourer for he received neither wages nor thanks for his work from Master Heathcliff, who was a cruel, hard, unforgiving man. It was the talk of the farms round here how from the grey of dawn to the onset of night and in all weathers, wind and wet, ice and snow, Hareton did all that was demanded of him, foddering cattle, milking cows, feeding pigs, repairing walls, sowing and reaping in harvest. Yet Master Heathcliff despised him for the meanness of his existence and took pleasure in thrashing him at the slightest excuse.'

'What kept him then at Wuthering Heights?'

'At first it was just his youth but when he came more of an age when flight was possible, there was another cause. On the rare occasions that Hareton saw me he would sometimes speak of how his love for his cousin Catherine kept him at the farmhouse. He told me she was the first person in his family who had ever spoken a kind word to him. Not that he ever thought she would love him. He knew he was far too ungainly and ill-educated to attract a lass of her beauty and upbringing.'

'What was Catherine like, Mr Hodges?'

He smiled as he recalled her. 'She was the prettiest of things. Hair the colour of newly cut straw and eyes the colour of blue butterflies. And she had the sweetest of natures. Everyone said she took after her mother, though I never knew her. Mrs Linton died giving birth to her daughter and that was long before I took up my post as a stable boy in the service of the family.'

'And what of Mr Linton?'

'He was a true gentleman. I never knew him say an unkind word to anyone and, unlike most masters, he treated his servants with kindness.

However, his wife's death left him a broken man and in all the time I worked for him I never heard him once laugh. I was not surprised when what happened at Wuthering Heights killed him. The news of the fire broke what little spirit he had left to live.'

'Was the fire at Wuthering Heights what destroyed Catherine?'

'Aye, and it killed Hareton too and Catherine's cousin, Linton Earnshaw.'

'Do you know much about the fire, Mr Hodges?'

'I should do. I was there and the memory of it still sometimes gives me a sleepless night.'

The news that he had actually been present at the fire was far more than I had ever expected in my wildest hopes and I could not believe my very good fortune. There were many digressions along the way but over the next hour or so I extracted from him all that had happened. He told me his tale with a number of lengthy digressions but what he said totally captured my imagination. Looking back, I now appreciate my visit was truly a timely one because had I waited even a month longer I would never have met him and discovered the truth of what happened on that August night in 1801. Not long after my visit Mr Grant had his way and Walter Hodges was taken into the workhouse that he had so long dreaded. I gather the poor man died within a few days of being within its unsympathetic walls. What follows is not his account but one that I have better worded for my readers, omitting the things that he said which were of no import. I dedicate it to his memory.

10

The Fire at Wuthering Heights

The shocking news brought by Nelly Dean that Catherine had eloped caused uproar at Thrushcross Grange. Edgar Linton could not bear the thought of history repeating itself and his precious daughter disgracing herself in the same way as had his sister. He roused himself from his sickbed and immediately sent out every able-bodied man in his employ to go to all the neighbouring houses and farms in order to see if anyone had any knowledge of the route that the couple might have taken. He said not one of them should return until they had secured some information or, better still, apprehended his daughter. As a consequence, his men continued their futile task across an ever-increasing area, because the response they received was always the same – none had seen the couple.

The only servant to return was Walter Hodges and that was because he had been sent to elicit further information from Heathcliff himself. Walter reported that Mr Earnshaw had told him that there was no point in his master making any further fuss because the couple had long since left for London. When he delivered this news to Mr Linton, he saw the wretched man's heart break. The fiery energy that had driven him to seek his erring daughter simply drained away as his hope withered. He looked like a man ready for the grave and he soon took to his bed, ordering Walter to tell the search parties when they eventually returned to cease their endeavours.

Later that evening Walter Hodges heard someone pounding at the main door. He assumed it must be the first of the search parties returning after a fruitless enquiry. However, when he opened the door, outside was Hareton, looking wild-eyed and terrified. It was evident that he had been subjected to the most savage beating because his clothes were torn and soaked with blood and his face was very badly bruised and cut. His nose had obviously been broken and his left eye was so bloody and swollen that it looked as if he might have permanently lost the sight in it. He asked him what on earth had happened to him and Hareton replied that his uncle had beaten him into unconsciousness for daring to challenge his authority. He knew not how long he had been dead to the world but when he had regained his senses he had found himself bound and tied and, to his great sorrow, without a letter that Catherine had entrusted to his care. Although he knew not its precise contents, he knew its message. She was being held prisoner at the farmhouse and she required rescue if she was not to be forced into a marriage against her will to Linton Earnshaw.

Hareton was terrified that his escape might have been already discovered and that his uncle might be riding in pursuit of him. Though Hareton's story ran counter to the story provided by Nelly Dean and by Heathcliff Earnshaw, Walter knew immediately whose version he should trust. Looking at the fiercely torn and frayed skin around Hareton's lacerated wrists, he could only surmise what appalling suffering the poor lad had endured to achieve his release. He took him straight to see Mr Linton. On the way Nelly Dean saw them and tried to block their path, but Walter had no difficulty brushing her aside. Had he known what she would later do, he would not have permitted her to escape.

Mr Linton was relieved to hear that Catherine had not deceived him in the way that he had feared but mortified that he had permitted himself to be so easily duped. Unfortunately the shocking news of Catherine's plight proved too much for his weakened state and he instantly collapsed when he tried to rise from his bed. He therefore urged Walter Hodges to return at once with Hareton and demand his daughter's release. Even such an evil man as Heathcliff Earnshaw, he argued, could not keep her prisoner once he knew her captivity was public knowledge. It would call down on him the whole wrath of the local authorities. To this unwise course of action both men assented, though Hareton had a far less optimistic view of what his crazed uncle might do in response, and Walter would have preferred to wait till some of the other servants had returned so they could then go in force.

The two young men made their way as quickly as they could to Wuthering Heights by both riding the one horse available for their use. There they found Heathcliff standing at his door, expecting their arrival. He bade them enter. To their amazement Nelly Dean was standing in a corner of the room with a look of contemptuous derision on her face. It was immediately apparent who had forewarned him of their coming. Walter said that he wished he had silenced her for good before she could do more evil, but she only laughed, saying that it would take more than a poor wretch like him to outwit her. Hareton voiced that she must be a witch to have so speedily arrived at the farmhouse, but this only served to further amuse her. She said that she had no need of magic. All she had done was to intercept Heathcliff, riding in search of his nephew, and he had brought her back to Wuthering Heights on his horse.

At this juncture Heathcliff beckoned her to leave the house so he could speak alone with his new guests. She scowled but left. Heathcliff then turned to Walter and told him to give whatever message his master had sent before he took a whip to him. To his credit, the lad refused to be browbeaten by such words, and bravely demanded Catherine's instant release. He said that if Heathcliff refused to comply he was under instructions to immediately leave so he could ride to tell the local magistrate of the kidnapping. The magistrate would then summon forces to not only free Catherine but also imprison her captor. In response Heathcliff appeared to play for time, saying he would have to give the matter careful consideration. Walter replied that he would brook no delay in securing his mistress's immediate release. Suddenly a shrill whistle came from outside. Heathcliff's cold eyes sparkled with amusement as he told them that the noise was Nelly's signal that she had just untied and driven off their horse. There would be no riding for help to any magistrate.

From behind a heavy book that had been resting on the table near him, Heathcliff pulled out a pistol and ordered Hareton and Walter to each sit on a chair. Knowing he would have no hesitation in shooting them, they reluctantly obeyed. Nelly entered the room bearing two ropes and she proceeded to tie up each of them so they could not escape. Once they were both bound, Heathcliff walked over to poor Hareton and clubbed him viciously with the butt of his pistol across his face. Walter heard the poor lad's nose and cheekbone shatter. Not content with inflicting such a harsh blow, Heathcliff struck him again. This time the blow knocked both him and the chair over. Hareton was probably unconscious before he hit the floor, but this did not prevent Heathcliff brutally kicking his body.

Walter thought that he would be next, but Nelly Dean intervened. She told Heathcliff that he must not murder his captives in such a way as to endanger himself or her. Heathcliff nodded his assent and bid her help him move both bound men into the inner room. While Nelly fetched the key to unlock the door that led to this, Heathcliff freed the unconscious Hareton from the rope that bound him to the chair. He picked up the body as if it weighed nothing and then flung it onto the floor of the other room. Shouts of alarm and horror from the room's occupants greeted this act. One voice was female and Walter immediately recognized it as belonging to Catherine. The other was male and he surmised rightly that it was the voice of her cousin Linton.

Heathcliff picked up Walter, still tied to the chair, and threw him also into the room, swearing that he would horsewhip anyone who tried to release him. Then he slammed shut the door and Nelly relocked it. Walter was knocked out by his fall and when he regained consciousness he found Catherine bathing a great gash to his forehead. He feebly acknowledged her assistance with a nod, though the movement caused him immense pain. She put her hand to his lips and whispered that he should remain as quiet as possible. She hoped that if Heathcliff could not hear him he would assume he was still unconscious. Walter turned to look across the room. The poor body of Hareton had been carefully laid out and partially covered but there was little sign of life, bar the sound of laboured breathing. The nature of this indicated that Heathcliff's savage kicks must have done great damage to the poor lad's rib-cage.

Catherine spoke very softly, telling Walter Hodges that she had done what she could for Hareton but unless he received proper medical care very quickly, she feared for his life. Walter urged her to release him from the ropes that bound him, but she said that was impossible because Linton would prevent her. She pointed over his shoulder. Turning his head round as best he could, Walter saw that Linton was sitting with his back to the locked door and with a knife in his hand. The poor trembling lad was scared out of his wits. It was obvious that all he could think about was obeying Heathcliff's every command lest he should face what had happened to his cousin.

It was then that Walter Hodges noted something odd. Strange wisps of smoke were beginning to emerge from the bottom of the locked door. At first these were so small as almost to be unnoticeable but with every passing second they grew in density. It was Catherine who was the first to realize what this signified. 'My God,' she said, ceasing to whisper, 'Heathcliff has set the house on fire. He means to burn us to death!' A most evil laugh resounded from outside. Heathcliff shouted out that he would put on such a good show of grief at their untimely end that no one would suspect him for a moment of causing their deaths. A most unfortunate fire, doubtless caused by a candle being accidentally knocked over! What a tragedy! Four young people so tragically killed! Walter yelled out that Mr Linton would make sure the truth was known. This only evoked more laughter from Heathcliff. 'I fear not,' he said. 'Nelly has done a good job ensuring he remained a sick man, and now she has gone back to Thrushcross to ensure that he dies in his bed long before any of the other servants get anywhere near him.'

By the time Heathcliff had finished speaking, Linton was in such a state of shock that Catherine was able to seize his knife. She hastily cut through the ropes that bound Walter and he then helped her swiftly move Hareton's body further away from the mounting fumes. Walter looked around in desperation. There seemed to be no way out because the one small window in the room was barred from the outside. Suddenly, to his amazement, Hareton spoke. They had thought him to be still unconscious. The voice was only just audible, not least because there were heart-rending gasps for air between each word. 'There is a passage out of this room. It's one family secret that my uncle has never discovered. My father told only me before he died.' Pain prevented him using his arms but he indicated where they should search by staring as hard as he could at one of the room's wooden panels.

Hampered by the mounting smoke in the room, Walter could not find anything that marked the panel as being different. Linton offered no assistance. He seemed to have retreated into some world of his own as if terror had deprived him of his sanity. It was Catherine's nimble fingers that eventually discovered a switch, which made the whole panel move. Behind it was a narrow staircase that led upwards. Walter urged her to run ahead, saying he and Linton would carry Hareton. Even as he said this, he felt Linton push him aside. Flames had begun to lick their way across the floor of the room and these had brought the poor lad out of his trance. They had also set fire to the bedding that partially covered Hareton. At that point Walter knew there was nothing he could do – trying to move such a badly broken figure unaided would have been difficult enough, but the rapidly enveloping flames made even attempting it impossible.

Walter therefore followed Catherine and Linton, slamming the panelled door shut behind him to delay the fire's spread and praying that the passage had another exit. If it did not, they had exchanged one tomb for another. Catherine was waiting at the top of the old staircase. She knew by the speed of his footsteps that he was carrying no burden and she tried to return to the room below. 'It's too late,' he said, holding her in his arms as they heard from below the sound of Hareton's tortured death throes. Mercifully these did not last long, but when his anguished screams ceased, Catherine broke down in a fit of the bitterest grief. 'Do not let him have died in vain,' said Walter, trying to comfort her. 'We must use the escape route he has given us. Only then can we bring justice to his cruel murderer!'

Whilst this was going on, Linton had been frantically searching at the top of the staircase for any lever that might open out into another room. With a cry of triumph, he now found it. There was a click and a thin gap appeared, but the exit was clearly blocked. Something had been placed against the door on the other side. He pushed as hard as his feeble frame permitted but to no success. Choking smoke was already rising up the staircase by the time that Walter Hodges added his more powerful weight to that of Linton. Slowly the gap widened, revealing a large wardrobe blocking their exit. They managed to move this aside and all three made their way into the room. It was Hareton's old bedroom. Walter turned to push the wardrobe back in place. He knew they had to delay the flames entering the room if they were to make their escape. Catherine assisted him.

When they turned round, having achieved their task, there was no sign of Linton. He had already run from the room. 'The stupid boy,' said Catherine. 'If he is not careful, he will alert Mr Earnshaw to our escape.' And that, of course, was exactly what Linton did. In his terror of being burned alive, he first ran down the main staircase, though it was smoke-filled, towards the living room below, only to quickly discover that it was a blazing inferno. Running back up the stairs he headed for Heathcliff's bedroom in the hope that he might be able to clamber from there onto the roof. As he looked out of the window he gazed straight down into the face of his uncle, who was surveying the fire in a transport of joy because he knew that he would be able to inherit all the Linton estate once they were destroyed.

Heathcliff immediately realized that by some miracle his enemies had escaped the inner room. Linton sprang back from the window and into the arms of Walter and Catherine, who had just entered the room. 'He's seen me. I'm doomed!' he screamed, quite hysterical with fright. 'Pull yourself together, man!' said Catherine and slapped him hard across the face. She knew much depended on whether they could find some way to escape from the building before the flames reached them again. Already they could feel the smoke burning their lungs as the fire took a destructive grip on the main staircase. 'If there is any escape route, it has to be in Hareton's room. Why else would the passageway lead there?' said Catherine. She turned to head back to the room from which they had just come. Walter followed, not liking to point out that it was far more likely that the passageway was a route intended to enable a person to escape from the bedroom. Linton refused to join them.

Walter and Catherine were shocked to discover that the entire wardrobe, which they had pushed back, was already ablaze and the floor timbers of the bedroom were smouldering. Catherine rushed to the window and opened it. The fresh air fuelled the advancing flames and set them soaring and crackling along the bedroom walls and ceiling. 'There's a way that leads across the roof,' she said. With Walter's assistance, she climbed out and he followed her. Even as they took their first tentative steps across the tiles, the window glass shattered with the heat, scattering thousands of tiny shards through he air. The left side of Catherine's face and body took the brunt of this, lacerating her skin and clothes. Her once beautiful face was reduced to that of a monster as blood poured from many cuts. Walter desperately urged her on. Such was her state of shock that she initially followed him as if oblivious of what had happened.

They staggered across the sloping roof. It was as if they were making their way through a deep London fog because smoke was coming out through every gap between the tiles. As they neared the far end of the roof, a single shot rang out. It was Heathcliff. He had seen them and was firing at them with his pistol. Walter turned to tell Catherine to lie down, but she was standing with a hole in her forehead where the bullet had struck her. Even as he gasped, she slumped lifeless at his feet. Another bullet whistled past Walter's ear and he dropped down. He felt as if his heart would break as he lay there, his eyes staring into the bloodied face of the dead girl. Then a grim determination seized him. Whatever else happened, Heathcliff Earnshaw would not get away with this!

He crawled away as best he could, keenly aware that behind him sections of the roof were now ablaze. He had very little time. He kept his head down in the hope that Heathcliff would think him either dead or wounded from the second shot. Once he reached the far edge, he peered down. At first he could see little because intense smoke seemed to billow everywhere, but then he caught a glimpse of the roof of the nearby barn, which, as yet, was unaffected by the fire. Somehow he had to get onto it! The one thing in his favour was that the increasing smoke now made it impossible for Heathcliff to see him.

Wuthering Heights was surrounded by trees, which had been planted generations earlier in a vain attempt to block out some of the cutting wind. Most were stunted and malformed but one, the nearest to the house, had defied the fate of its brothers and sisters and had grown almost to embrace sections of the farmhouse. It was one of its big boughs that offered Walter an escape route. It ran near enough to the section of roof on which he stood to justify him jumping out towards it. For a moment he thought he had misjudged his leap as his body moved rapidly through a mass of leaves and lesser branches. However, he did not plummet to the ground. His fall was stopped by a firmer branch, which momentarily knocked out all his breath.

Once he had recovered, he edged his way along it, conscious that the tree would soon be caught up in flames, a victim of the house it had so long protected. Suddenly, a section of the branch snapped and he fell again, but this time onto the aged roof of the barn. Long in need of renewal, it could not withstand the impact. It held his weight only momentarily and then he found himself tumbling through it into the barn itself. When he landed on the floor of an upper gallery, he was completely winded and just for a moment or two he wondered if he dare move because he was convinced that he must have broken something.

It seemed only seconds later that he heard the barn door being opened. Glimpsing through the gaps between the beams on which he lay, he saw it was Heathcliff. He had somehow seen his escape, despite all the smoke and flames! 'You cannot escape me, Hodges. You know that,' declared this fiend in human form. 'I know you are in here somewhere.' Walter looked again. There was no sign of any gun. Presumably Heathcliff had discarded it once he had fired those shots at him and poor Catherine. In his hand, however, there was a large blade. Given this weapon and his natural strength, Heathcliff had all the advantages. The monster laughed. He was clearly enjoying the hunt. Walter watched as Heathcliff methodically began searching the ground level of the barn. So intent was the poor stable boy's gaze that he did not notice that above him the roof of the barn was now on fire. Sparks from the flaming house had fallen onto it. It was Heathcliff who noticed first what was happening. He looked upwards and, as he did so, he spotted where Walter was. 'It's me or the fire,' he laughed. 'Choose your death!'

However, from his vantage point, Walter saw another figure enter the barn. The crackling flames of the inferno that was consuming the farmhouse made the sound of his entry unnoticeable. At first he wondered whether it was some strange creature from hell because nothing so black and misshapen could possibly be human, but then something about the manner of its movement made him realize it was Linton. Somehow he too had managed to escape the fire, but not without a terrible cost. He was almost naked because most of his clothes had been burnt away. He had no hair for that too had been consumed by the flames. There was scarce an inch of his body that was not covered with the most horrific of burns. But in his hand was Heathcliff's pistol. He raised it and pointed it at the back of the man who had so destroyed his life. Some strange sixth sense made Heathcliff turn around. If he was startled, he did not show it. 'Linton, is it you?' he said. The figure nodded its mutilated head.

What follows is their conversation as Walter Hodges told it to me:

'What did my mother do to deserve what you did to her?' croaked Linton. 'And what did I ever do? And how did poor Hareton or Catherine earn your hatred?'

'Your mother was the sister of Edgar Linton, the man who stole away my Cathy,' snapped back Heathcliff. 'And to that crime she added the stupidity of loving me. How could I feel anything but loathing for such a creature or for her offspring.'

'But you are my father!'

'So she claimed. But look at you, man. Your feeble spirit shows you are descended from the Lintons, and it speaks nothing of any physical link to me. And if, by some strange quirk of fate, my raping of your mother produced you, then take my word for it, you were born entirely out of the hatred in my loins and not from any scrap of love. As was your alleged cousin Hareton. I seduced his stupid mother to spite Hindley Earnshaw. Why should I therefore love either of you two bastards, who remind me only that I can never have proper sons with Cathy!'

'If Cathy was so precious to you, how could you destroy her daughter?'

'You call that light-headed creature Cathy's daughter! She was a Linton through and through. The way she behaved, the way she thought, the way she dressed, everything about her proclaimed that she was entirely a product of Edgar Linton's upbringing. I would not have had her near me for an instant if I had not seen that, in breaking her, I could cause as much pain to him as he caused to me. I rejoiced watching her burn on the roof!'

'She is dead, like Hareton, then?'

'Of course, and just as painfully.'

'Then I alone am left,' uttered the totally dejected Linton.

'But not for long, you contemptible little bastard!' jeered Heathcliff.

'It is I who have the gun.'

'But not the courage to use it!' was the mocking reply.

Ever since his mother's death, Linton had been nothing except the butt of his father's cruelty. It was Heathcliff who had taunted him, laughed at him and reviled him. It was Heathcliff who had spat at him, punched him and kicked him. And it was Heathcliff who had made him do things that he hated and, in the process, destroyed every ounce of his self-esteem. In seeking to avoid the physical punishments he saw lavished on Hareton, Linton had become the worthless creature that Heathcliff had always held him to be. Now, for the very first time, he did what Heathcliff had never expected. He fired the gun. But he was no marksman, even at close range. The shot hit Heathcliff in his right thigh but struck no mortal blow. Linton stood like a small black chimney boy trapped in a flue, unable to move, as Heathcliff staggered towards him. He made no attempt to escape, even when Heathcliff drew his sharp knife across the boy's blackened throat. I think poor Linton was happy to depart his sad and tormented life.

It was at that point Walter Hodges was driven down from the gallery by the flames that were now threatening to consume the entire barn. He knew that he had but one distinct advantage over the injured Heathcliff and that was speed. He ran outside, turned, and began to shut its huge door. Realizing his intention, Heathcliff moved to stop him, but the injury in his thigh was sufficient to make him stumble and fall. This provided the precious seconds that Walter required. He pushed the long wooden bar down that bolted the barn shut. Heathcliff began to bang at the door, screaming to be let out. Now that he was safe, Walter sank down on his knees and yelled back at him, 'Burn, you son of Satan! Burn as you would have had us burn!' Then he broke down into the bitterest of tears as he remembered the resigned look that had spread across Linton's blackened features as his life-blood poured from his opened throat. Worse still was recalling poor Hareton's fate, beaten to such a helpless state that he could not even flee the flames that agonizingly consumed him. And then there was innocent, brave, beautiful Catherine!

It was the memory of Catherine that made Walter suddenly realize he had another task. He had to get back and prevent Nelly Dean killing Edgar Linton. Ignoring Heathcliff's screams for help, he began to run towards Thrushcross Grange as fast as the terrain and his strength permitted, though his body, after all its exertions, was clamouring for rest. By the time he got to the mansion there was no sign of Nelly Dean and Edgar Linton was lying virtually dead in his bed. Walter could not say whether this was a product of her handiwork or whether the anxiety generated by events had proved too much for the poor father's frail form. He spent about an hour seeing if he could revive him and then decided he must go for a doctor. Having stripped, washed and donned fresh clothes, he set off, running as quickly as he could, sheer determination overcoming his exhaustion. The doctor, once roused, rode to the mansion, leaving the exhausted messenger to walk back as best he could.

By the time Walter reached Thrushcross for the second time, other servants were in command, having finally returned from their fruitless searches. He was told the doctor was saying that he could do nothing for their master. The news destroyed the sole hope that alone had kept him functioning and Walter collapsed. For many days it was thought he also might not survive. During that time Edgar Linton passed away and the burnt remains of three young bodies were removed from the ashes of Wuthering Heights and interred.

A fresh horror awaited Walter when he regained consciousness because the first person he saw hovering over him was Nelly Dean. She informed him with delight that Heathcliff Earnshaw, though very badly burnt, was still alive. Moreover, her testimony had led to him being hailed as a hero. Nelly had been quick to appreciate that she could write her own version of events. Walter, in his shattered state, had only told the doctor that Catherine had died in a fire and that Edgar Linton was near to death. Nelly had therefore felt free to inform the authorities that Heathcliff had managed to find the eloping couple and bring them back to Wuthering Heights, and that the fire had started accidentally from an upturned candle. Heathcliff had sent her to ride for help to Thrushcross, whilst he tried to rescue Catherine, Hareton and Linton, who were trapped upstairs. Unused to riding, she had fallen from the horse and so been forced to make the rest of the way by foot. She had found no one in the house but Mr Linton, who was clearly dying. Unsure what to do, she had returned to Wuthering Heights, only to find a charred and smoking ruin with Heathcliff's cruelly burned body lying not far from it.

She told Walter that any attempt by him to tell the truth was pointless. Her word as to what had happened would be believed before that of a common stable boy. She had destroyed the evidence of his burnt clothes and put out that the bruises and cuts on his body were a product of injuries incurred whilst drunk, so Hodges could offer no proof. She threatened that, if he persisted in talking about what happened, she would ensure that he never worked again. However, if he kept his tongue, she would give him enough money to set himself up in a smallholding. She added that there was no reason for him to seek vengeance because Heathcliff's injuries were so horrific that he had lost his reason and would spend the rest of his life locked away in some asylum for the insane should he manage to survive.

In his weakened state, Walter Hodges surrendered and took the proffered bribe to remain silent. It was a decision in which he took no pride. For that reason, once he had recovered his health, he went to visit Heathcliff in the asylum in which he was being kept with the intention of murdering him for what he had done. However, when Walter saw the terrible burns that Heathcliff had suffered and listened to his lunatic ramblings, he changed his mind. He thought letting the fiend face a living death was a far greater punishment.

11

The Return of Heathcliff

Walter Hodges' account still left me with the mystery of what had subsequently happened to Heathcliff. Had he spent the rest of his life locked away in some home for the insane? Hodges simply did not know. Through all the passing years he had just assumed that was the case. But I thought Heathcliff might have recovered. As far as I knew, Emily had got the initial idea of writing *Wuthering Heights* from Charlotte and so I thought it might be possible that Charlotte had somehow come across Heathcliff and heard his version of his love for Cathy. If that were the case, it offered a possible explanation of why she featured both insanity and a fire in her own novel, *Jane Eyre*. Most of what Charlotte wrote had some autobiographical origin. Tradition has it that the idea for Bertha Rochester's insanity in the novel came from Charlotte hearing of a poor woman locked in an attic in a house near Ripon, but was it stretching the realms of the credible to surmise that she might also have been given this idea by knowing what had happened to Heathcliff and turning the fire that had caused his temporary insanity into the means of destroying Rochester's unwanted wife? Certainly her description of the cruel scars and injuries inflicted on Rochester in the fire might well have been drawn from seeing Heathcliff's injuries.

Fortunately Hodges had given me a means of pursuing my investigations further because he had told me the name of the asylum to which Heathcliff had been eventually taken. It was in York and not unknown to me, because my brother George had suffered a nervous breakdown and been placed in it for a time. I wrote to the institution requesting any information they might have on a Mr Heathcliff Earnshaw and on any visitors who had come to see him. It was just a few days later that I received a reply. It read as follows:

3 May 1854

Dear Miss Nussey,

I remember you well from the time when you used to visit your brother. I was intrigued to receive your letter requesting information about a patient here called Heathcliff Earnshaw, because you are not the first person to seek such information. Many years ago a young man came to see me on exactly the same issue. I had just been in this post a few weeks and so I could tell him nothing from any first-hand knowledge, but it was simple for me to look up the records kept by my predecessor and to talk to some of the nurses. I therefore compiled a brief report for my visitor and I am happy to pass on that same report to you. It was originally written in the autumn of 1839:

'Mr Heathcliff Earnshaw was admitted here in 1802. The previous year he had been seriously burned while heroically trying to rescue his son and a nephew and niece from a fire that had raged through his farmhouse. Unfortunately, his efforts were to no avail and they all perished. A combination of seeing them all burn to death and sustaining horrific injuries temporarily deprived the poor man of his senses. His burns were very extensive and it was a miracle he survived them. His notes say that at first all he kept muttering over and over again was the name "Cathy". I believe this was the name of the unfortunate niece who died in the fire. As his physical strength returned, he became increasingly more aggressive in manner until he had to be restrained. Fortunately after a few years this phase came to an end and he then became altogether calmer. He began to talk about what had happened, at first hesitantly and then with more courage, and from then on his mental recovery became daily clearer. He was released in 1812. There is no record of where he went when he left here.'

You also ask me in your letter about any visitors who came to see the patient. The records show that he only had one – a Miss

Dean. She saw him every three months at first but then ceased visiting altogether when he entered his violent phase. I am not surprised. It would have been very distressing for her to see him. We had no address to inform her of his eventual recovery and I can find no record of anyone coming here to meet him when he was released. The first interest shown in him was therefore the visit of the young man to me. He told me his name was Branwell Patrick Brontë and that he believed he might be a relative of Mr Earnshaw. I have had no contact from him since.

I hope that you find this information helpful.

Yours faithfully

Dr Timothy Harris

The surprise in this letter was not so much the proof that Heathcliff had recovered, but that Branwell had been making enquiries about him rather than Charlotte or Emily. What had led to his interest? Had he met Heathcliff and if so where? If Heathcliff had returned to his birthplace then one possible answer was Liverpool because I knew Branwell had visited that city in the summer of 1839. He had gone there with some of his old boyhood friends, ostensibly to hear the evangelical preaching of a then famous minister called the Reverend McNeille at St Jude's Church. I remember Charlotte telling me at the time it was all an excuse. The young men simply wanted a good time free from parental control. I suspect Mr Brontë also had his questions about the visit because not so very long afterwards Branwell had been made to take up a steady form of employment. In the spring of 1840 he had become a private tutor to the two sons of a large landowner called Mr Robert Postlethwaite, who lived at Broughton House in Westmorland. It was his failure in that post that had signalled the start of his serious decline.

I determined to find out more about what had happened during Branwell's visit to Liverpool and, knowing his main confidante had always been Charlotte, the obvious source was his letters to her. That Charlotte still possessed these was not in doubt because I knew that she had never destroyed anything he had written. I decided that I had to gain unauthorized access to his letters whilst Charlotte was absent from Haworth. She had told me that she was going on a tour of some of her friends and would visit me at Brookroyd in the second week of May. I think she felt the need to win our support for her forthcoming marriage. I therefore went immediately to Haworth, confident I could gain unaccompanied access to her room.

Mr Brontë was surprised to see me but I pretended that an unexpected journey had led me to pass close to the parsonage and that I had decided to call just so I could congratulate him on his daughter's forthcoming marriage. He told me Charlotte was in Manchester discussing wedding plans with Mrs Gaskell and other friends and then to my surprise commented, 'It's my hope that she and her betrothed both have the unhappiness they deserve.'

'Surely, sir, you want your daughter to be happy?' I replied.

'She should have placed her father's wishes above that of his curate. Her place is by my side, not his.'

'If you will forgive me, sir, I think that does not sound very Christian.'

'Does not the Bible say, Miss Nussey, it is our Christian duty to honour our parents?'

I was tempted to say that I thought the Bible also tells us that a man will join with a woman and for that reason both will leave their parents, but I feared he would take offence and that I would jeopardize my mission. Instead, I tried to woo his favour by saying what I truthfully believed. 'I confess, sir,' I said, 'I am puzzled why Charlotte is marrying him. I cannot find in him any qualities that justify her sacrifice.'

'The man is a talentless fool with no ambition,' he muttered. 'Charlotte tells me I should be content with the fact he is high principled and affectionate, but she herself has arranged this marriage to be as quiet as possible. She knows the world will judge her to have thrown herself away on this man.'

After further venting his spleen against his prospective son-in-law, Mr Brontë retreated into his study, leaving me to await my return transport. This gave me the time I required. I quickly entered Charlotte's room. I had been her friend long enough to know where she kept Branwell's letters. To my delight I found her methodical approach meant that they were in a box in chronological order. I rapidly scanned the few letters that dated back to 1839 and 1840 and I found two that gave me all the answers I wanted. These I quickly copied and then I returned them to the box so that Charlotte would not know what I had done. Shortly afterwards I took my leave. Here at last I can reveal what the two letters contained. The first dates from the spring of 1840 but relays what happened in Liverpool the year before. It is very long but it is so important that I give it in its entirety:

Broughton House
Broughton-in-Furness
11 March 1840

Dearest Charlotte,
How much longer must I endure this miserable little retired seashore town! Oh for angel wings that I might rise above the wild woody hills that surround me and escape to the cream-white clouds that cap the nearby peaks! Oh to free myself from mankind's sordid nature so that I might talk with the seraphim! Here there is company fit for none of my intellect and intelligence. My landlord may be deemed by the world to be a respectable surgeon, but he is a drunkard six days out of seven. Even the inane prattle of his bustling, chattering, kind-hearted and long-suffering wife is preferable to talking with such a sot. She, poor woman, attempts to hide the evidence of his drinking, judging me to be a most calm, sedate, sober, abstemious, patient, mild-hearted and virtuous young man – and doubtless, therefore, a prospective husband for her eighteen-year-old daughter. For the latter's benefit until now I have dressed in black and smiled like a martyr and pretended to dislike wine and spirits, but she has yet to surrender anything of value. If her mother could see into my real soul and know the lustful thoughts that dwell there, she would certainly lock up her daughter more securely than her husband's drink!

I do not mind telling you, Charlotte, that I sometimes dream of going to the Royal Hotel and downing a few hot as hell whisky-toddies till my senses reel and the candles in the room dance before my eyes and then returning to my lodgings to shock them all! But what would you say to such folly? You keep telling me that I have every reason to be happy, though it is not so many weeks ago that you were saying that no one of any spirit could endure a tutor's lot! Why should I be happy educating the high-spirited but moronic sons of a retired magistrate? Because my wealthy employer happens to have a right hearty and generous disposition? Because his wife is an amiable enough woman? Because I can flirt with Agnes Riley, one of the servants here, knowing she is stupid enough to believe that I love her? Why should I be grateful for such small mercies as these? Tutoring is not the life that you or I ever envisaged for one of my many talents.

I know this may all sound melodramatic but as each day passes my misery increases because I now know why I am doomed to failure. In fact I begin to think that I am not even worthy to fulfil my current role. I keep looking at my master's two boys and thinking that, far from learning anything from me, they should eschew my sin-bound presence. I have often complained to you in the past about the way fate has denied me recognition, but what I have kept hidden from you in recent weeks is that I have discovered why that should be so. Now I want you to know. I cannot carry the burden alone any more. I have no doubt that the rest of the family would shun me if I told them what I am about to write to you, but you have always been my closest confidante and greatest supporter. When you hear what I have to say, you will realize that I do not even deserve this station in life because, Charlotte, I am a fornicator, a murderer and a bastard.

As you know, last summer I went with some friends to Liverpool. We listened to the stupid meanderings of a dim evangelical of the worst kind so that we could dutifully report back his words, and then took ourselves off to happier and less moral pursuits in the dock area of the city. I will not seek to shock you by giving a detailed account of the debaucheries in which we engaged. Suffice it to say that money will purchase anything you require in that godforsaken hole. We took cheap lodgings to recover from the worst of our excesses before returning home, and it was there that my slumbers were disturbed by the news that my company was sought by a man who dwelt in one of the taverns that we had visited. I thought in my naivety that he must want to seek address for damage that we had drunkenly incurred and, fearing lest he seek his compensation through contacting our father, I went reluctantly to see him. It is since meeting him that I have known why I am truly cursed and why I shall never achieve fame, only condemnation and ignominy.

The man turned out to be far older than I expected because he looked to be at least in his seventies. However, he was still a powerful-looking person and the hand that gripped mine was uncomfortably firm and strong. I could see from his features that as a young man he must have been quite handsome, but his appearance had been marred not just by age but by the most vicious scarring. This marked the entire right-hand side of his face and neck and, on looking closer, I noticed that his right hand was equally badly scarred. From this I surmised that his clothes might cover other injuries. Though his lodgings were in a very unsavoury place, there was something about his manner that spoke of better days and his deep voice was not without evidence of him having received an education at some stage. He certainly did not speak with the common language of the docks. What struck me most were his deep black eyes. These seemed to bore a hole into my very soul, so fierce was their unflinching gaze, and yet I could see in them no ounce of humanity.

Before I could begin protesting my willingness to pay for any damage we had inadvertently caused, he commanded I accompany him upstairs to his room so we could speak in private. A wiser man might have resisted such a suggestion but I found myself immediately obeying him. Like the snake is said to sometimes hypnotize its victim before striking, his manner countenanced no resistance. The room into which he led me was surprisingly clean but very scarcely furnished. This was clearly a man who took no interest in his creature comforts. He directed me to an antique chair by a rough-hewn table and then pulled up another opposite me. He again looked at me in such an intense way that I thought he wished to etch every feature of my countenance into his mind. 'You are not what I expected,' he said. 'I had hoped that you would be a fine-looking man.'

I responded to this rude affront by saying that those who set store by appearance are often disappointed and that what matters is not the body but the mind that drives it. I assured him that I had a great future ahead of me and that it was only a matter of time before my story-writing skills brought me the acclaim of the literary world. I admit this sounds very pompous but it was my response to the man's insolent manner. Unfortunately, it did nothing to earn his approval. On the contrary, he spat with contempt and muttered that, in producing a son like me, his blood must have turned to water. I told him I was no son of his and he had obviously lost his senses. I give you verbatim what next passed between us because it is indelibly written on my mind:

'Aye, I lost my senses once to the extent that I was locked away and men did not know whether I was a beast or a human being. Although I was covered with clothing, I bore little semblance to a man. I grovelled on all fours, and I snatched and growled like some strange, wild animal. A quantity of dark, grizzled hair, wild as a mane, hid my head and face. If I chose to stand on my hind feet to stare at some poor visitor, I looked like a clothed hyena. Few could face my purple scarred features and red-balled eyes. On one occasion I sprang and attacked a man and I laid bare his cheek with my teeth. After that few were allowed to visit unless I was first pinioned to a chair.'

I unconsciously put my hand to my face as if I feared a repeat of this barbaric act, and he, seeing the gesture, laughed. 'I'm not mad now, I can assure you,' he said, 'but I have things to say that some might count insane. Look not to leave. You must bear me out.' His lips curled up in more of a sneer than a smile and he added, 'Humour my madness, if you like to think of it that way.'

Inhibited by his brutal manner, I nodded my acquiescence and he continued. 'Years ago I was the victim of a fire that destroyed my home and my family. Most men would have died from the burns I suffered, but I survived. However, I was left not only with these horrible scars but also with a mind that had temporarily lost its reason. Once I had physically recovered from my burns, I was moved to a ward for the insane and there I was put on display to

G.M. BEST

the curious. They could take pleasure in witnessing both my facial
deformity and my mental incapacity. What I said earlier about my
condition is true and I did attack one of those who particularly
mocked me. After that, I was more closely confined.'

He paused and shuddered at the memory of that bad time.
Then he resumed his story. 'Fortunately after the passage of many
years my mind grew gradually calmer with each passing day and
there eventually came a time when I no longer amused anyone
with wild antics. As a consequence I was released, but please be not
deceived, this was no charitable act. After ten years of incarcera-
tion, there was no one to greet me or assist me. My jailers let me
go in the sure knowledge that I would either be arrested as a
vagrant or die in the streets. However, neither happened. I defied
the odds against me and I took up work again, but I was no
happier here than in the days of my madness. You see, I now knew
again who I was and who I had lost.'

'Who are you, sir?' I said, seeing the obvious agony in his mind.

'My name is Heathcliff Earnshaw and the person I lost was
Cathy, the only woman I have ever loved. She was taken from me
by a cursed scoundrel called Mr Edgar Linton. He deceived her
into marrying him whilst I was away making my fortune. You can
imagine the pain of returning home a wealthy man only to find the
woman you love beyond your reach! I begged my Cathy to run
away with me, but she refused because she was by then pregnant
with twins. She died giving birth to two daughters. Edgar Linton
took one and I stole the other. He named his child Catherine after
her mother and he brought her up in his image – proud and
haughty and deceitful. In contrast I had Cathy's other daughter
brought up by friends in Cornwall to be a most loving and kind
girl. She was called Maria. I did not bring her up myself because I
did not wish her ever to look on me as her father. Instead I hoped
to win her as my bride once she had reached the same age as her
mother had been when I lost her.'

He paused and looked to see my reaction. I could hardly believe
such an outrageous story but the manner in which he told it left
me in no doubt that he was telling the truth, and, looking at the

154

grim determination in his visage, I feared what insanity I might hear next. I tried to smile and so indicate I was listening with sympathy to his tale, but my face gave more of a rictus grin. Nevertheless, this seemed sufficient for him to continue:

'The year before I was to summon my new bride, I realized that I must first remove all evidence of my previous relationships. By then Edgar Linton was a dying man so all that was required was the elimination of the daughter he had corrupted and my two pathetic sons. One of these was born legally and named Linton. I had married his mother, who was Edgar's sister, simply out of revenge and not love, and this hapless creature was the sole outcome of that undesirable union. He was a poor imitation of a young man and already half in his grave through a weak constitution. My other son was a half-wit that the world mistakenly called my nephew, a lad called Hareton. I had seduced his mother with ease because of her unhappy life with my half-brother, a man I detested. I gathered Hareton and Linton and Catherine into my home with their destruction in mind. Only my desire to first hear that Edgar Linton had died in an agony of despair at his daughter's loss made me postpone their immediate murder. That was a mistake because Hareton escaped and brought assistance in the form of a stable boy to rescue the other two. In the struggle that ensued I set my farm-house alight with the intention of destroying all my enemies. Unfortunately, the stupid interfering stable boy locked me into the barn and so I found myself also plunged into the flaming inferno. Hence my injuries and hence my resulting madness.'

I thought that madness must have affected him before the fire if there was even a scrap of truth in his appalling story, but I feared to make any comment and let him continue with his narrative.

'Once I recalled who I was, I became obsessed with discovering how long I had been in the asylum and what had happened to the others. It did not take me long to discover that the fire had taken place many years before and that Catherine, Linton and Hareton had died in the blaze. When I was released, I tried to put all the past behind me but after the passage of a couple of years I came to a gradual determination to discover what had happened to my proposed bride. To my surprise I discovered Maria had left Cornwall and come to Yorkshire, not to join me as I had originally planned but to assist some relatives of those who had brought her up. These people lived in a new school created at ...'

Before he could finish the sentence my mind had made the jump to what he would say. Surely the bride he had hoped to marry could not be my mother! I think he saw the look of startled recognition on my face. 'Aye, lad,' he said. 'The name she had been given was Maria Branwell. The people she thought were her relatives were a schoolmaster and his wife named Fennell. He had taken up a post at Woodhouse Grove. A spineless Irish minister named Patrick Brontë – the man you call Father – had married my Maria in the December of 1812. When I heard, I knew that history had repeated itself. Once again my intended bride had been snatched from me and given to an unworthy man. I knew Cathy would turn in her grave if I did not rescue her child from the sour-faced cleric. Though I was much older than her husband and, as you can see, very badly scarred, I was still twice the man that he was. I did not doubt that I could win Maria's love.'

He said this with such conviction that, although my mind reeled, I doubted not that he thought he spoke the truth, even if he did not.

'When I first saw your mother,' he continued, 'I confess that I was very taken aback because she was so short in stature and she looked nothing like Cathy, but I soon recognized that she had the same natural vivacity and gaiety. In a strange way her lack of beauty made her a better choice because it made us well matched. After all, I had none of my former good looks. Using wealth that I had retained from my earlier existence as a revenue man, I set up home near to where she and her husband lived, but under an assumed name, so none might recall my past. I was confident that my disfigurement would prevent anyone recognizing me, and I evoked sympathy by making out that my scarred visage stemmed from injuries sustained in fighting for my country. It did not take me long to appreciate that Maria had been brought up to be more religious than is to my taste, and so I determined that I should not permit my feelings to rush me into any precipitate action that might cause her to reject my advances. Although the world saw them as being a successful and happy couple because she had borne her husband two daughters, I saw otherwise. It was obvious to me that Maria was very unhappy in her marriage.'

'I don't believe you,' I interrupted. 'My parents were very happily married.'

'Patrick Brontë may have given you that impression,' he replied, 'but I can assure you that the man only married her because he wrongly assumed she came from a family of some wealth that would ensure his promotion within the Church. When he first married her, he satisfied his lusts on her but there was no love. She knew that and it caused her much pain. She, who was used to the concert hall and assembly rooms of Penzance, found herself trapped in a grimy, small town that consisted of little more than one grey terraced street, devoid of culture, society and beauty. Worse still, she found she had married a man who professed Christianity yet was domineering and self-centred. I found as an older man it was easy to win her confidence and to let her pour out her sorrows to a sympathetic ear. It was but a short step to win first her affection and then, as the months passed, her love. Ours was a true passion.'

'True passion!' I exclaimed. 'I'll not believe a word of it. My mother would never have succumbed to your embraces or the sick seducement of such a warped mind as yours!'

'Believe that, if you prefer,' he said. 'But I assure you that when she finally permitted me to gather her in my arms she experienced the kind of lovemaking that her hypocritical husband had never offered. And surely you would prefer to be a love-child than the product of a loveless match?'

'You are not my father!' I screamed.

'I am and, in your heart, I believe you already know it. What have you got in common with that poor specimen you have called your father?'

'More than I have in common with you!'

He laughed. 'You are indeed not the son that I had imagined but that's the influence of that damned Brontë. He has brought you up to be the effeminate creature that you are. Had I been the master of your fate, I would have turned you into a son worthy of me and of your mother.'

'So where have you been all these years?'

'Until recently I was in a prison cell, entirely due to the slanderous lies of your so-called father. When I heard your name last night, I could scarce believe it. Branwell Brontë. I knew there could not be another. Fortune has brought us together and this time it will not separate us.'

Though most of my mind told me I should leave the place and never see this monster again, my curiosity bade me to stay. I found myself saying, almost despite myself, 'So what happened all those years ago?'

'Maria found she was pregnant and she believed the child could only be ours because at that time her husband had decided to abstain from further carnal knowledge of her. He did not wish to see his family grow so large that it might prevent him advancing his career. I urged her to flee away with me but she refused to be parted from her two daughters. Without my knowledge she sought to hide her infidelity by deliberately seducing her own husband in the hope he would think the third child was his. I was angry when I heard what she had done and began to think of ways in which I could ensure Brontë's demise. With him dead she would be free to marry me and retain all her children.'

'There is no way that my mother would have contemplated linking herself to a murderer!' I shouted.

'I recognized that and so I knew I would have to act carefully to disguise my actions. Our daughter was born and named Charlotte and our affair continued. Once again Maria became pregnant – this time with a son, with you. Once again she seduced her husband into making love, but this time she left matters too late and Brontë was suspicious that he could not be the father. I know not what he did to your mother but she was forced to admit her love for me. He took swift action. At the time there had been much mob violence from those opposed to new machinery in the mills and he had me arrested as a leader of this. Despite my protestations of innocence, I was condemned and sent to prison. The only way that I could have proved myself free of the charge would have been to uncover my true identity and I dared not do that.'

'Why not, sir?'

'Because there was enough in my past to warrant a hanging. Once I was imprisoned, your poor mother was forced to bear the brunt of her husband's anger. I am sure this included raping her on more than one occasion for I cannot believe she would have willingly given herself to him yet I heard they had two more children before she died. In my worst moments I fear he was responsible also for her untimely death.'

'No more! No more!' I sobbed. 'I cannot bear to hear any more evil from your mouth! You have destroyed all my certainties and all my peace of mind!'

'Your suffering is nothing compared to mine!' he snarled. 'What do you know of passion? I watched your pathetic behaviour with the sluts whose services you paid for last night. Maybe I should destroy you as I have destroyed my other children.'

I ignored this threat and yelled back at him, 'What do you want? Why tell me all this if I matter nothing to you!'

'Because I want you to bring your sister Charlotte to me. She is Maria's daughter and Cathy's granddaughter. With her I can begin again!'

'Begin again?' I muttered questioningly. He did not reply but, looking at his lustful face, the enormity of what he meant suddenly hit me and I was stunned to my innermost depths. The man was totally insane! Did he now want to marry his own daughter? What perverse logic dominated this man's sick mind? I thrust him from me, shouting, 'Keep away from my sister!', and I grabbed a knife from the table that lay between us.

'Hareton did what I told him. Linton did what I told him. And you will do what I tell you to do or, like them, you will feel the lash of my fist,' he threatened.

He dived towards me and I in my panic and terror lashed out at him. The knife was in my hand and, without my intending it, it sliced across his throat. With a sudden look of shock, he held his hand to the gaping wound and watched the red blood begin trickling through his scarred fingers. He made as if to seize me but his much-vaunted strength failed him and he sank to his knees. A strange gurgling sound escaped from his mouth as he tried to speak and then he crashed to the floor. A red pool began to form around his body as his life-blood flowed out. I watched the man who claimed to be my father slowly but surely die and in that moment, despite all the horror, I believed all that he had told me.

You know, Charlotte, what the man the world calls our father is like. He is cold and unfeeling beneath the veneer of his respectability. How could our mother have received the affection from him that was her due? I now saw his insistence on my always sleeping in his room for what it was – his way of keeping a bastard from contaminating his true children. Maybe Heathcliff Earnshaw was wrong in thinking that you were his child because our mother clearly was still fulfilling all the duties of a wife, but I am sure he was right in saying that I am his son.

I fled the scene of murder and vowed never to disclose these events to anyone, especially you. I dosed myself with opium in the hope that it would remove all memory of what had happened, but it gave only temporary relief. When I returned to Haworth I tried to behave as if nothing had happened whilst constantly fearing a knock on the door would single the arrival of those who had come to arrest me for my crime. Even worse, I began imagining that maybe the lunatic man I had killed was right in thinking that our mother's death was a product of her husband's revenge for her infidelity. You know as well as I how quickly after her death your father (for I no longer can call him mine) sought to remarry, though he could find none to take him. In my worst imaginings I feared even that Aunt Elizabeth might have had a hand in what happened. Who knows what he may have promised to her in order to engage her assistance in her stepsister's demise? Was her love for us just penitence at her earlier crime?

Not surprisingly, I found I could not bear to be within the same walls as the man I no longer saw as my father and that is why I took the post here, though it ran counter to all my earlier expressed ambitions. I simply had to escape. What a joke! Escape! The past weeks have taught me there is no escape. Wherever I choose to go, I am still a bastard, still the child of a maniac and a sadly duped woman. Wherever I go, I am still the murderer of my own father. What hope is there for me? Before I could scream against the injustice of a fate that denied my talents, but now my miserable existence can only be seen as the rightful lifestyle for a man who must be cursed and condemned for all eternity. All the majestic beauty of the hills and lakes that surround here cannot bring peace to a tortured soul like mine!

I know that I will have brought you much pain by what I have revealed, especially the behaviour of our mother and therefore the uncertainty of your own birth. I know also that I will have made you think less of the man you so affectionately call brother by revealing my own illegitimacy and my unworthy and criminal action. All I can ask is that you forgive me and pray for me. I know not what to do to escape my current situation! I look on all my cherished wishes, yesterday so blooming and glowing, as now no more than just stark, chill, livid corpses that can never revive.

Your forever damned but still loving half-brother,
Branwell

12

Branwell's Infernal World

I have thought much about Branwell's letter in the years since I first read it and I believe Charlotte must have taken it deeply to heart. I say this because I can see echoes of its contents in her subsequent writing of *Jane Eyre*. Heathcliff's description of his mad behaviour is used almost verbatim in Charlotte's account of Bertha Rochester's insanity. Branwell's comment on his unhappy state is used to describe Jane's shattered life after her discovery that Rochester has a mad wife. The blinding and maiming of Rochester – so reminiscent of Heathcliff's sufferings – is presented as a fitting punishment for a man who has desired an unacceptable relationship. I think the novel also reflects Charlotte's feelings about what had been uncovered. When Jane Eyre recognizes that Rochester is 'not what I had thought him', she responds by saying, 'I had now put love out of the question and thought only of duty.' Was not that how Charlotte behaved towards Patrick Brontë once she knew he might not be her father? Above all, I suspect that the conclusion of *Jane Eyre* may well have been taken from what she wrote in reply to Branwell because it is a clarion call to face up to traumatic events that have wrecked one's dreams:

> Do not look forward to an uninterrupted flow of happiness. That is not the position of mortals this side of eternity ... When the young fancy is warm, it sees nothing but a gay prospect before it. But sage experience removes the delusion, and teaches more moderate expectations. Let me advise you ... to be fully resigned to the Divine will, constantly preserving a tranquil equanimity. Let each look upon the other as the best earthly friend. And be not

blind to faults on either side, but cover them with a mantle of charity ... Let not the sun go down upon your wrath.

Back in 1854, my response was less complex. I simply appreciated for the first time why Charlotte had often been so sympathetic to her brother when his hopes of a sparkling career came to naught. She alone knew and understood the cause of his emotional collapse. The other letter I copied from Branwell, which is much shorter, shows how her initial attempts to help him came to naught because of another flaw in his character:

Broughton House
Broughton-in-Furness
26 June 1840

Dearest Charlotte,

All is undone! My attempt to heed your advice and resume seeking a future for myself has proved fruitless!

In response to your encouragement I composed a letter to Hartley Coleridge at his cottage on the banks of Rydal Water and enclosed some of my verse. I told him that I had devoted my energies to literary composition since childhood, that I had never shown the outcome to any discerning mind, and that I would value his judgement on my skill or lack of it. To my amazement he agreed to see me and the day fixed for that was yesterday. You can imagine my pride when I shook the hand of the son of the great Coleridge, a man who associates with Wordsworth, Southey and many others of note. He looked older than his years, but I found his mind sharp enough, despite the reputation that he has earned for over-drinking. We discovered that we had certain interests in common, not least that he too writes of imaginary worlds like us. For the first time in weeks I felt happy again. He kindly promised to assist me in whatever way he could and I said that I would send him a copy of my translation of some of Horace's verse. I felt the curse of Heathcliff had been lifted and I rejoiced.

But that was yesterday and today I have again accepted the

certainty that any ambition is a complete waste of time. Today I discovered that the servant girl Agnes Riley was even more stupid than I had thought. She is with child. She came to see me with red-rimmed but hopeful eyes, expecting me to do the honourable thing. I told her that I was sorry to hear of her condition but that I would rather die than marry her. She threatened to inform Mr Postlethwaite. I told her that neither he nor any other man had the authority to make me wed a slut. I suppose that was not kind, but what matters unkindness when the sinner is already burdened with a far greater crime? Will God forgive fornication as well as murder? I think not. My life is stained by sins that can neither be forgiven in this life nor the next. Truly Heathcliff Earnshaw's blood flows in my veins!

Mr Postlethwaite summoned me to his room and he confronted me with Agnes Riley's accusations. What could I say? I immediately tendered my resignation. Poor Agnes wept throughout. That did not, of course, prevent Mr Postlethwaite dismissing her. I promised I would send her some money. I can only hope that our child will not survive. The thought of Heathcliff Earnshaw's blood entering another generation chills me. I now have to return home and somehow explain to Father why I have left my post. I cannot possibly tell him the truth. I know you will say that I am overreacting but I have determined that in future a man of my ignobility should have no contact with the young lest I corrupt them. I will abandon tutoring in favour of some menial post, where I can be a danger to none.

My only concern at taking such a step is that I know my own weaknesses and I fear that such a course of action may lead me to drown my sorrows in alcohol or, worse still, make me turn to opium again. If I am so weak as to resort to such foul measures, then do not seek to stop me. They may be the means of an early death. Whatever you say to the contrary, I know you will be far better off without my sinful presence.

Your loving but unworthy admirer whom once you called brother,
Branwell

Like many, I had been very surprised when Branwell had become a mere railway worker in the autumn of 1840. This letter made the reason very clear. It also made me realize why Charlotte had refused to abandon her desire to go to Brussels, even though he had pleaded with her to remain in Haworth to help him. Why should she stay to help a man who had shown such unworthy behaviour to Agnes Riley? It was ironic that, once abroad, she had behaved almost as badly. However, I knew that Charlotte would never accept this comparison. She viewed her passionate feelings for Professor Héger as a product of a genuine and irresistible love but I knew from her comments to me that she saw Branwell's immoral doings as just a product of mindless lust – hence her strong disapproval of his distraught behaviour at the ending of his affair with Mrs Robinson in 1845. Given how Branwell had damned himself for his passing affair with Agnes Riley, I doubted not that he would have thought himself even more condemned by adding adultery to his crimes.

After reading both letters, I was sure that the key to the tragic family deaths in 1848 and 1849 rested with what had happened in 1839. Branwell had never recovered from the overwhelming emotional impact of his ill-fated meeting with Heathcliff. Instead his life had become ever more degraded and dissolute. It seemed to me Charlotte's mounting concern over his behaviour offered a perfect explanation as to why she had become so obsessed with remaining anonymous when *Jane Eyre* became such a success. Alcohol loosens the tongue but unless the drunkard is noteworthy no one really listens. It is a different matter if the drunkard happens to be the brother of a famous authoress. Then the world would relish the scandal if, in a drunken state, Branwell spoke of what Heathcliff had revealed about her parentage. Had that happened, I did not doubt that her reputation would have been destroyed overnight. Had therefore Anne been right after all in speculating that Charlotte had had a hand in Branwell's early death? If so, and Emily had been suspicious, did that also explain her quick demise? And had Anne's agitation over Emily's death made her the next target? It all seemed to make sense of what until then had been inexplicable.

The one thing I found hard to explain was why Charlotte encouraged Emily to write *Wuthering Heights*. Surely she would have wanted the name of Heathcliff forgotten, not immortalized? I could only assume that she had hoped that, by making Heathcliff fictional, no one would take seriously any drunken comments inadvertently made about him.

Understandably I hoped that all my speculation was wrong, and yet I feared the worst and that my surmises might be correct. I can assure you that it is not a happy experience to think that the person you have loved for so many years as your closest friend might be a murderer. As a consequence I knew that I had no option but to be open with Charlotte about what I had uncovered, even if I feared a very angry reaction, especially when she heard that I had dared search her papers in order to read some of Branwell's letters. I decided to strike while the iron was hot and to discuss everything with her during her imminent planned visit to my home in May. It was my hope that she would reveal to me all that had actually happened, even if that meant admitting to crimes that she had hoped would always remain hidden.

For the first two days of her stay at Brookroyd I could not bring myself to initiate the conversation that I dreaded. Instead I let her speak at length about her forthcoming wedding. Her comments did little to convince me that she should be marrying Mr Nicholls, but I did what she requested in helping her prepare for her forthcoming wedding day, even accompanying her while she chose her dress. On the third day of her visit I engineered it so that we went out together for a quiet walk. I thought that perhaps the happy memories of earlier outings might put her into a better frame of mind to hear my disclosures. Once I had commenced, she listened with mounting displeasure as I recounted all that I had undertaken: my reading of Cathy's manuscript so at variance with Emily's novel, my finding of the entry in Dr Wroughton's journal that revealed a second child; my search for Cathy's missing daughter that led me, via discussions at Woodhouse Grove and the confession of John Reynolds, to the unpalatable truth that the lost child was Maria Branwell; my unearthing of the letters of Catherine Linton and my meeting with Walter Hodges that informed me of the tragedy that had destroyed the lives of three innocent young people; and, finally (and most painfully), my treachery of her trust in searching her letters to find the two written by Branwell in which he had disclosed his and possibly her true parentage and his murder of Heathcliff. Then I stopped, not daring to say what terrible conclusions

I had drawn about the subsequent deaths of Branwell, Emily and Anne.

'My God,' she said when I had finished, 'I think I have underestimated you, Nell. All these years I thought you were no more than a useful glove – something to be taken out and used whenever that was desirable and then rapidly set aside when no longer required. Now I see you are quite a force in your own right and I respect you the more for it. But what do you propose to do with all this information? Sell it to the press so they can take pleasure in destroying our family's reputation?'

'Charlotte, how can you think that of me? I would never do anything to hurt you or your family's reputation!'

'Then why else have you gone behind my back, ignored by distinct advice, and wormed out all this family sewage?'

'I love the truth, Charlotte.'

'You may be clever but you still know just a fraction of the truth, Nell.'

'I know enough that it has made me look with fresh eyes at the self-destruction that seized your brother. I am now sympathetic towards him in a way I never was while he was still alive.'

'And is the implication that I was not sympathetic? Let me remind you that it was I and not you who had to contend with the drunkard who inhabited Branwell's frame in the later years of his life. There was not a day that passed that I did not mourn the passing of the brother with whom I had grown up, the Branwell who had enlivened my life and inspired my imagination. You express sympathy for the later man and he deserves none. Whilst I worked tirelessly to drag this family out of obscurity, he let his emotions squander his greater talents. Whilst I took my destiny into my own hands, he whined that fate was against him and did nothing. When I weep for my dead brother – and I still do – I weep for a man who died on the day he met Heathcliff, not the man who died nine years later.'

Tears trickled down her cheek and I did not think her emotion feigned. She wiped them away with a gesture of frustration at her weakness. 'Tell me, Ellen, what did all his suffering and talk of damnation initially stem from? Just two things. That he was born a bastard and that, in a moment of terror, he accidentally killed a man. Yet in response to those things he abandoned all hope of a distinguished future and sought to humiliate himself by taking on the menial role of a booking clerk at Sowerby Bridge Station. We all tried to put a brave face on his new employment, saying it was a role that held prospects because of the growing success of railway companies, but the truth was that the station was no more than a wooden shed and its stationmaster was a renowned sot. How could a man of Branwell's talents and education endure such a place and such a master? I am not surprised he soon engaged in excessive drinking. We used contacts to achieve his promotion to the post of stationmaster at Luddenden Foot but that was scarce better. A man who could wax lyrical on the sweet strains of a nightingale was doomed to the company of amoral bargees and rowdy millworkers who were far his inferior and to whom his intellect meant absolutely nothing!'

'But he did retain some of his former friends,' I interjected.

'A few but he saw them only intermittently. He would walk with them through the beautiful valley scenery, displaying his wondrous knowledge upon subjects moral, intellectual and philosophical, and temporarily recapture the feel of earlier and happier days. On such occasions he would repent of his malignant debauchery but once they were gone he would resume the path that had only one destination – his ultimate self-destruction. As you well know, the depths to which he sank were soon made public when he was dismissed from the Leeds and Manchester Railway for a serious discrepancy in his station's accounts. Eleven pounds went missing.'

'I cannot prove that he did not take the money, Charlotte, but I prefer to give him the benefit of the doubt. You know that he often left the station in the hands of one or other of the station's two porters and one of these may well have been the guilty party for the money's disappearance.'

'It matters not whether it was incompetence or theft that lay behind the loss, because either way he returned to Haworth in humiliating and public disgrace. I saw there was now no belief in his mind that he would ever publish anything of worth. Despair consumed him. And do you know the saddest thing of all? He could not bring himself to enter a church yet amid his scribbles I found repeated the one name that he hoped one day might bring him absolution from his innate sinfulness – Jesu … Jesu … Jesu.'

'Yet you left him, Charlotte. You deserted him to go with Emily to Brussels, leaving him undefended against your father's stern disapproval. Nor did you help him come to terms with the death of your aunt, who had so idolized him in happier times. You returned only for her funeral and then, because of your passion for Professor Héger, you left him again.'

'Yes, I left him, but you have read the letter in which he describes his disgusting behaviour with Agnes Riley. In the light of that, for the first time in my life I put myself first and him second. And when I returned to Haworth, I was happy to leave him again for Brussels because I was sickened by what he had done to Aunt Elizabeth.'

'What on earth do you mean?'

'The stupid doctor said that she had died of exhaustion after suffering from severe constipation but Branwell told me otherwise. He had deliberately killed her.'

'He had no cause, Charlotte.'

'That is where you are wrong. Branwell wanted Emily and me back. Making our aunt severely ill was a sure way of securing that.'

'He cannot have been so evil.'

'Like me, he was ready to use any means in order to effect what he wanted. Why should he worry about the consequences when he knew he was already damned? It only took a few powders secretly administered to make her bowels seize up. Can you imagine it, Ellen? He sat by her bed and secretly smiled at the thought of my return as he watched her writhe in agony for a fortnight. Our so-called father was touched by what he saw as Branwell's devotion and left her entirely to his care, while he took to his prayers for her recovery. Branwell let no one else tend her, least of all our servant Tabby, who, though old and crippled, might have suspected things were not as they should be. The medicine prescribed by the doctor never touched her lips, only the poison which daily was dripped into her parched mouth. Branwell told me only towards the end did our aunt look at him with doubt in her face as if she finally understood that the boy on whom she had lavished her affection had no love for her and was indeed the cause of her vile sickness. But by then she was too weak to speak out or do anything.'

'Then he is truly worthy of damnation,' I said. 'Please, Charlotte, be silent. I can bear no more revelations!'

'But I thought you wanted the truth, Ellen,' she replied with a grim smile.

As I looked at her harsh and cruel face, I suddenly thought of Anne's conjectures that I had dismissed five years before. For the first time I believed them possibly to be true. I could see the young Charlotte deter- minedly ensuring that her older sisters should not stand in the way of what she wanted. I could see her as a young girl of eight poisoning them till her father took them and her back home. I recognized that the time had come for me to ask her directly whether she had been the cause of Maria and Elizabeth's untimely deaths, and I replied, 'Yes, I want the truth. It will surprise you to learn that I have in my care some documents written by Anne in which she thought you poisoned your elder sisters, Maria and Elizabeth, just to escape school. Were you guilty of the same crime as Branwell? Is that also the truth? Is that why, when we were young, you wrote a letter to me saying that you felt yourself to be one of the damned?'

If my words took her by surprise, she did not show it, but calmly answered, 'I loved my eldest sisters, Ellen, but they were not prepared to support my demand that we should return home. They tolerated the appalling conditions in that school, but for me it was not just the cold and the damp and the terrible food that made life impossible. I could have borne those. The difference was that I was always being condemned. I strove to fulfil every duty yet I was daily termed naughty and tiresome, sullen and sneaking, a useless and wicked creature. I could never please or win anyone's favour. When I wrote about Lowood School in *Jane Eyre* I based it entirely on my horrid experiences at Cowan Bridge so please understand, Ellen, that when Mr Brocklehurst places Jane on a chair in front of the entire school and publicly humiliates her, that was what the Reverend Carus Wilson used to do to me. His cruelty is etched on my brain.'

Charlotte appeared to enter a trance as she spoke the following in a tone that was not hers and which I took to be a copy of her former teacher's voice:

'You see she is yet young; you observe she possesses the ordinary form of childhood ... no single deformity points her out as a marked character. Who would think that the Evil One had already found a servant and agent in her? Yet such, I grieve to say, is the case ... My dear children ... this is a sad, a melancholy occasion; for it becomes my duty to warn you that this girl, who might be one of God's little lambs, is a little castaway – not a member of the true flock, but evidently an interloper and an alien. You must be on guard against her; you must shun her example – if necessary, avoid her company, exclude her from your sports, and shut her out of your converse. Teachers, you must watch her; keep your eyes on her movements, weigh well her words, scrutinize her actions, punish her body to save her soul – if indeed, such salvation be possible for ... this girl is a liar.'

I recognized the words from the book but only now did I appreciate their full significance. I think she had expected them to evoke my pity, but instead they raised a series of questions in my mind that would have horrified her had I voiced them. What on earth had Charlotte done as a schoolgirl to incur such a description of herself? Surely, if her behaviour had remotely warranted such words, was she not indeed the spawn of Satan himself? Was she not truly Heathcliff's child – a monstrous cuckoo in the Brontë nest? I knew how determined and ruthless Charlotte could be, even against those she professed to love. She had not specifically answered my question, but I doubted not she had poisoned her two older sisters and that, years later, she had similarly poisoned Emily and Anne to escape Roe Head. I knew that she and Branwell deserved to be exposed, but had I the stomach to do it? And would anyone believe me?

'Branwell always talked as if he was the only person who suffered,' continued Charlotte, oblivious of my discomfiture, 'but I suffered far more than him as a child. I saw no reason to turn my back on a chance of happiness in Brussels in order to comfort my murderous brother. No, Ellen, I did the right thing. I demanded that he undertake appropriate employment or face having his crimes made known to the rest of the family and, in response, he quickly agreed that he should take up a post as tutor in the household in which Anne had served as a governess for almost two years. If that left me free to return to Brussels, did it not leave him free to carve a new life for himself under Anne's watchful eye?'

'But you must have known it would not work,' I interrupted. 'The

Reverend Edward Robinson might have been a clergyman of wealthy means but he led a quiet and relatively remote life because he was an invalid. The pedestrian lifestyle at Thorp Green Hall was bound to soon bore Branwell and, in that situation, there was no way he would heed any advice proffered by Anne, who was so much younger than him and, in his opinion, the least talented of the family.'

'You say that, Ellen, but at first, all went well. Branwell took up residence in an old building in the grounds and he informed me that he saw his new life as being a very appropriate punishment for his sins. How could I have foreseen that his employer's wife would seduce him?'

'Mrs Lydia Robinson had a husband who was a sick and emaciated man and who brought her no pleasure. Is it so surprising that she should find in Branwell an interesting diversion in what had become a tedious existence?'

'It was not just sweet talk that was exchanged, Ellen. I know what happened because after their affair was uncovered and my brother was dismissed, he told me everything about it in the most nauseating detail. From the outset Mrs Robinson made clear that she wished not for mere dalliance but for him to go on to extremities. I do not find fault with him for giving in to her lewd wishes. He was seventeen years her junior and he found her attentions both flattering and arousing. She introduced him to erotic practices that I would blush to tell you. If I blame him for anything it is that he thought she actually loved him when in fact theirs was a relationship built entirely on carnal lust! Once the gardener reported to her husband how he had seen them locked in a passionate embrace in the boathouse, she dropped my brother as if he had never existed.'

'Anne did not look at the matter like you,' I responded. 'She resigned when she saw what was happening. She knew that Branwell should have resisted Mrs Robinson's advances.'

'There speaks a true spinster! Do you have any understanding of passion, Ellen? Am I so different from my brother? You more than anyone know of my affair with Constantin Héger! At one level, my actions were no better than Branwell's licentious fumblings with Lydia Robinson or with that slut he impregnated. The difference between us is that he let a dismissal from an invalid husband ruin his life. Branwell lacked the capacity to fight for what he wanted. That is not true of me. I have taken pleasure in opposing those who have stood in my way and I have always delighted in seeing an enemy – or if necessary a friend – removed from blocking my chosen path. Why else, for example, did I take so calmly the death of poor Martha Taylor in Brussels?'

'Martha Taylor?'

'Yes, sweet little Martha Taylor, despite her ugliness, threatened to draw Constantin's affections away from me. That's a truth you have never uncovered, Ellen, despite all your supposed cleverness.'

'I think you are mistaken, Charlotte. I am sure that Martha would not have been interested in your professor. And, if he showed any interest in her, it would have been simply because, like all of us, he found her vivacity attractive and her prattle engaging.'

'It was for that very reason I feared she might steal the heart of the man I had come to love. I knew I lacked her natural wit and that my ugliness was plain for all to see when contrasted with her beauty. Although she was the sister of one of my oldest and closest friends, no one was happier than I when she unexpectedly became ill and died.'

My stomach churned at these words. I could not stop my mind wondering whether Charlotte had had a hand in her death. It would have been but the work of a moment to pour some poison into a glass of fruit juice that Martha was drinking. My courage failed me and I did not ask whether this had been the case. I only hoped that I was wrong. Death can come in many forms and none but God knows the hour at which any of us will be summoned to depart our earthly existence. Recovering my composure as quickly as I could, I made only a simple comment. 'I now appreciate that until recently I knew very little of the truth about your life or Branwell's,' I said.

'There is little more to know about my brother. When I had to cope with the loss of my true love, I did not indulge in such loud-mouthed self-pity as did he, though my loss was infinitely greater than his. He had lost a conniving and duplicitous woman who never loved him, whereas I had lost a man of incalculable worth who genuinely adored me. His response was to become mindlessly drunk and destroy his gifts. Mine was to throw myself into writing and to encourage my sisters to similarly use their talents. You know the outcome of our labours. We put behind us the juvenile productions of the past and showed our true worth. In contrast, Branwell's only achievement was to make life at Haworth intolerable. All he could do was talk endlessly of Mrs Robinson. He even kept his pockets full of her love letters so that he might continue to read of the passion they had once shared.

'Whenever I challenged him to stop being sorry for himself and to take up worthwhile employment, he would feebly mutter about how "Heathcliff's curse" was an immovable block to God's forgiveness and how it damned him of any chance of attaining worldly success. The passing months saw him produce only a few nondescript poems and some badly written fantastical fiction. The only inventiveness he showed was in the various reasons he gave to con my father out of money so he could fund his dissolute lifestyle.'

'And what did he make of Emily writing about Heathcliff in *Wuthering Heights*?'

'He never knew because, as you well know, we never told him that we were having our books published. That would have been too cruel. It was easy to deceive him because he was too wrapped up in his own world. He largely kept to his studio while I wrote in the dining room and Emily wrote in her room.'

'I cannot understand why you encouraged Emily to write about Heathcliff in the first place, given his relationship to your family.'

'Unlike Branwell, I am not obsessed with the man. I never met him and I have no way of knowing whether he did in fact father me. What did it matter if I had him transformed into fiction? If anything, it made him less real. When we sisters agreed to write, it was easy for Anne and me. Both of us turned to our recent experience for inspiration. Emily was not so fortunately placed. I gave her the idea of writing a romance about Heathcliff because I got the idea from my brother. Not directly, of course. Some of his friends had been encouraging him to write and they had agreed to meet him at the Cross Roads Inn, which is about halfway between Keighley and Haworth. It was expected that he would read some of his work to them. Typically he had done nothing but, not wanting to lose face, he rapidly scribbled some notes before going there. In his haste for inspiration he chose to write about the man who dominated his thoughts and so devised a foolish tale on Heathcliff's early life.

When he returned home, the notes were cast aside. I found them. At first I confess I was horrified that Branwell should be mentioning Heathcliff to anyone, but then I realized it was better if people did think of him as being a fictional figure.'

I nodded my assent and she continued. 'Reading my brother's notes, I sensed they could be developed into a strong novel, but I did not care for the author to be Branwell. He was too unpredictable in what he might write. I knew it was safer if it was written by someone who had no idea that there was a real Heathcliff. I therefore passed some of the ideas contained in his notes on to Emily and she did a superb job with them. She created a sweeping drama that incorporated not only all her knowledge of this area and its people but also her own special love for the moors. I was not concerned that anyone might judge the novel to have any foundation in fact. Why should I have been? Most of the novel's set pieces draw entirely from Emily's imagination – Cathy's ghost haunting the wintry moors, Heathcliff getting the sexton to open her coffin seven years after her burial and, of course, Lockwood's discovery of Heathcliff's corpse. Why should I take anything other than pride in what she produced? I have no doubt that as each decade passes, it will be of our books the one most remembered.'

'Did you not fear that Branwell might one day reveal to the world that Heathcliff was not just a fictional character but a real person?'

'No. There was always a danger that whilst drunk he might talk of Heathcliff, but usually his speech was so slurred people did not bother to listen. When he was sober he had no desire to reveal our family's guilty secret. His death certificate says he died from chronic bronchitis and wasting of the body, but you and I know his true spirit died that day he met and killed Heathcliff. From then the brother I had known was replaced by a doom-ridden failure. As I have said to you on more than one occasion, I shed my tears for the loss of the brother I loved long before his flesh finally gave way. It was only his death that released me to love him again. Looking at his body as it lay in his coffin I saw a marble calm over his features and I felt there was peace and forgiveness for him in heaven. All his errors, all his crimes, even that of murdering Aunt Elizabeth, seemed to me nothing in that moment. Every wrong he had done, every pain he had caused, vanished and I recalled only his wondrous promise, his natural family affection, and his many sufferings. And if I can forgive him, surely so will God? He who knew no peace in life is now at rest, and had his sins been scarlet in their dye, I believe now they are as white as snow.'

Moved by her eloquence, I could not bring myself to ask whether she had hastened his death – and whether that had led her to also seek the destruction of Emily and Anne. Instead I found myself saying, 'God bless you for that, Charlotte, and may God be equally merciful towards you and me.' We said nothing more that day. The next morning she was due to return to Haworth. At breakfast I vowed to her that I would keep quiet about what I had discovered and she graciously accepted that, almost certainly because it was her assumption that my investigations had come to an end. I am not sure she would have made such a misjudgement had not her mind been centred on her imminent marriage. In fact I had no intention of letting matters drop. Charlotte had sounded very convincing and I wanted to believe all that she had said, but I also recognized that she could fabricate the truth when she chose. Had she not deceived me for months that she was wasting her talents at the very time she was writing *The Professor* and *Jane Eyre*! Charlotte might have told me some of the truth but the more I thought about it the more I doubted that she had told me all of it. In the space of a few months it was not just Branwell who had died. So too had both Emily and Anne. Could I safely assume Charlotte had had no hand in those deaths? I felt I could not, however much she genuinely grieved for their loss.

13

A Marriage and a Meeting

Charlotte's wedding took place at 8.00 a.m. on 29 June 1854. I was her bridesmaid and so I helped escort her into the church where a small group of people awaited us. Charlotte looked very pale. She was dressed in a white muslin dress with delicate green embroidery and she wore a white bonnet that was trimmed in flowers and lace. Our former headmistress, Miss Wooler, gave her away because, at the last minute, her father refused to attend the service. It was given out that this was because he had been taken ill, but in my mind I thought there must be other reasons. The minister officiating was the Reverend Sutcliffe Snowdon, who was a friend of the bridegroom. He kept the service brief and afterwards we all went to a modest wedding breakfast. Along with others, I threw flowers over the couple. A carriage then arrived to take the couple to Keighley station, from whence Charlotte and her new husband were to travel by train to North Wales for their honeymoon.

Once they had gone I made my excuses to the other guests as fast as I could, saying that I needed to attend to Charlotte's father. It seemed the perfect opportunity to question him without fear of interruption. His eyesight was very poor, despite his having had an operation a few years before, and so I was careful to let him know who had entered his room. 'It is Miss Nussey,' I said.

'Is it done then,' he muttered. 'Charlotte is married?'

'Yes.' He gave a snort of disapproval, which I ignored. 'Over recent months, sir,' I said, 'I have discovered much about your family and it has left me deeply troubled. I would have you help me know whether what I have heard is true?'

'There has always been too much gossip about this family, Miss Nussey. It is almost certainly untrue,' he replied dismissively.

'I am not speaking of what the outside world says.'

'Then say what you must. I am no Roman priest who delights in hearing confession but if you wish to talk to me about your concerns, please go on,' he snapped. Then he added ungraciously, 'I have nothing better to do this day.'

'Some of what I say may cause you pain, sir.'

'Believe me, Miss Nussey, nothing you can say can cause me anything like the pain I have suffered in this godforsaken spot.'

'I fear you may be wrong, sir, because what I say may evoke the most painful of memories. You see, I have discovered much about a man called Heathcliff Earnshaw.'

The old man's blind eyes gave away no secrets, but I noted that a spasm passed through his body. 'A creature of fiction,' he mumbled.

'But also, I believe, a real man whose evil nature caused havoc within families.'

I admired his control. He turned his virtually sightless eyes towards me as if somehow they could see into my soul. 'Speak on, Miss Nussey. I am not so old and feeble that I cannot face whatever you have to say.'

I spoke at length of what I had uncovered – of Heathcliff's origins and his obsessive love for his half-sister Cathy, of his destructive impact on the Earnshaw and Linton households and his machinations with Nelly Dean, of their abduction of one of Cathy's children and how that child became Maria Branwell. Then I paused, fearing that the impact of my words might cause too much distress to a man in his seventies. He was visibly shaken but he indicated with a nod of his head that I should proceed and so I did. I spoke of the fire at Wuthering Heights and its tragic outcome and how Heathcliff had been prevented from receiving and marrying Maria only because he was locked away.

'And I married her instead,' he interrupted, 'and it was an ill day that I did. Our marriage was not a happy one and it has prevented me having the clerical career that I once hoped would be mine. It is the reason why I am still here in this remote spot.'

'But you must have loved her.'

'Maria Branwell set her cap at me, Miss Nussey. I was thirty-five and had not yet known a woman. Almost from our first meeting she told me I had won her warmest esteem and that I had stirred feelings in her that exceeded the bounds of propriety. She said that God had brought us together and that she would do anything that I desired. Is it any wonder I fell like a fly into her web? Like a fool, I turned from writing religious verse to producing romantic poetry to our love and, after just a few weeks of courtship, I agreed to make her my wife. You may call it love but it was but a mix of folly and lust and I view now our wedding as an evil day.'

'I may be wrong, sir, but I suspect you have chosen to forget the early days of your marriage. Say rather that it was an evil day when Heathcliff Earnshaw was released from his asylum because it was he who destroyed your happiness. He was no more prepared to accept your marriage to Maria than he had been to accept that of Edgar Linton to Cathy and, just as he had destroyed Edgar Linton's happiness, he was determined to destroy yours. In that he succeeded though modesty makes it difficult for me to say how.'

''Tis a false modesty, Miss Nussey, but I will save you the labour. He seduced my wife and turned her into his whore. She then tried to foist on me the product of their fornication, thinking I would take such pleasure in the birth of a son that I would not notice he was not mine! Do I look such a fool?'

'And so you took your revenge,' I said, ignoring his question.

'No. Had I taken my revenge I would have had both of them stripped naked and beaten through the streets of every town in this land so the whole world could know of their disgusting behaviour and see them justly punished. Instead, I acted as a Christian minister of God. I told no man of my wife's infidelity and I adopted the bastard child as my own, and I contented myself with securing the man's imprisonment so he could seduce no other.'

'But did you forgive your wife?'

He made no reply so I repeated the question. His virtually sightless eyes seemed to burn with the fire of hell as he finally made his bitter reply. 'She was not worthy of forgiveness. God took his rightful vengeance. He ensured that her womb should be destroyed and I told her, as she suffered in agony, she should accept that was just a foretaste of the eternal punishment that she would face. I sat by our marital bed and listened to her moans and I thanked God. Had it not been for her sister's intervention I would have prevented her from taking the laudanum prescribed by the doctor. Why should he seek to reduce her suffering? My wife heeded what I told her. She accepted there was no point seeking God's mercy for herself. I was pleased that when she took the medicine it did not prevent her experiencing nightmare visions. When she began praying for her children, I told her it was a waste of time. God does not listen to a harlot's prayers and the sins of the parents fall upon their children. I knew that they must inevitably suffer as a result of her sins – and have they not done so? All are now dead except Charlotte and all of them died in pain and suffering.'

'You paint a grim picture of God's justice, sir.'

'I have never seen reason to disguise the truth, Miss Nussey. When Maria lay screaming in agony in her deathbed, I took the children into her presence. I wanted them to see what happens to those who turn their backs on God's commandments. I like to think it has helped some of them do sufficient that their souls will go heavenwards, though that is certainly not true of Branwell. Despite all my efforts, he turned out as bad as his mother and father.'

I know some readers may find it shocking and say that I am showing too much tolerance towards an adulteress but at that moment my heart bled for poor Maria Branwell. Bound by her children to stay in a love-less marriage with this hard, unforgiving man, I dreaded to think of what agony, mental and physical, she must have suffered. Though he could not see my expression, he must somehow have sensed what I was thinking because he added: 'Save your pity for others. Pity poor Elizabeth, who foolishly vowed to her dying sister that she would care for the children. It was a promise that she came to bitterly regret for it brought her scant affection and kept her imprisoned here, far removed from all that she held dear in Penzance. Pity me because I had to bring up the monster's child as if it was my own and, worse still, then watch that child become the agent of increasing unhappiness within my family.'

'How did you so easily have Heathcliff imprisoned?'

'The year I was married there was huge unrest in this area against industrial change. The new textile factories were replacing the old way of spinning and weaving at home and machines were replacing men. Many feared their families would starve. That unrest was transformed into rioting by a shadowy figure whom the people nicknamed "King Ludd". The lily-livered magistrates refused in their cowardice to take on the rioting Luddites and this encouraged the mob to believe they could destroy both the mills and the machines. I know you have read Charlotte's historical novel which depicts these events.'

'Yes, I have, and I am aware that Charlotte used your memories as one of her sources. She told me that she found your account of the attack on Mr Cartwright's mill at Rawsfold particularly helpful.'

'Yes she did and named it Hollow's Mill in her book. At the time I was working at Hartshead cum Clifton, just a couple of miles from Mr Cartwright's mill, and the night of the attack I was woken from my bed by some of my parishioners who had foolishly joined the rioters and now sought sanctuary in their church. I soon gathered that the mill's master had armed himself and his household well. The Luddites had been repelled after a bloody struggle in which a number had been injured, some very seriously. They carried with them two such men and these they laid down in the box pews. They begged me to hide them from the authorities. I refused to offer my aid, even though some then threatened my life. I told them I was loyal to my Church and King and that I would have no truck with those who turned their hand to violence and who led my flock astray.'

I recalled how I had been told once that Mr Brontë in his youth always carried a pistol on his person, even when going to bed. Now I knew why. 'Had you no compassion for the wounded?' I asked.

'Not for men such as these, who encourage violence and looting. They took the two men away on litters and I afterwards learned they died in the Star Inn at Robertstown. The authorities had seventeen others executed in York. Some were my parishioners. I did not wish to have those buried in my churchyard, but there were threats that Maria would be harmed if I did not permit that. For her sake I acceded and maybe what happened afterwards is God's punishment for that sin. Those rioters deserved no place in sanctified ground.'

I was tempted to say that I thought Jesus had been the friend of sinners but I thought there would be no point in challenging his intransigent beliefs. So instead I merely asked, 'But what has this to do with Heathcliff's arrest five years later? He was not involved in that incident.'

'The authorities were rightly determined to root out more of the ringleaders. It was very easy for me to suggest that Heathcliff was one of those. The man was such an outspoken blackguard that the authorities had no problem in accepting my story. I said that I thought he had been one of those involved in murdering a woollen manufacturer from Marsden called William Horsfall. Three men had already been hung for his murder and I hoped they would hang Heathcliff as a fourth, but unfortunately I could not devise sufficient evidence to justify that, especially as the passage of time since the riots meant that there was not the same desire to make public examples. However, he was imprisoned and for enough years that I hoped he would never emerge from his gaol.'

'But he did emerge twenty years later and, once released from prison, found Branwell?'

'Yes, though at first Branwell hid that from me. He came back from a visit to Liverpool strangely excited but I did not take that amiss. He was always a strange boy in terms of his moods. The fact he had met his real father only emerged after he came back home with his tail between his legs over having resigned his post in the Lake District. At first he tried to give a variety of nonsensical reasons for his action but, when I pressed him, he confessed to being in a state of confusion because of what he had discovered from a man called Heathcliff Earnshaw in Liverpool and how he had murdered the man. I was shocked because I thought Heathcliff had long since died in prison, but I also drew pleasure from the news of his death at the hands of his bastard son.'

'And what happened then?'

'Branwell, of course, wanted me to tell him that it was all a lie. He said that I was his father, that he had always worshipped me, that a person of his talents could not possibly be illegitimate. I laughed in his face! I told him the real truth – that his mother was a whore, that his father was a murdering lunatic, that I had always hated him. He asked me why I had encouraged his education and made him believe he was destined for greatness if I had no love for him. I told him that I had hoped to undo the evil of his birth but that with each passing year it had become ever clearer his blood was irredeemably tainted. That is why he was a failure as an artist, a failure as a writer, a failure as a man. I pointed out that even when he had murdered someone he had done so by accident and not by design.'

'What happened between Heathcliff and your wife was not his fault!' I exclaimed, angered that he should have been so cruel to a young man as sensitive as Branwell.

'I have told you already, Miss Nussey, the sins of the fathers shall be upon their sons.'

For the first time I fully understood why all the promise shown by Charlotte's youthful brother had suddenly come to naught, why Branwell had turned to drink and drugs to ease his deeply troubled mind, why he had become increasingly insistent to Charlotte that he was a damned soul, why he had sought and found comfort in the arms of an older woman. It was not just the meeting with Heathcliff. It was Patrick Brontë's response. Branwell had often poked fun at religious people in the way that young boys often do, but he was no atheist. Mr Brontë had turned the young man's faith into a conviction of damnation that had torn him apart.

'Branwell was not Heathcliff,' I said.

'Like father, like son. He seduced another man's wife. Or is that a secret of which you are unaware?'

'I know of what happened at Thorp Green Hall.'

'Then do not take up the cause of a fornicator! He has no right to anyone's sympathies. Please remember, Miss Nussey, I saw it as my Christian duty to treat Branwell as my son, but I received no reward for my efforts, not even the consolation of acquiring a helpmeet. No woman was prepared to take on my family and I have had to stay a widower. As for Branwell, he squandered all the opportunities that I gave him to make a name for himself and never produced a painting or book of any worth. Believe me, there was no finer day than when I heard the earth fall on his coffin!'

'So if you hated him so much, why did you let him stay?'

'Because his sisters begged me to let him stay. They still loved him, despite all his manifold weaknesses. I let him stay and I prayed to the Lord to give me grace and strength sufficient for each day.'

'And what was Charlotte's response?'

'Ask her. Are not you and she the best of friends?'

'I have spoken with her but I am not sure that she is telling me the entire truth. I fear, sir, that it is not just Branwell whose behaviour is open to judgement. As you know, I have known your children for twenty years and loved them all, especially Charlotte. But recently I have come to know secrets about her that have deeply shocked me. I have no desire to share those secrets with the wider world but I fear that it would be wrong for them not to be known by you, if only so that you can take steps to ensure that Charlotte can commit no more harm.'

'You begin to alarm me, Miss Nussey. Speak what you must. Let me be the judge of what happens next.'

'As you well know, Charlotte is a person who likes to get what she wants. Once she wants something, she lets nothing and no one stand in her way, even a friend, even a member of her family. When you sent her away to become a teacher so that Emily and Anne could receive a good education, she was bitterly resentful. That was not the career she envisaged for herself. I have read a secret account that Anne wrote and in it she expresses her fear that the reason why first Emily and then she were taken so ill at school was that Charlotte had poisoned them. Their illness forced you to have them back here and thus made Charlotte's continued stay at the school unnecessary. Anne was suspicious that this might also be the explanation as to why years earlier her older sisters, Maria and Elizabeth, were taken so violently ill after Charlotte joined them at their school. It was Charlotte's way of getting them all returned home. Unfortunately, Charlotte, being so young, gave them too much poison and thus ensured not just their illness, but their death.'

'This is just mere silly supposition, Miss Nussey. I would have hoped better from Anne than to write such nonsense.'

'I fear, sir, it is true. I challenged Charlotte with this and she did not deny the charge.'

For years Mr Brontë had learned to get around the parsonage without relying on the use of sight. He had been able to do this because everything within the house had its fixed place. In the same way he had moved without fear of losing his direction through the lives of his children, each having their assigned role. Now my words were upturning his world and I could see for the first time he knew not which way to turn. I felt genuinely sorry for him as he struggled to come to terms with the implications of what I had told him. All his certainty had been removed. The man who had so harshly condemned Branwell struggled to apply the same damnation to his daughter. I gave him time to gather his chaotic thoughts into some semblance of order.

'What you tell me is deeply shocking and extremely painful,' he said, 'but I must not lose sight of the fact that Charlotte was but a child herself when Maria and Elizabeth died.'

'I am afraid there is worse. I suspect that Charlotte may have deliberately poisoned Martha Taylor in Brussels.'

'For what reason?'

'Charlotte was attracted to Professor Héger and felt that Martha was becoming her rival.'

'But the professor was a married man!'

'I am afraid that did not stop Charlotte wanting to have an affair with him.'

'Then she is no daughter of mine!' he stormed. The words were said with one meaning in mind but once spoken took on another. Fears that he had long repressed came to the fore. 'Have I all these years brought up not one but two bastards?' he said. 'Does Heathcliff's poisonous blood flow also through her veins?'

His obvious shock and the vehemence with which he asked this question made it obvious that, until then, Mr Brontë had not seen Charlotte as Heathcliff's child. This made me question whether I was doing the right thing. What proof did I have that Charlotte was not Mr Brontë's child? Only the word of Heathcliff and even then it was possible that Maria had been mistaken and that Charlotte was her husband's child and not her lover's. 'I do not know for certain if Heathcliff's poisonous blood runs in Charlotte's veins, sir,' I said. 'I only fear that it might. You see, the reason why I have come here today is that I keep questioning how Branwell, Emily and Anne all died in such a short space of time and I think Charlotte may have had a hand in that – certainly that is what Anne thought before she died.'

'God help me. I would rather have died than live to hear what you are telling me. It cannot be so.'

'Then prove it is not so,' I replied. 'Give me your account of the deaths of your children. Start with how Branwell drank himself to death.'

'Well, for a start, Miss Nussey, he certainly did not drink himself to death. Although he had many other vices, he was not totally addicted to the bottle, even if there were days and sometimes weeks when he seriously overindulged. It was one of the foolish and annoying ways in which he felt he was getting back at me. I may be blind but my other senses are sharp enough to detect when a man has had too much to drink. I know on which days he returned home in a disgraceful condition and, whenever that happened, he faced my wrath. However, he was no permanently drunken sot and there was a good reason for that.'

'What good reason?'

'Drinking alcohol sometimes caused him to have fits. This made it an activity in which he could not always take pleasure.'

'So why does the outside world believe he became a total drunkard?' I asked.

'Because when he was very depressed he did at times drink far too much and because people mistakenly thought his occasional fits were evidence of him being drunk.'

'You have left out the most important reason,' I said.

'And what may that be?'

'Charlotte told us all he was leading such a dissolute life that he was more or less permanently under the influence of either alcohol or opium – and she said this not once but repeatedly.'

'I cannot imagine why she would say that. It is not true.'

'I think I can.' As I said this, I recalled Anne's accusation about Emily's illness – that it had not dated from the time that Charlotte had said. Had Charlotte also been preparing the world for Branwell's demise by depicting him as being in a worse state than he was? 'Mr Brontë, it may have suited Charlotte to tell the world that Branwell was drinking himself to death if she planned to kill him.'

'Surely even the spawn of Satan himself could not be so evil? I will not believe it!'

'Tell me what Branwell was doing in those last three years of his life.'

'Nothing of worth. Some of the time he simply hung about the house, sometimes he went out to see friends – sometimes for days or weeks at a time. Often he helped his sisters with what they were writing. I confess I thought all that scribbling a waste of time. I had no idea – and nor did Branwell – that any of what was being written would ever be published. As you know, Charlotte deceived both me and Branwell on that front.'

'Were you ever party to exactly what Branwell and the others were writing?'

'No. To be honest, their scribblemania irritated me. They therefore preferred to discuss their writing when I was not around. The only thing of which I am certain is that Branwell frequently talked with Anne about what eventually became her novel, *The Tenant of Wildfell Hall*.'

'What makes you say that?' I asked.

'Because it is not a book I admire. Think about it, Miss Nussey. Does not the novel both begin and end with a male narrator and does that narrator not remind you forcefully of Branwell himself? He is a man who is infatuated with a married woman. Moreover, he gets her in the end once her husband has died. That was, of course, Branwell's dream. For months he had tried to persuade us all that the wretched wife would come and seek him out, once she was freed from her husband.'

Though I had not thought about it before, I knew he was right. *The Tenant of Wildfell Hall* was indeed bound up with Branwell's love affair with Mrs Robinson. Faced with writing another novel – and this time one that could not rely so much on her personal experiences as had *Agnes Grey* – it did not surprise me that Anne might have looked to her brother for ideas and inspiration. For years all the sisters had got used to writing with him and often taken their lead from him. Given her moral objections to her brother's sexual behaviour at Thorp Green Hall, Anne had, of course, then adjusted the story. How much the book was hers and how much it was his would now be impossible to judge.

'Charlotte was also very unhappy about Anne's book,' continued Mr Brontë. 'She thought its subject matter was inappropriate. She told me that she had tried to persuade Anne to abandon its publication and was aggrieved when Anne refused.'

'What about Emily? What was she writing?'

'I have told you that I took no interest in my daughters' writing. All I can recall is that Branwell helped her when she started writing her second book. Emily told me that the book was about family betrayal and that it would be far more shocking than *Wuthering Heights*.'

'When did she tell you that?'

'I cannot recall but it would have been after I discovered that my daughters were having their books published because, prior to that, I would not have known about her first novel's existence.'

'How did you discover Charlotte was publishing books?'

'Only when Charlotte chose to tell me. One day she entered my study and said, "Papa, I have been writing a book." "Have you, my dear?" I said. "Yes, and I want you to look at it," she replied. I told her that I could not risk tiring my eyes by attempting to decipher her manuscript and she said that I need not be concerned because it was printed. "I hope you have not been involving yourself in silly expenses," I said. She replied, "No, Papa. I think I shall gain some money by it. May I read you some reviews?" I nodded and then called for Emily and Anne to join us so they could hear too, not realizing they were also authors in print.'

'Why did you not also call Branwell?'

'He was not in the house and my daughters all judged it was the wrong time to tell him. Charlotte said it would lower his self-esteem to think his sisters had work published whilst he did not. She said she would encourage him also to write a novel and, once that was published, their secret could then be told.'

'And so he never found out? That is what Charlotte has told me.'

'Then she lies. He found out a few days later and from another source. He met two men in The Black Bull asking for Currer Bell, the author of *Jane Eyre*. It did not take much conversation for him to realize they were speaking of Charlotte.'

'And what was his reaction?'

'He stormed back here, saying Charlotte had bitterly deceived him. They had an argument. It was to be the first of many.'

'What happened next?'

'He went to see friends in Halifax and threw himself into a round of drunken debauchery. When he suffered some serious fits, his friends brought him back here. He was in such a bad state that I feared for my daughters' safety and so insisted on having him confined to my room. The doctor thought that he was suffering from delirium tremens brought on by intoxication, but I believe that was not the case. He knew he was a damned soul and he was seeing all the demons of hell that awaited him. I heard him repeat endlessly, "It's her fault. It's her fault." I assumed he was referring to Mrs Robinson.'

'But he could have been referring to Charlotte?'

'I suppose so.'

'And when did he recover?'

'I don't think he ever did entirely. But his fits gradually reduced and by April he was helping Emily in particular with her writing. The two of them spent hours scribbling together, especially in July when Charlotte and Anne went to London to hold meetings with their publishers. Charlotte was annoyed that Emily would not go.'

I knew all about that trip. Charlotte had told me how she and Anne had spent their entire time in London in a state of constant excitement. They had used the opportunity of being there to visit the Royal Academy, the National Gallery and, most thrillingly, the theatre, attending a performance of *The Barber of Seville*. 'Tell me what happened after Charlotte and Anne returned,' I said.

'Life went on much as it always had until Branwell died.'

'Tell me about the manner of his death.'

'There is not much to tell. On 22 September he left the house to go into Haworth. He said he was going to the post office. William Brown, the sexton's brother, subsequently found him lying on the ground in the lane between the parsonage and the church. He brought him here and we put him to bed and called the doctor. My vision is limited but I am told that he looked dreadful. His cheeks were yellow and sunken, his lips were shaking, and his eyes had the glint of madness. He never rallied and he died in my arms two days later. Much though I had reason to hate him, Miss Nussey, I carried out my role as a priest in seeking to grant him absolution of his sins and, for the sake of my daughters, I gave a public pretence of mourning.'

'What was on the death certificate?'

'Chronic bronchitis and marasmus.'

'Marasmus?'

'Wasting of the body.'

'And then what happened?'

'My daughters grieved and each seemed to retreat within a shell of their own, emerging from their rooms only for those times when they discussed the reviews still appearing about their work.'

'There must be something else, sir. Please think more carefully. Was there anything that caused any ill-feeling?'

He racked his brain and then finally came up with something that made me sit up. 'Charlotte went through Branwell's papers and burnt many of them that she judged unsuitable,' he said, 'and then she and Emily had an argument. Emily alleged that Charlotte had destroyed the manuscript of the novel that she and Branwell had been writing. Charlotte denied doing so and said that Branwell had probably destroyed it in one of his drunken states. Emily vowed to rewrite the missing novel and Charlotte said that she was too ill to undertake such work and that she should rest instead.'

'And then Emily was taken ill and died on 19 December,' I said. 'How very convenient!'

'What do you mean?'

'Emily and Branwell produce a book of which Charlotte disapproves. She tries to get them to stop writing it and fails. Then Branwell dies and the manuscript disappears. Soon after Emily challenges Charlotte about its disappearance, she also dies. Is there not something alarming in that sequence of events? Tell me, Mr Brontë, did you think Emily was seriously ill that autumn or did her death come as a shock?'

'I certainly did not think she had a fatal illness, but I am old and my eyesight is poor. We all had colds. It was not just Emily that was coughing.'

'And what do you feel now?'

'God help me. I don't know what I believe. Do you really think everything hinges on Emily's second novel?'

'Yes, I do, sir.'

'If so, there is one more thing I can offer you.'

'What is that, Mr Brontë?'

'I have just remembered something that I had forgotten. I said that Branwell left this house to go to the post office. When he was brought back here, we undressed him. His clothes were placed in a pile in his room. I looked to see if there was anything that might indicate what he had been doing and I discovered to my horror that his pockets were still full of love letters from his adulterous relationship. Among these was a new letter that he had not posted. I burned the love letters but put the other letter away, intending to look at it later. My daughters' grief at his dramatic decline made me delay and, once he had died, the whole thing seemed pointless. I never opened that letter, Miss Nussey. I still have it. It was not among the papers that Charlotte looked at. It may contain nothing but it just might also contain information about the novel.'

'Where is it?' I said, scarce able to contain my excitement at this sudden turn of events.

'In the book I was reading at the time. That one over there,' he said, pointing to a book of sermons on his bookshelf.

I rose and pulled out the book. I opened its pages and there was the unopened envelope. I turned its face towards me. It was addressed to his friend, Joseph Leyland. I hesitated what to do next. Had I the right to open a letter addressed to another? My thoughts were interrupted by a command from Charlotte's father: 'What are you waiting for, Miss Nussey? Open it and read it to me.' I opened it and this is what I read:

Dear Joseph,

I thank you for all the patience you have shown to me. I know that I have been but a poor friend these past months. If I tell you all now, then perhaps you will understand why. Do not worry. I am not going to talk yet again of my former love. You know already how much agony her desertion has caused me. You also know how much I have tried to drink myself to oblivion and how much that has destroyed my capacities.

No, I have another tale to tell. And, hearing it, maybe some of your pity for your friend will be revived. Not that I pen this letter to win your sympathy. I write because the whole story will shortly become known to the world and I want you to hear from me and not from others. By the time you read this, I will have handed over a parcel to be posted to a publisher in London. It is a sequel to *Wuthering Heights*. Emily has written it with my help. It will be called *Wuthering Heights Revisited*. Not very original perhaps, but very apt.

Can you recall that almost six years ago I was writing a novel of my own? It concerned a house called Wuthering Heights and a man called Heathcliff and his determination to possess a woman called Cathy, a determination that made him destroy the lives of others. I think you thought the theme had potential. I never completed it because my sister Charlotte persuaded me to abandon it in favour of taking up a post at Thorp Green Hall. She said that the role would give new meaning to my life. Well, she was right.

Until January of this year I gave the manuscript I had abandoned no thought. So imagine my surprise when I overheard two men speaking in the Black Bull and one of them was talking about a book called *Wuthering Heights*. I interrupted them, seeking to know what they were talking about. 'We have come here to try and find Currer Bell, the author of *Jane Eyre*,' they said. 'We know she lives near here and we hope to find someone to introduce us to her.' 'I know no one called Currer Bell,' I said. 'That's only a pseudonym,' they said. 'We have discovered through her publishers that the author's real name is Charlotte Brontë.' I tried not to show my shock. 'A pseudonym?' I said. 'Oh yes!' was their reply. 'And not the only one she uses. She is also known as Ellis Bell and Acton Bell – you may not yet have heard of the books recently published under those names, *Wuthering Heights* and *Agnes Grey*?' They opened the bag that rested on their table and pulled out copies of the three books. I picked them up and looked at the titles. Three books published by Charlotte and one of them about my Wuthering Heights! My mind reeled.

You sometimes used to say that I should go on stage with my ability to mimic others. Believe me, my finest acting hour came at that time. I had no desire to let them see that I had been kept in such ignorance. They would have thought me a fool. I therefore showed none of my inner turmoil. Instead I introduced myself as Charlotte's brother and I let them gain the impression that I knew all about my sister's writing. I even managed to persuade them that she was a recluse and that there was no point in them trying to see her. You would have been proud of me if you had witnessed my performance. And then I offered to take the three books and obtain my sister's autograph on each of them. They were delighted to accept. I warned them that they might have to be patient about when the books were returned to them. I said that my sister hated the idea of being famous and so I would have to seize the right moment to ask her to sign them. However, if they left their home address, I would post the books back to them once she had autographed them. To this they agreed, thanking me most profusely.

I ran home with the three books hidden under my coat. I went to my room and began to read them one by one. First *Jane Eyre*, then *Agnes Grey*, and finally, left deliberately to last, *Wuthering Heights*. I did not eat and I did not sleep until I had read all three. My family were used to my odd behaviour and thought nothing of my absence. Once I had finished all of them, I went to see Charlotte and flung the books down in front of her. We had the most terrible row. What hurt me most was what she had done with my story. She had turned the monstrous Heathcliff into a romantic figure. You may not think, Joseph, it matters. But it mattered to me because Heathcliff was not just a fictional character. He was a real living and breathing monster who seduced my mother. I am the product of their adulterous affair. He came back into my life when I was twenty-two and I slit his throat with a knife. I know this all sounds insane, but it is the truth.

The row we had was long and bitter after I confronted Charlotte with her crime. Cruel things were said on both sides. The main thrust of her argument was that she had abandoned all hope of me ever making anything of my life and so she had been forced to write for publication herself. That I could concede to some extent – but not the fact she had plagiarized and distorted my work in order to make a sensational tale. Eventually I could take no more. I stormed out of the house and left for Halifax. I almost killed myself in acts of debauchery in an attempt to forget what had happened. It was only on my return to Haworth that I discovered Charlotte had not written all three books. She had penned only *Jane Eyre*. However, she had persuaded Anne to write *Agnes Grey* and she had given the ideas from my manuscript to Emily to encourage her to write *Wuthering Heights*.

Emily was as much a victim as me. In talking with her, it quickly became obvious that she had been told nothing of the facts that lay behind my manuscript. She had assumed it was entirely fictional. She was horrified at Charlotte's duplicity and at how her novel had caused me such pain, not least because she had never wanted to have the book published anyway. Over these past few months Emily and I have plotted our revenge and we have made the punishment fit the crime. We have written a fictional novel that is based entirely on fact – on Charlotte's betrayal. In *Wuthering Heights Revisited* the world will read how Heathcliff's story is a very different one. Those who know the family will soon guess the truth and Charlotte will win a notoriety far greater than the fame she currently possesses. Our novel will destroy her reputation and, in the process, the literary acclaim given to her work. If it also plunges Emily's *Wuthering Heights* into oblivion, that does not matter.

I do not think the publicity will be easy when *Wuthering Heights Revisited* is published but Emily and I are not afraid of facing it. If we have any concern, it is for poor Anne. She will hate this division in the family, but she loves Emily and I know whose side she will be on. There are enough reasons in Anne's past for her to appreciate Charlotte's ruthless nature.

I write this in haste but in the deepest regard for your friendship. I will need that friendship to help me face what lies ahead.

Your most loving friend

Branwell

As I finished speaking, I looked with triumph at Mr Brontë. We had our answer! There was no corresponding look of delight on his face, only the deepest of sorrows. His pain silenced me. It was he who eventually broke the silence. 'Charlotte must have discovered their plot and there is no way she would have permitted that book to be published. I think, Miss Nussey, we now know what happened if not the detail.'

'Yes. Charlotte ensured Branwell's death and destroyed the manuscript. And then, because she feared Emily might still betray her secret, she also removed her. Only Anne, who knew nothing about the real Heathcliff, was permitted to survive until she began asking questions about Emily's death. Then Charlotte deliberately advanced the disease that would destroy her one remaining sister.'

'Then what are we to do?' he muttered.

'As yet I do not think we can do anything. We have not the slightest shred of evidence except for this letter. I need time to reflect.'

'And until you find a way forward?'

'Charlotte must not know what we have discovered. If she has the slightest indicator that we have information that might be used against her, we know what the outcome will be. You are an old man, Mr Brontë, and you have now buried five of your six children. Would anyone have a second thought if you now died? As for me, I am a nobody and I am sure Charlotte can effect my removal without anyone thinking she might be responsible – after all, am I not her greatest friend? We therefore both have to behave to her as if our conversation today had never happened. I know that will be harder for you because she will return to this house, but you have to be strong.'

He seemed to visibly age before me and tears began to fall from his face, but he nodded his assent. I folded up Branwell's letter, placed it in my bag and left him to his grief.

14

The Death of Charlotte

Charlotte's honeymoon lasted almost a month. The couple spent the first few days exploring the beauties of Snowdonia before taking a packet steamer to Dublin, where she met her new husband's brother and some of his cousins. From there Charlotte went to his family home in Banagher. She was keen to communicate to her friends that Mr Nicholls' Irish relatives were well educated and very 'English' in their manners. After spending some time with members of his family, the newlyweds then explored more of Ireland, including Limerick and the magnificent west coast and such beauty spots as Tarbert, Tralee, Killarney, Glengariff and Cork. Some of the scenery exceeded all her expectations.

In early August, about a week after her return to Haworth, Charlotte wrote to me, saying that she felt marriage had changed the colour of her thoughts because she knew more of the realities of life. She had come to understand that it was a strange and perilous thing for a woman to become a wife. I was not sure what she meant by this. It was obvious from the letter that she felt the role of being a minister's wife placed more demands on her, but this she judged to be a marvellous thing. More difficult was the expectation that a wife should have no opinion but that of her husband. I could not begin to imagine how Charlotte could possibly be happy subordinating her sharp mind to Mr Nicholls' pedestrian thought processes. It was obvious from her letters that Charlotte knew nothing of my discussion with her father so I assumed that he had kept our meeting to himself. All she said was that he appeared to have become much frailer and was obviously not well, preferring to keep out of her company.

In September Charlotte invited me to join her at Haworth and I duly obliged, arriving there on the 25th. I had determined in my own mind that I should face her with Branwell's final letter, whatever the outcome to our former friendship, and so I did exactly that. I told her how I had talked further with her father because of my doubts over the way Branwell, Emily and Anne had died. I was prepared to face her anger but this was not the response that my confession produced. Instead she expressed her total mystification. She swore that she had had nothing to do with the deaths of any of them. She looked me straight in the face and challenged me. 'How can you say you are my friend, Ellen, and believe that for one moment I would deliberately destroy those that I love?'

'But did you not destroy your sisters Maria and Elizabeth?'

'I was but a child. I took action that I thought would make them sick so I could return home from the hell in which I found myself. I never intended them to die! I loved them and, God knows, I have mourned my part in what happened and bitterly repented my action.'

'And did you not poison Martha Taylor?'

'No. I was beside myself with passion and I wickedly did not mourn her death but I did not kill her. I am very sorry if I gave you that impression.'

'Could not your passion lie behind actions that destroyed first Branwell, then Emily, and finally Anne?'

'Passion for what?'

'For fame, for literary recognition, for a place in the world beyond what is possible here in Haworth. You had no conscience to prevent you striking down those who stood in the way of those things because, as you have told me on more than one occasion, you are already by your birth and previous actions a damned soul.'

'Yes, I thought then that I was one of the damned, Ellen, though my husband has since encouraged me to begin thinking otherwise. And yes, I wanted those things you describe but I can assure you not at the cost of losing my brother or my sisters. God knows how much I loved them and how much I have mourned their passing. I cannot see why you should even begin to think I might have had a hand in their deaths.'

'Because there was no obvious reason, Charlotte, why Branwell died when he did. He had no fatal illness at the time and he was not the drunken sot that you have portrayed. Equally I think Emily's death was unusually sudden.'

'But we are surrounded by death. Its uninvited knock is heard almost daily here in Haworth. I myself almost died three years ago. Indeed, it was only your love that pulled me back from the grave.'

I knew the event to which Charlotte referred. As I mentioned earlier in this narrative, she thought she had contracted the same disease as her sisters in 1851 and I had nursed her for a week. 'I think you exaggerate my role, Charlotte.' I said, 'You suffered from depression, not a life-threatening illness.'

'No, I do not. Your role in my recovery was to show me a love that made life seem worth living. I was fortunate, but Branwell lacked any reason to want to live.'

'But you are wrong, Charlotte. He had a real reason to want to live. He and Emily were about to send a joint book for publication.'

'Are you referring to the pathetic notes that I destroyed after Emily's death? They were certainly not worth publication by anyone's standard.'

'I am referring to the novel, *Wuthering Heights Revisited*.'

'*Wuthering Heights Revisited*? I know of no such book!'

'Then how do you account for this?'

I waved in front of her Branwell's letter and, having explained to her amazement how it had come into my possession, I read out to her its contents. Either Charlotte was a consummate actress or else she genuinely was taken aback. When she had recovered some composure, she said, 'If I had known of the book, I grant you that I would have done all in my power to prevent its publication. But, believe me, Ellen, I knew nothing about it. I had not the slightest idea that Branwell and Emily were writing such an exposure. I thought they were writing something else. That is what they led me to believe. They even showed me extracts. It was all nonsense set in an imaginary world. I destroyed it as worthless after Emily's death.'

'Then where is the manuscript of *Wuthering Heights Revisited*? And was it pure coincidence that Branwell died on the eve of seeking its publication? I find that hard to believe!'

'So do I, Ellen. You have shattered all my assumptions about Branwell's death.'

'And what of Emily's death? Was that also not convenient? Anne thought Emily's death highly suspicious. She did not share your view that Emily had been seriously ill for some time.'

'Emily never looked after herself properly. I genuinely thought her health was in a precarious state and that she should be receiving medical attention, but Emily was determined to run counter to my every wish. She could not forgive me for having given her the Heathcliff story when I knew the eventual pain it would cause Branwell. The very fact that I was urging her to see a doctor made her all the more determined to refuse to see one – until it was too late. You have to also remember that Emily was a real stoic when it came to suffering. She would not yield a step before pain or sickness until forced. She hated it when people showed sympathy towards her and she was annoyed if anyone suggested she might require any help, even if that help was medical. The fact Anne did not share my concerns about Emily's health did not help. I swear to you, Ellen, I thought Emily's death was entirely the product of tuberculosis. She had all the signs – a deep tight cough, rapid panting after exertion of any kind, pain in the chest and side. I saw nothing suspicious in her dying when she did, though she was in the prime of her life. Now you are making me less sure that her death was natural.'

'And Anne's death? Did you not deliberately keep her here to the detriment of her health?'

'I had lost my brother. I had lost a sister. I desperately wanted to keep Anne alive. Surely you know that, Ellen? I kept her here only because I wanted to tend her myself. I feared to expose her to the strain of travel. If I did wrong, God forgive me. Our trip to Scarborough gave her pleasure but it ended in destroying her. She might have lived longer if she had stayed here. What kind of monster do you think I am? What has happened to your love of me?'

'What kind of monster do you think you are?' I mercilessly countered.

'I know that I am a woman in whom may flow the blood of a fiendish villain who blighted the life of his wife, who destroyed the woman he allegedly loved, who murdered his two eldest sons, one of whom was illegitimately conceived in hate, and who wrecked the lives of two innocent women, murdering one and seducing the other. What kind of monster does that make me? Is the reason that few can love me because most sense the wickedness that I have inherited? Does the presence of Heathcliff's blood in my veins explain why as a child I was so often treated as the worst of sinners and why I was responsible for the deaths of two sisters and, if truth be told, for also making both Emily and Anne ill at Roe Head? Does it not also explain why I could not help myself burning with such lustful passion for a married man that I took satisfaction in the death of a friend's sister? And why, in my desire for this family to achieve literary fame, I gave my brother's notes to Emily, deceiving her and betraying him? This is the monster that I am, Ellen. But I swear to you that I never had anything to do with the deaths of Branwell, Emily or Anne. It was their love – and until now your friendship – that alone made my life worth living. You know that! You have seen me marry a man whom I did not love because, without my brother and sisters, my life had become completely and utterly pointless.'

Charlotte's words threw my mind into utter confusion. All my investigations had pointed to her being responsible for the destruction within her family, and now she was asking me to believe otherwise. However, if my brain could not find an answer to the dilemma, my heart could. My heart told me that she was telling me the truth and, even before I spoke, I think she saw that in my eyes because she began to weep. 'Charlotte,' I said, 'I believe that Anne was right to think that both Branwell's and Emily's deaths were suspicious and it is not difficult to see what led her to fear your hand in what had happened. Her earlier experience at Roe Head and her earlier conjectures about your possible role in the deaths of Maria and Elizabeth account for that. However, what you have said makes me think she was wrong. You have done many things that were evil and which I cannot condone, but I now truly believe you are innocent of any involvement in the deaths of Branwell and Emily. I also accept that your treatment of Anne was designed to help her and not, as she feared, to destroy her.'

Charlotte's face lit up at my declaration and she flung herself into my arms, crying, 'Nell! Nell! Thank God you believe me!' My tears mixed with hers because I had reclaimed the friend that I thought I had lost. Once we had calmed ourselves, Charlotte resumed our conversation, asking, 'What makes you still so sure, Nell, that Anne was so right about the death of Branwell and Emily being suspicious?'

'The missing manuscript. You destroyed all Emily's papers that you thought worthless yet you never found *Wuthering Heights Revisited* among them. Nor was it found on Branwell's body. So someone took it – and that someone may well have had a hand in his death.'

'But the manuscript threatened no one but me,' said Charlotte. 'It was written to expose my failings and my treachery.'

'So who would want to protect you?'

'My father if he is my father. He took pride in the publication of our books and he would not have wished to have the family's secrets revealed.'

'But it was Mr Brontë who gave me Branwell's letter. Why should he do that if he had any hand in his death? It does not make sense.'

'There is another, Nell, who would not have wished to see me hurt, but I dare not say his name.'

'You must, Charlotte. The blood of Branwell and Emily cries out for the truth to be known.'

Charlotte's sobbing had subsided, but now it intensified again. I held her in my arms and tried to soothe her. Finally she uttered what she had feared to say. It was just two words: 'My husband.'

The Reverend Arthur Bell Nicholls! He who had worshipped Charlotte ever since becoming her father's curate. He who had constantly sought her hand in marriage, despite all her attempts to drive him away. He who had revelled in her fame as an authoress and delighted in her depiction of him in one of her novels. Charlotte was right! He would not have wished to see the reputation of the woman he worshipped be destroyed by a book – especially a book that stemmed from the pen of a known fornicator, who was oft besotted with drink, a man who had wrecked the peace of the family for years. And Mr Nicholls was the one person so intimate with the family that he might have discovered what was being written, even though Charlotte was ignorant of it herself.

'I fear you are right. I fear it might indeed have been him,' I said, 'but I have jumped to hasty conclusions already and I do not wish to repeat my mistake. He may be entirely innocent. Indeed, I hope for your sake that he is.'

After she had composed herself, Charlotte said she alone had to take on the responsibility of challenging her husband with our newfound suspicions. She made me promise to do nothing. I reluctantly agreed, though I feared for her safety should he indeed prove to have had a hand in the deaths of Branwell and Emily.

As you can imagine, I waited at home for a letter that would tell me the outcome of Charlotte's talk with her husband. Letters arrived but none referred to the matter. However, the reason was obvious. A clearly upset Charlotte had to inform me that not only was her husband trying to make her write less frequently to her friends, but also he was censoring what she said on the grounds that her letters might contain thoughts that were as dangerous as lucifer matches. I was informed that she had been told that in future she could only write to those who promised to immediately destroy whatever she wrote. She said that if I wanted to remain in touch, I would have to accept her husband's terms. I agreed but without any intention of carrying out such a ludicrous step. I wrote the following missive to him:

My dear Mr Nicholls,
As you seem to hold in great horror the ardentia verba of feminine epistles, I pledge myself to the destruction of Charlotte's epistles, henceforth, if you pledge yourself to no censorship in the matter communicated.
  Yours very truly
  Ellen Nussey

I knew that he would continue to censor her writing and that my pledge to destroy her letters was therefore null and void. Friends told me that Charlotte's letters to them conveyed that she had never been so well or so happy, but was that just what he was dictating her to say?

I did the one thing that offered a chance of my discovering the truth. I invited Charlotte to my home. She quickly agreed but when the time came she did not come, ostensibly because my sister was ill and her husband feared to expose her to any danger. This is an extract from the letter I received from her, dated 7 December:

For my own part I really should have no fear – and if it just depended on me I should come – but these matters are not quite in my power now – another must be consulted – and where his wish and judgement have a decided bias to a particular course – I make no stir, but just adopt it. Arthur is sorry to disappoint both you and me, but it is his fixed wish that a few weeks should elapse before we meet.

What was I to make of this but that he had deliberately prevented us meeting! What made the matter worse was when I received a note from her at Christmas in which she described her husband as 'her dear boy' and said that he was 'dearer now than he was six months ago'. In my mind I could not help imagining him standing over poor Charlotte and dictating this! I wrote asking her to come to my home in the New Year, but received the following reply, written on 19 January:

I very much wish to come to Brookroyd – and I hoped to be able to write with certainty and fix Wednesday the 31 January as the day, but the fact is I am not sure whether I shall be well enough to leave home. At present I should be a most tedious visitor. My health has been really very good ever since my return from Ireland till about ten days ago, when the stomach seemed quite suddenly to lose its tone – indigestion and continual sickness have been my portion ever since. Don't conjecture – dear Nell – for it is too soon yet – though I certainly never before felt as I have done lately. But keep the matter wholly to yourself ... Dear Ellen, I want to see you and I hope I shall see you well.

I begged that I should be permitted to visit her but I received a curt refusal from her husband, who said his wife was not up to the excitement of entertaining any visitor. I then sent letter after letter seeking to know what was happening but received no reply until mid February when Mr Nicholls sent me a brief note saying that I must accept I could not see Charlotte because she was completely prostrated with weakness and sickness and frequent fever. In answer to my continued letters, I received a short letter from Charlotte, dated 21 February. In it she wrote:

My dear Ellen, I must write one line from my weary bed ... I am not going to talk about my sufferings as it would be useless and painful. I want to give you an assurance which I know will comfort you – and that is that I find in my husband the tenderest nurse, the kindest support, the best earthly comfort that ever woman had. His patience never fails and it is tried by sad days and broken nights ... May God comfort and help you.

I doubted not that his hand lay behind the words of praise. Had I not been coping at the time with problems within my own family I would have dropped everything to go to Haworth, despite her husband's ban on me visiting her. Now I wish that I had gone because a final letter came from her saying that she was reduced to greater weakness. Then I received two letters. One, written on 30 March, was from her father, informing me that Charlotte was very ill and on the verge of the grave and asking me to pass on that information to Miss Wooler and other of our friends. The other was from her husband, written on 31 March. This is what it said and I give it in its entirety:

Dear Miss Nussey,
Mr Brontë's letter would prepare you for the sad intelligence I have to communicate. Our dear Charlotte is no more. She died last night of exhaustion. For the last two or three weeks we had become very uneasy about her, but it was not until Sunday evening that it became apparent that her sojourn with us was likely to be short. We intend to bury her on Wednesday morning.
    Believe me sincerely yours,
    A.B. Nicholls

I immediately went to Haworth and demanded entrance. My presence was obviously not wanted. Mr Nicholls was quite rude and his only concern was to try to make me promise that I would burn all Charlotte's correspondence with me. I was told that Charlotte's father was too prostrate with grief to see me. It was left to the maid Martha to take me upstairs to where my dearest friend's body lay. I looked down on the face that I had known so well, but now all the vitality and intelligence that had so given it shape and form was absent. This was not the Charlotte I had known but her pale imitation, a mere empty shell. Her drawn features, pallid and wax-like, had an artificial beauty, but the inner spirit, which had so gloriously charged her tiny frame, had gone. Martha had provided me with a tray full of evergreens and such flowers as she had been able to procure so that I could scatter them over Charlotte. This I willingly did, and their God-given glory and sweet scent somehow partially dissipated the sight and smell of death. I tried to say to myself that my dearest friend was now in the arms of He who loves us far more than the lilies of the field. However, I could not help but recall the world's loss and that it was just nine months earlier that I had been throwing flowers at her marriage and therefore I wept bitterly anew. And what distressed me even more when I ceased to focus on her lifeless body and began to look around was the state of the room in which her coffin lay. Someone – and I could only surmise it was her husband – had been going through all her papers and the room looked as if it had been ransacked. I found this premature desecration very difficult to accept.

I was given a room so I could be present at the funeral but both Charlotte's father and husband studiously avoided me. I asked to see the death certificate. It gave as the cause of death 'Phthisis' – a phrase often used in cases of tuberculosis. Having little faith in Charlotte's doctor, I was not convinced that was an accurate assessment and, with the passage of time, others have felt the same. There has been much speculation that her death arose from complications that sprang from pregnancy, but I do not believe that Charlotte would have kept such an event from me and even her inept doctor could not have missed the fact she was bearing a child. Mr Nicholls never said that was the cause.

On Wednesday 4 April I accompanied the funeral cortege that escorted her coffin to her final resting place in the graveyard that she had so often passed. A crowd had gathered for the occasion. Mr Sowden, who had married her those nine months earlier, led the service. As the coffin was lowered into the grave, I said prayers for my lost friend. I prayed that she might be forgiven for the sins she had committed and find release from all the inner torment that had so troubled her soul throughout most of her life. I prayed that she might forgive me for the false suspicions that I had held about her. And I prayed that she might once again be in the company of those she had loved most – Branwell, Emily and Anne. As I write this, though over forty years have passed, the memory still brings tears to my eyes and I draw comfort from the poem that Matthew Arnold wrote as his tribute to Charlotte:

> *Strew with roses the grave*
> *Of the earl-dying. Alas!*
> *Early she goes on the path*
> *To the Silent Country, and leaves*
> *Half her laurels unwon,*
> *Dying too soon, yet green*
> *Laurels she had, and a course*
> *Short, yet redoubled by Fame.*

However, less happy is the memory of what happened next. As we made our way back to the parsonage, Mr Nicholls moved alongside me and whispered in my ear, 'Now leave this place within the hour and never return!' Knowing not what else to do, I did as I was bid.

My discomfiture was completed when the terms of Charlotte's will were released. She had talked to me about making a will at the time of her wedding. She had been very specific. If she died childless, she did not want any of her money from her books to pass to her husband. She wanted it to go to her father. If she had any children, the money was to be held in trust until they came of age. Again it was not to go to her husband. Imagine my surprise when I learned that a new will handing over her entire estate to Mr Nicholls had been made in February at the height of her illness. Surely this was something forced upon her by him! His obsession with controlling what she wrote and destroying her earlier correspondence, his ransacking of her room, his treatment of me at the funeral, and now the will, all made me certain that her death had stemmed from his actions. But I knew that I did not possess one ounce of proof that would stand up in any court of law. What was I to do?

15

Where Lies the Truth?

I f Charlotte's husband hoped that the funeral would bring an end to interest in his wife, he was badly mistaken. News of her death was broadcast by the stationer in Haworth, a man called John Greenwood, and by the novelist Harriet Martineau, who wrote a lengthy if rather lurid tribute to Charlotte in the *Daily News*. Extracts from this were published in other newspapers and many stories told, some true and some false. Following this, I received a curt letter from Mr Nicholls reiterating his demand that I should destroy all the letters that I had received from his wife. To this I declined to reply and, to my amazement, he came to Brookroyd to see me. As it happened I was out when he called. He left a message inviting me to stay with some friends of his. Mistrustful of his intent, I wrote declining his offer and making clear that I did not take orders from him. I also told him how shocked I had been that he had ransacked his wife's possessions so shortly after her death and that such action seemed unworthy of a man of his profession.

In June an article appeared about Charlotte in *Sharpe's London Magazine* and I was shocked by its misrepresentation of her father. Though I had never liked him, I thought the article ought not to go unchallenged. I wrote to Mr Nicholls saying that he should not let malignant lies be circulated about his father-in-law and that he should seek the assistance of the great writer, Mrs Gaskell, who had come to know Charlotte well in recent years and who was sufficiently acquainted with her life at the parsonage to distil the untruths. She had the literary skills, the national reputation and the necessary contacts to write a strong rebuttal. He replied that Charlotte's character stood too high to be damaged by a magazine of little circulation and little influence and that he had no intention of encouraging any response because it would only serve to give the malicious article an importance it otherwise would lack. He alleged that, unlike me, Charlotte's father had not taken offence at what had been written because it was so laughably inaccurate.

I did not accept this and wrote direct to Charlotte's father, taking care to disguise my handwriting lest my letter be intercepted. Mr Brontë's response was totally different from that of his son-in-law. He thanked me for bringing the matter to his attention. He said that he had not previously been aware of the magazine's attack on him and that he shared my view entirely on the need to rebut its lies. Whilst I was not party to the resulting row that took place between him and Mr Nicholls, I saw the outcome. Mr Brontë wrote to Mrs Gaskell and asked if she would be willing to produce a short account of Charlotte's life, together with some comments on her novels, in order to squash the inaccuracies that were beginning to circulate. She agreed, although she recognized that this was not going to be an easy task because she knew enough about Charlotte to have her own reservations about the character of both Mr Brontë and Mr Nicholls. I heard from Mrs Gaskell that she went to Haworth at the end of July to discuss how she would research the biography and both men, according to her, appeared outwardly quite desolate. Mr Brontë told her that so deep was his grief that he found it difficult to dwell on his sad privation. Mr Nicholls made it clear that he was only bowing to the idea of a biography because of the insistence of his father-in-law.

They both very reluctantly agreed that no biography could be produced without reference to me, Charlotte's longest-standing friend, but they warned her that I was prone to silly imaginings. Shortly afterwards I received another letter from Mr Nicholls. He reiterated his own opposition to the idea of producing a biography but asked me to cooperate with Mrs Gaskell's research by sending him any letters that I might have from her in order that he might select what could be appropriately included. I agreed to cooperate but insisted that we meet before I did so. He reluctantly agreed but on the condition that no one should be informed of our meeting or of what passed between us. In secret and for the last time I therefore made my way to the Haworth parsonage. As I dismounted from the gig and approached the parsonage, I could not help but recall my first visit over twenty years before. Then Charlotte had greeted me so warmly. Now I faced at best her husband's indifference and, at worst, his open dislike.

Mr Nicholls had dismissed the servant for the day and so he opened the door when I knocked. He greeted me coldly and ushered me into the parlour and, after a few polite formalities, he made clear his feelings about having to see me. 'Meeting you is not easy because I am very much aware, Miss Nussey, that you have never approved of me becoming my beloved Charlotte's husband. Indeed, you did much to try and prevent our marriage.'

'It is true, sir, that I thought you lacked the qualities to make her a happy wife,' I replied, deciding to be equally candid.

'But you were wrong, Miss Nussey. From the outset, our marriage was blessed. In Ireland on our honeymoon she heard members of my family speak very highly of me and I think that made her realize that she had married a worthy and honourable gentleman. Until then all she had heard was your constant belittling of my character and abilities. Moreover, she found herself no longer looked upon as an old maid but as a beloved wife. That is a state that you will never attain, I suspect.'

'Be warned, Mr Nicholls, I will not stay here to be insulted,' I snapped back at him, rising to my feet from my chair.

'At least what I say is said openly to your face and not behind your back as were your derogatory comments about me to Charlotte. But you are right to be angered. I will not be rude to you. It is not gentlemanly.' He beckoned me to sit down again, and I did because I was desperate somehow to gain information that would help me resolve the mysteries that still beset me. 'What I want you to hear,' he continued, 'is how happy I made Charlotte. Her tendency to express morbid opinions about herself disappeared and, as she thought less intensely about herself, she became more considerate and open to others. As each day passed I could see her relaxing more and, as a consequence, she no longer suffered from the headaches that had so often beset her prior to our marriage. I sensed that she was growing daily fonder of me and I began to talk to her of all the parish work we could do together when we returned to Haworth. She said that she had feared the submission expected from a wife, but now realized that she had found a new freedom. A life devoted to serving me offered far more rewards than her previous devotion to writing books. I basked in her growing admiration and was never more tranquil and content in all my life.'

'I do not doubt, sir, that Charlotte had the capacity to be a fine wife. She had many, many talents.'

'And she began putting them to good use. When we returned to the parsonage Charlotte organized a tea-and-supper party for five hundred of our parishioners in the schoolroom and it was very well received. She was so proud of me when the assembled throng acclaimed me as a consistent Christian and a kind gentleman. She said such praise for her husband mattered more than all the fame she had won through her writing. She willingly began to undertake the tasks that I directed, such as teaching in the Sunday school and visiting the sick. Yet I thought that all the good achieved during our four weeks away was going to be undone because Charlotte's father was in a most strange and agitated state. He refused to even let Charlotte enter his room. She took this to mean that he had not forgiven her for proceeding with her marriage to me and she was understandably very upset. I promised her that I would resolve the situation and I demanded that he give me a proper audience. To this he eventually agreed. It was only then that I discovered that his behaviour stemmed not from our wedding but from a meeting that he had held with you after our departure. You had filled his mind with all kinds of nonsense.'

'I can assure you, sir, that our conversation was concerned only with uncovering the truth,' I interjected.

'Then you have a strange idea of truth, Miss Nussey, and one that bears no relation to mine. You revealed to Mr Brontë that you had uncovered something that he had long sought to bury – that his wife had been unfaithful and that Branwell was not his son. What right had you to speak of this? The poor man had hidden his suffering from the world and even nursed the woman who had betrayed him when she took ill. He had brought up the illegitimate boy as one of his own family, indeed lavished more care on him than on his rightful daughters. He had done his best to give the lad a Christian upbringing and borne – as only a true Christian can – the pain of seeing the boy's bad blood increasingly rise to the surface. Have you any idea at all of what it must be like to watch a young man, on whom you have nurtured nothing but care, throw away all his opportunities and turn to drink and to whoring and to worse? Branwell rejected all that his adopted father had done for him and became just a living copy of his real father. Is it any wonder that Mr Brontë spent so much time on his own in his room? He was on his knees praying for forgiveness for a bastard child who deserved none.'

'I think you err, sir, in your depiction of Mr Brontë's upbringing of Branwell. It was undertaken out of duty and his heart was not in it. He gave him a good education but not any love, and when Branwell discovered his true parentage Mr Brontë showed no pity. He told him his mother was a whore and his father was a murdering lunatic.'

Mr Nicholls glared at me and coldly declared, 'So they were.'

I refused to be silenced by his attitude and I continued speaking. 'He told Branwell that he had always hated him. He made him believe that his blood was irredeemably tainted and that he was destined for failure in everything he undertook. Is it any wonder that Branwell sought solace in drink or lost his way?'

'You cannot blame Mr Brontë for the sins of Branwell. Each of us is responsible for our own actions, Miss Nussey, and Branwell trod the path he chose in life – a path that ran counter to everything that he had been taught. I think that before you say anything critical about Charlotte's father, you should examine your own actions because, in my opinion, they do not bear much scrutiny. You led Mr Brontë to believe that Charlotte might also not be his child and that she shared instead the parentage of Branwell. What evidence do you have for making such a cruel and slanderous statement? You alleged that Charlotte murdered her two eldest sisters. What made you spread such a calumny about a person whom you claim is your dearest friend? I would rather have your enmity than such friendship! At least I would then be on the lookout for treachery.'

'I cannot prove what I said, but I said no more than Charlotte believed herself.'

'Do you understand anything about Charlotte, Miss Nussey?' he almost shouted. 'She adored Branwell and if Branwell said she was his true sister, she would have totally accepted that – but there is no certainty that she was. I believe she was the child of Maria Branwell and Patrick Brontë, and that there was not a drop of Heathcliff's blood in her. How did Branwell know this alleged fact – because of the ramblings of a monster, a man who had spent years in an asylum and in prison! Any court in the land would scorn your so-called proof!'

'I admit, sir, that there can be no certainty over the matter and I, like you, would much prefer to think that Charlotte was not Heathcliff's child. But you cannot deny the sinfulness of some of her behaviour.'

'What sinfulness? The alleged murder of her sisters that you so preposterously described to Mr Brontë? What nonsense! She was a child suffering abuse at the hands of a heartless teacher and is it any wonder that she wished for something to happen that might result in her returning home? When something did happen – the tragic illnesses of her sisters – she blamed herself. I doubt whether anything she did caused either their sickness or their death. It was the insanitary and harsh conditions in the school which sadly caused the death of not only Maria and Elizabeth Branwell but also many other young children.'

'But why was she singled out as being such a wicked child whilst she was at the school?' I countered.

'Have you not read any of the writings of the Reverend Carus Wilson, who founded the school at Cowan Bridge? Do so and you will see that he rejoiced in the fact that most children die in infancy! He believed it prevented them from committing the sins that would inevitably condemn them to the wrath to come. He thought all children are ripe at an early age for every act of sin and so every hour of their existence leads them step by step towards hell, unless they are made to feel the extent of their inherent wickedness. He saw it as his role at Cowan Bridge to make each girl recognize her monstrous sinfulness. What was said to Charlotte was said to all the others at the school! He hoped this would make them turn to God in repentance. However, in Charlotte's case, it made her believe that she was so sinful that she was doomed to damnation because God had turned his back on her. Painful impressions sink deep into the hearts of children, especially one as imaginative and sensitive as Charlotte.'

'I did not realize that the Reverend Wilson was so cruel,' I said, regretting that I had not thought to examine the man's character.

'That is because you have undertaken the role of investigator into Charlotte's life without committing yourself to the necessary research.

If you had, you would also have discovered that the school at Cowan Bridge was underfunded. The fees paid by the parents were barely sufficient for food and lodging, let alone an education. The cook was a careless woman who kept a dirty and disorderly kitchen and her meals often caused food poisoning among the girls. Maria and Elizabeth were particularly susceptible because they were recovering from having had both the measles and hooping cough. Add to this the fact that attendance at church involved a four-mile return trip, often in wet and cold conditions, and is it any wonder that so many girls fell ill and, in some instances, fatally so? The doctors were quite clear, Miss Nussey, that both Maria and Elizabeth died from consumption, not from some poison given by Charlotte! The truth is that Charlotte was always far too harsh on herself – a product I think not only of the Reverend Carus Wilson's preaching but also of listening too much to her aunt's daily prattling about hellfire and damnation. Yet far from challenging her ridiculous beliefs, you chose to confirm them. You even accepted Anne's crazed illness-induced meanderings and believed that Charlotte had poisoned her and Emily. I find that contemptible! In reality Charlotte saved both her younger sisters' lives by making her father take them away from the school when they were ill. She feared to see history repeat itself.'

'If what you say is true, sir, I confess I have erred badly, but you are wrong in thinking that I have ever wished to encourage Charlotte's obsession with being damned. It was I who for many years encouraged Charlotte to believe in the power of God's forgiveness. I made her wish she was a better person and I helped her see glimpses of holy, inexpressible things.'

'But, Miss Nussey, don't you see that your homilies served too often only to open her eyes to further stings of conscience and further visitings of remorse? Listening to your pious prattling, she foolishly thought herself morally and spiritually your inferior. Why do you think that I have been so keen to censor Charlotte's letters and to ask her friends to burn all her prior correspondence? Because I fear what nonsense Charlotte might have written about herself to you and others – nonsense that a foolish world might wrongly take to have some grain of truth. As children at Roe Head your apparent piety made her feel even more wretched about herself and, throughout recent months, all your actions have had only one consequence – to confirm in Charlotte's mind that she was born inherently wicked.'

'That was not my intent, sir.'

'Yet you gave the same lie about her evil nature to her aged father, whose mind was no longer agile enough to dismiss your imaginings. I gather, for example, that it was you who told him that she had become the mistress of Professor Heger in Brussels. May I ask what evidence did you ever have of that?'

'I blush to say it but Charlotte shared her secrets about her passion with me.' I replied, finally feeling on firmer ground.

'And you, in your wicked imagination, read an illicit relationship into her schoolgirl crush for her teacher. It was no more than that, Miss Nussey. Branwell had corrupted her poor mind into seeking for a grand romance. Quite sensibly, Mr and Mrs Heger quickly packed her off home before she made a complete fool of herself. It was not passion but hurt pride that made the memory of Brussels so painful to her. Her alleged affair with the professor was no more a reality than her misguided belief that Mr Smith, her young publisher, was romantically attached to her – and that too caused her much suffering. It was you, Miss Nussey, who fed Charlotte's foolishness. It was you who encouraged her to flirt with the Reverend Weightman and suggested that she was treating him badly when she had the good sense to recognize the man's failings. It was you who made her dwell on what happened in Brussels. It was you constantly made fun of any idea that she might marry me. You portrayed my honesty as dullness, my integrity as stupidity, my faith as lack of intelligence. You made out that marriage to a man of the cloth would diminish her.'

'I spoke only the truth as I saw it and I think you are wrong about Charlotte and Mr Heger. There was far more to what happened in Brussels than an innocent schoolgirl infatuation. And I still judge that to be happy, Charlotte required a far greater man than you. If you will forgive me, sir, your mind has not a drop of poetic imagination, not an ounce of her finer sensibilities.'

'What you mean, Miss Nussey, is that you wanted Charlotte never to marry because a husband of any kind threatened your position as

Charlotte's main confidante. It was only after she had that argument with you that for a few blessed months she was free of your pernicious influence. Then she began to look at me in a new light. I saw her begin to reappraise my qualities and turn slowly but surely towards the true love I had always offered her. And yet such was your influence that she still feared she might be demeaning herself by marrying me. How do you think it made me feel to know that Charlotte was writing to friends in order to justify why she should marry me? And all because of you! Our love needed no justification – and only when we were married did Charlotte fully appreciate that fact.'

'You do me wrong, sir,' I protested.

'No, Miss Nussey, you have done this family much wrong! When we got back here from our honeymoon Charlotte found her father not only no longer viewed her as his daughter but also believed she had had a hand in murdering Branwell, Emily and Anne. That was your doing – seeds sown by your evil hand. And what was your evidence for this? Your stupid assumption that Charlotte had discovered that there existed a manuscript novel called *Wuthering Heights Revisited* which had been written by Emily under Branwell's influence. Your belief that this posed such a threat to Charlotte that it would lead her to murder the three people she loved most in the world.'

So far I felt that Mr Nicholls had possessed the stronger hand in most of his arguments, but now I felt the time had come to reassert what I had uncovered and so my voice took on a greater certainty. 'I made no assumption, sir. *Wuthering Heights Revisited* is no figment of my imagination. I know it existed. I have Branwell's letter. I know such a book would have destroyed Charlotte's reputation. It would overnight have undone all her efforts to create a name for herself. The only mistake I have made was to think that it was Charlotte who had uncovered its existence. After I had spoken with Mr Brontë, I spoke with Charlotte and she made me realize that I had been totally wrong and that she was entirely innocent of an involvement in the deaths of Branwell, Emily and Anne. I therefore bitterly regret the unnecessary pain I caused her father – and indeed Charlotte herself. However, the fact remains that *Wuthering Heights Revisited* did exist and that it was destroyed and that its creators died in circumstances that are, to say the least, open to question.'

'I am aware of your conversation with Charlotte and that this led both of you to look in my direction. Had it not occurred to you before that I might have played some role? I lived only across from the parsonage and I was a regular visitor to it. I saw more closely than could Charlotte's virtually blind father the impact of Branwell's debauched behaviour on the family.'

'No, it did not occur to me, Mr Nicholls. The thought never crossed my mind. It was Charlotte who first guessed that you might have found out about the manuscript novel. To me you were always rather a non-entity. Charlotte told me that she would have to raise with you whether the deaths of Branwell and Emily owed something to your intervention.' I paused to add weight to what I said next. 'She died before she could tell me the outcome of your conversation.'

'Then I had better enlighten you about my role lest you engage in yet more wild imaginings, Miss Nussey. You seem to specialize in fantasy rather than reality. *Wuthering Heights Revisited* might well have been published before I knew of its existence had matters been left to Emily. She was always adept at hiding what she was doing. I think that is why Charlotte's reading of her private poetry caused her such initial distress. I had no inkling – and nor did Charlotte – of the true nature of the book that she was writing with her brother. However, Branwell lacked Emily's talent for deceit. When he was the worse for drink, he was not able to keep any matter private. Witness his appalling behaviour in proclaiming to the entire world his affair with the wife of his former employer. Charlotte tended to avoid him on those occasions when he was under alcohol's influence because the sight of him destroying himself was far too painful to her. She had worshipped him for so many years and placed him on such a high pedestal that his terrible fall from grace wounded her deeply. It was often therefore left to others in the household to either restrain his behaviour or put him to bed and, of course, that lot occasionally fell to me. It was on one such occasion that he boasted to me about *Wuthering Heights Revisited*. He told me how he and Emily were writing a book that would expose Charlotte's sanctimonious piety and reveal her true origin and nature. At first I thought he was spouting nonsense but gradually he revealed to me all about Heathcliff. It was only then that I began to appreciate the depth of hatred he felt towards Charlotte for encouraging Emily to write *Wuthering Heights*.'

'And so what was your response, sir, to your discovery?'

'At first I did all I could to persuade him in his sober moments to abandon the project. I said that only harm could flow from writing a book about the family's secrets. He just laughed in my face. I also spoke with Emily but she said she owed it to Branwell to do penance for her unwitting injury to him and that Charlotte should never have encouraged her to write her original novel. Whatever pain the new version caused Charlotte would be deserved. I next threatened both of them that I would tell their father and Charlotte about what was happening but they somehow rightly guessed that I had not the stomach to be the bearer of such ill news.

'They knew I feared to be the instrument of causing Charlotte pain and that I still hoped somehow to resolve the matter without her even knowing what danger had hung over her.'

'So what did you do?'

'I turned to Him who controls all our fates and prayed that God would intervene to save Charlotte from Branwell's insane desire for revenge and Emily's ill-considered willingness to go along with it.'

The tone in which he said this had the self-righteous ring that I detest in clerics, and I quickly interposed, 'And did you therefore act as God's agent, Mr Nicholls, and ensure Branwell's death?' I hoped to trick him into a confession.

'My dear Miss Nussey, you have read too many melodramas. Believe what you like, but I did not kill Branwell. God struck him down. All I did in the confusion that followed was to search his room, find the manuscript of the novel, and destroy it. Had I known of the letter in his pocket I would also have destroyed that.'

'But Emily must have questioned you about its disappearance?'

'Once her initial grief was over, she did, but I simply claimed no knowledge of its whereabouts. She assumed that before he had died Branwell must have sent *Wuthering Heights Revisited* to a publisher but, not knowing which one, she was at a loss what to do other than await a potential reply. None came. What might have happened next, I am not sure. She began to be more suspicious about the novel's disappearance and challenged not only me but also Charlotte about what had happened to it. My wife was so ignorant of its contents that she would have encouraged Emily to rewrite it had she not been concerned about her sister's health. She told Emily that the most important thing for her to do was rest.'

'But did you not think that Emily would rewrite the book, even if she was not well? Did you not see that as a real danger?'

'At first, yes, but not on reflection. It was my hope that, without Branwell's insistent voice to drive her, the idea of publishing the family's secret would eventually seem less desirable and that she would abandon any idea of rewriting the lost manuscript. In the event, her own illness then intervened and, as you know, she was dead within less than three months of her brother's death. It saddens me that Anne lived the last months of her life believing that Charlotte might have had some hand in her death, but Anne was always the most introverted of the sisters. Had she for one moment voiced her concerns, they could have been swiftly allayed.'

His words sounded very plausible and they placed all that I had uncovered in a totally different light. At one level I welcomed this because it restored Charlotte's position to one of complete innocence, even in the matter of the deaths of Maria and Elizabeth – children do have a tendency to wrongly blame themselves for bad things that happen within families. I recognized that my own investigative skills had been shown to be inadequate and that I had often permitted myself to make conclusions on very limited evidence. I therefore found myself saying words that I would never have thought possible before our meeting. 'I think, Mr Nicholls, that I have been foolishly hasty. And I deeply regret the needless pain I caused Mr Brontë and Charlotte by sharing with them conclusions that were faulty.'

'I am pleased to hear you say that, Miss Nussey,' he replied, sounding far more courteous in his tone. 'It makes it far easier for me to accept some very limited involvement by you in the forthcoming biography of Charlotte.'

He might have been less gracious if he could have read my mind. Part of me was deeply unsure that I was being told the entire truth. The deaths of both Branwell and Emily had been highly convenient to say the least and, even if Charlotte had had no hand in that (as I now believed was the case), could I be certain that Mr Nicholls had not murdered one or both of them? Indeed, if he had committed such a terrible act, then might it not also be possible that he had poisoned Charlotte once she knew of his role? This thought was the most unsettling of all. Had my investigations only had one outcome – making Charlotte challenge a murderer and, as a consequence, be murdered?

'I want you,' he continued, 'to help undo the damage you have caused by assisting Mrs Gaskell obtain information for the biography of my wife. I may not approve of this book being written but if it is to happen it must accurately depict Charlotte's many qualities. I will read her finished manuscript before it goes for publication and I warn you now that whatever has been your input will be closely checked by me. Now I want you to take your leave and never darken the door of this house again.'

I wanted to voice my new fear but lacked the courage. After all, I had not a shred of evidence and, if my conclusions were justified, I risked him deciding that he ought also to secure my demise. I therefore gave a curt assent to assist Mrs Gaskell and then departed as he had bid. However, I did not let him select whatever might suit him from Charlotte's correspondence with me. Instead I chose some 300 letters, just over half of the correspondence that I had retained, and asked Mrs Gaskell to collect them from me in person. I gave her all the contacts that I thought might help her research and even persuaded Miss Wooler to release some of the letters that she had received from Charlotte, though Mr Nicholls had asked her not to. More importantly, I used my meetings with Mrs Gaskell to provide many stories about Charlotte and to draw her attention to certain things that had adversely affected her, most notably Mr Wilson's treatment of her at Cowan Bridge. Mrs Gaskell twice came to Brookroyd as part of her extensive researches that autumn. I got away with all this participation because the one person who was refusing to cooperate in her investigations was Mr Nicholls and he made sure that access to Mr Brontë was also denied.

Nevertheless, I was careful to restrict the information that I gave to Mrs Gaskell. I told her nothing of the Brontë family's link to Heathcliff Earnshaw and the true story of Wuthering Heights, nothing of

Charlotte's belief that she might have had a hand in the deaths of her two eldest sisters, nothing of my investigations that had led me to wrongly fear Charlotte had been responsible for the deaths of Branwell, Emily and Anne, and nothing of the lost manuscript, *Wuthering Heights Revisited*. I was convinced that my original views on what had happened were inaccurate and I felt to raise all these matters would only jeopardize Charlotte's literary reputation and those of her sisters. It was safer to let Heathcliff remain a fictional character. The one thing I could not hide was Charlotte's affair with Constantin Heger, but fortunately Mrs Gaskell took the decision to play this down by glossing over what had happened.

The hard part was deciding what to say about Charlotte's father and husband. In the end I opted not to disguise my dislike for certain aspects of Mr Brontë's character or my antipathy towards Charlotte's husband, but I said nothing about my fear that Mr Nicholls might have been responsible for the sudden deaths of Branwell and Emily and, indeed, of Charlotte herself. Without revealing the one-time existence of *Wuthering Heights Revisited*. I felt I lacked the necessary proof to make my opinions sound remotely credible – and, of course, I had no objective evidence of the sequel ever having existed other than Branwell's letter. It would be easy for people to dismiss it as a mere product of his diseased mind.

Mrs Gaskell was impressively thorough in her research and the biography took longer than I had expected, but she had completed a considerable part of it by the summer of 1856. She made an unexpected visit to Haworth to try and obtain more cooperation from Mr Nicholls but got little response, other than persuading him that Charlotte's *The Professor* should be published. He did not even express a desire to see a pre-publication draft of the biography. His one demand was that she should not show a copy to me before publication lest I desire to have sections changed. He told her that he wanted no input from me at all. She therefore continued to hide from him the extent to which she had already used me in the production of the biography. However, his demand placed her in a dilemma because she had used so much of what I had given her that she felt she ought to let me see how she had incorporated my material before the book was published. She got round this by summoning me to her house and reading her manuscript to me, instead of letting me 'see' it.

I was delighted with Mrs Gaskell's draft, especially the section that implied what a poor choice of husband Charlotte had made. What made it particularly impressive was her judicious use of quotations from many letters but this posed a problem that neither she nor I had envisaged. Her publisher pointed out that all Charlotte's correspondence legally belonged to her husband and so his permission was necessary for any of it to be included. Such permission would certainly be refused once Mr Nicholls knew about the content of some of the book. It was Mr George Smith who came to the rescue. He wrote to Charlotte's husband saying that it would be normal business practice for him to sign over the copyright of the materials of the biography to Mrs Gaskell. Mr Nicholls resisted doing this but Mr Smith overcame his opposition by suggesting that if he did not sign he would be judged to have reneged on his original request to the writer. I have seen the letter that Mr Nicholls wrote, handing over the copyright. It lacks grace. He said that he felt he had been dragged into sanctioning a biography that was bound to be repugnant to him.

The Life of Charlotte Brontë appeared in a two-volume set in March 1857 and was an instant and sensational success. For what was said in the book Mrs Robinson threatened to sue, and so did the Reverend Carus Wilson. But neither did. Most people were fulsome in its praise. The famous Charles Kingsley, for example, said it had given the world a vivid portrayal of a valiant woman made perfect by suffering. Mr Brontë wrote to the publisher saying he found the biography to be full of truth and life, though he felt it was unfair in its portrayal of him. He urged only a few corrections in later editions. Needless to say, Mr Nicholls was less happy. He said it contained things that should never have been published and he spent the next few years trying to prevent any further investigation into his wife's life. His constant cry became 'Beware of the designs of prejudiced or reckless informants'.

Privately, of course, neither Charlotte's father nor husband forgave me for some of the biography's contents. They rightly saw my handiwork in the book's adverse comments about them. Moreover, my foolish conclusions that had so understandably upset Mr Brontë obviously still rankled. We never saw each other again. Mr Brontë died on 7 June 1861. As far as I can tell, he was virtually the prisoner of his son-in-law, who prevented people seeing him. Not surprisingly, Mr Nicholls developed an increasingly bad reputation. He was rude to the visitors who flocked to Haworth, refusing to let strangers visit his wife's grave or, more strangely, show respect to her memory as a writer. When Mr Brontë died. the trustees of the church refused to appoint Mr Nicholls as his successor as curate, even though for sixteen years he had been undertaking most and then all of his father-in-law's duties. There has been much speculation over the reasons for this decision and the fact there was no public testimonial, no parting gift from a grateful school and congregation. I will not add to it, but I am certain it reflects on the man's often bizarre behaviour.

Mr Nicholls was given just a few days to pack up and leave and he took the decision to return to Ireland. He made sure that he took with him not only all the family manuscripts but also all Charlotte's possessions, even her clothes. Was this the action of a man determined to outdo souvenir hunters or a man terrified that there might still be some clue hidden away as to his real role in the tragedies that beset the Brontës? He never sought another clerical appointment, choosing to live in poverty and obscurity. Was this his penitence? I am told that he has married again but that his home still looks like a shrine to Charlotte's memory. I told Charlotte that I wanted the full truth but I have had to learn to live without it. I now accept that I will die no clearer in my mind about what actually happened than I was forty years ago.

But the questions are still in my head. Were the deaths of both Branwell and Emily natural events – or even, as Mr Nicholls argued, willed by God? If so, they were highly convenient. Branwell's death enabled Mr Nicholls to destroy the manuscript of *Wuthering Heights Revisited* and Emily's death ensured that the book would never be rewritten. Or did Anne's conjectures have some basis in fact? She wrongly assumed that the murderer was Charlotte, but the killer could easily have been Mr Nicholls. Although I hate the man. I acknowledge that he certainly was passionately in love with Charlotte. He would have done anything for her – including murder. And I suspect he may have had another motive beyond her protection. As long as Charlotte had her brother and sisters with her, his chances of winning her hand in marriage were non-existent. It was only once she was reduced to a lonely and solitary figure at Haworth that she turned to him. For all I know, he may even have been the one who most persuaded Charlotte of the necessity of keeping Anne at home.

In my own mind these matters pale into insignificance beside the question that still causes me most pain. Did I contribute to Charlotte's death by encouraging her to speak to her husband about his role in the deaths of Branwell and Emily? Did Mr Nicholls kill her rather than risk her exposing his crimes? Much as he loved her, he would have recognized that I had sown seeds that could only destroy their relationship. Or am I once again drawing the wrong conclusions? Was Charlotte's death also a natural one?

I leave you, as reader, to judge. All I can say with any certainty is that Heathcliff's malignant presence destroyed four families. He first shattered the lives of all those connected to the Earnshaws and the Lintons – Hindley and Cathy, Edgar and Isabella, and then Catherine, Linton and Hareton. His impact on the Bramwell family was equally destructive in other ways. He encouraged Thomas Branwell to indirectly assist in the wrecking of a ship, murdered his daughter and, through his influence on Branwell Brontë, caused the cruel demise of Elizabeth Branwell. Finally he devastated the Brontë family. He seduced Maria, wrecking her marriage and causing such pain to her husband that it put pay to his career advancement and prevented him being a proper father to his children. He wrecked Branwell's life and, through the devastating impact of that, the lives of Charlotte, Emily and Anne. Only Mr Brontë might have altered the course of events if he had been able to respond lovingly to Branwell in his hour of greatest need – but that act proved beyond him. In one harsh moment he undid all the years of sacrifice he had made in treating Branwell as his son. Which of them is to be pitied most? Or should we reserve our sorrow for the three sisters, who strove in vain to ride the whirlwind of Branwell's emotional volatility and whose early deaths robbed this country of three of its brightest talents?

The nearer I get to death the more I want to forget the sadness of Charlotte's life and remember only that young girl that I first met all those years ago at Roe Head, the one who lacked looks and fine clothes and friends but who turned to me and offered me her companionship and who thrilled me from then on with her prodigious talent. She and her sisters gave me insights into the wonders of this world that I have never forgotten and I am eternally grateful for that. I look forward to seeing them again and to no longer having to rely on my faulty judgement to know the truth of what really happened. God washes not only our hearts but also our minds in heaven. *Wuthering Heights* will then be revisited for the final time. All I pray for is that God will forgive me for any pain that my actions have caused.

Before he died, Mr Brontë asked the world to stop focusing on his family and he wrote the following. I end my account by repeating it because I now make his words my own:

> As for myself, I wish to live in unnoticed and quiet retirement; setting my mind on things above in heaven, and not on things on the earth beneath … esteeming myself but an unprofitable servant, and resting my hopes of salvation on the all-prevailing merits of the Saviour of a lost world, and considering that the passing affairs of this life – which too much occupy the attention of passing mortal man, are but dust and ashes when compared with the concerns of Eternity.